CAT'S CRADLE

CAT'S CRADLE

Nick Green

www.stridentpublishing.co.uk

Published by
Strident Publishing Ltd
22 Strathwhillan Drive
The Orchard
Hairmyres
East Kilbride
G75 8GT

Tel: +44 (0)1355 220588
info@stridentpublishing.co.uk
www.stridentpublishing.co.uk

Published by Strident Publishing Limited, 2012
Text © Nick Green, 2012
Cover art and design by LawrenceMann.co.uk

ISBN 978-1-905537-88-4

Typeset in Garamond by oscarkills

The publisher acknowledges support from
Creative Scotland towards the publication of this title.

the publisher acknowledges investment from
Creative Scotland toward the publication of this book

For Henry

NICK GREEN

1
CATASTROPHE

They were burning in there, and only he could save them. From behind the locked door came Mum's muffled cries, overpowered by the shriek of the smoke alarm.

'Ben! Ben, what's happening?'

Smoke darkened the kitchen windows, a greying of the air that pinched his throat. Ben coughed his way through it to the sideboard, unplugged the toaster and chiselled out the blackened crumpets with a knife. He was too late. Mum burst from the bathroom, wrapped in a towel.

'Oh, well done. Still not housetrained, Benjamin.' Wincing at the alarm, she dripped into the lounge to fetch the chair for standing on. While she wasn't looking, Ben jumped up and pressed the alarm's reset button. The noise stopped. Mum reappeared.

'How did you do that?' Her glance took in the height of the smoke detector and the height of her son.

'I blew on it. Always works.'

'Really?' Mum frowned. 'I'll try that next time.'

Ben pushed the windows wide and the breeze poured in, clearing the air. Mum gently confiscated the two fresh crumpets he picked up, to toast them herself. Dad popped his shower-tousled head around the kitchen door to share a grin with Ben behind her back.

Ben lived for Saturday mornings. Waking up slowly, stretching in the day's first sunbeam, listening to the sounds of two people, not one, padding around the flat. Then the best part: sitting down to a family breakfast. For nearly eight years there had been Mum, or there had been Dad, but never both. Watching them share the same butter knife was weird, a feeling like the first day of the holidays.

The only thing better than Saturday breakfast was Sunday lunch.

They'd all go out to the Rose & Crown, and Dad would kiss Mum in front of the whole bar and Ben would pretend to die of embarrassment. But even better than that, maybe, was their weekly family treat: ten-pin bowling or the latest big film, a muse around an art gallery or craft fair to make Mum happy, or a match at the nearby Emirates stadium if she let the two males have their turn. Whenever his mates from school called him out, Ben was usually out already with Mum and Dad. They took the mickey mercilessly, but he didn't mind – after all, they were his parents. They could tease him all they liked.

'Dunno what to make of this one,' Dad was fond of saying. 'Nearly fifteen and still under our feet all day. Shouldn't you be sulking in your room?'

'Never any time to ourselves,' Mum would join in, with a pretend sigh. 'Other people's sons join gangs and leave them in peace.'

'Yeah, yeah.' Ben had to salvage his cool. 'I only hang around here for the food. Who are you people, anyway? You'd better not walk near me in the street, someone might think I'm being attacked by the living dead.'

They seemed bemused yet delighted that he wasn't a rebellious teen. Ben found that funny. The way he saw it, he *was* a rebel. He'd had a bellyful of time away from his parents, seven bleak years of Mum and Dad living apart, half a lifetime of missing either one or the other. He was glad to rebel against that.

Dad finished his toast and went downstairs to check the mailbox. On his return he passed Mum an envelope, to her faintly exasperated smile.

'You do know my birthday's *next* Saturday, not today?'

Dad covered his mouth, mortified with shame. Play-acting. 'Open it anyway.'

She pulled out three tickets to a show in the West End, the smash-hit *Falling Star*. Here were two things Ben knew about his mother: that she was nutty about musicals, and that the last time she had gone to see one, he had been nine. She danced Dad around the kitchen.

'Nice birthday treat, I thought.' Dad made light of it. 'A night out for the three of us. Right, Ben?'

'Uh?' He was still shielding his eyes from the scene. 'Next Saturday night?' An awkward thought pounced on him. 'I've got my pashki club.'

'Never mind.' Dad's smile didn't waver – of course Ben would miss the class.

'Thought your club meets on Fridays?' said Mum.

'Normally, yeah.' Ben chewed his lip. 'This is a… special meeting.'

'But not this special.' Just a hint of warning there, from Dad. Neither he nor Mum knew what pashki really was, only that it might be somewhere between yoga and kung-fu. However, they would tense up if Ben mentioned it, a shadow falling across them, as if they both deeply disliked the word but didn't know why.

'Okay.' It was the only possible answer. 'West End show, yeah, brilliant. No problem. I'll tell the others I can't make it.'

'I don't care if you've got tickets to see Elvis supporting the Beatles,' Tiffany shouted. 'You be there next Saturday, or, or…' Unable to think of a bad enough *or*, she flung her phone into the sofa cushions. Her dad, clearing away lunch plates, called from the dining room.

'Stop chucking that thing around. Do you want it to get lost?'

She glared at him through the dividing archway. 'Not *it*, no.'

'I beg your pardon? What is that supposed to mean?'

Already she had switched him off, made him invisible again. She dug out the phone to delete Ben's number forever, but Rufus jumped onto her lap with a jingle of his bell collar, butted her face affectionately and swept his tail in the way of her fingers. She shoved him off with unnecessary force and he fled, trailing lost hairs and dignity. The cat flap banged. At once she felt bad, which made her even crosser.

No, no, he couldn't do this! Ben absolutely had to come. Next

3

week would be D-Day, the payoff for all their hard work. All *her* hard work. For this one chance she had slaved away morning and night, running herself ragged, for months. Another such opportunity might never come. Did they dare attempt it without Ben?

Her mother invaded the lounge. 'Tiffany, we should have –'

'Not now!' she screamed.

'– a talk.' Mum stood her ground, holding a sheet of paper like a shield. 'This is from Ms Braby. Your new form teacher.'

'I know who she is.'

'You do? I gather she sees very little of you.'

Tiffany sprang off the sofa, so as not to be cornered, and stormed to the more strategic doorway.

'I missed *one* register! I was late, okay? Is that a capital offence? All right –' she could see Mum trying to interrupt, 'all right, two. And I lost a bit of homework. Ms Braby *wrote* you a *letter*? Let me see that.'

Mum drew it out of reach. 'More than a bit, she says. It's not just about this term, it's last year too. All your teachers have had words. You hardly give them a thing! And when you do, your marks…' She shook her head. 'Mr Sykes said you fell asleep during his class!'

'Hello? Chemistry! Molar equations! He was talking about iron moles. What would you have done?'

It was no use trying to escape. Mum followed her up the stairs.

'Tiffany, I don't understand. You used to be top of your class.'

Such an outrageous claim had to be crushed. 'Mum, that was *one* mark for *one* English essay on *I Capture The Castle*.' A book she could almost recite by heart.

'Still…' Mum rallied, 'you came top!'

Tiffany marched to her bedroom.

'Sweetheart,' said Mum, 'I'm not having a go at you. I'm trying to help. Tell me what's wrong.' She blocked the closing door. 'You spend so much time up here by yourself. I thought you must be studying. You've got your exams next year.'

'I completely forgot that, because you haven't mentioned it for at least thirty seconds.'

'I don't mind.' Mum wilted, plaintive. 'I don't mind if you fail your exams. If you quit school at sixteen and have to work a supermarket checkout, I would never think any less of you.' She sounded like she was really trying to mean that. 'You'll always be my Tiffany. All I care about is that you're happy. And I don't think you are.'

'I am happy.' It was only three words. Why did the strain of saying them almost kill her? 'Mum, leave me alone. Please.'

'If there was something the matter, you would tell me, wouldn't you? You would tell mummy first?'

Last, or never, thought Tiffany. 'Yes.'

'Because I worry.' Mum blinked her eyes dry. 'Sometimes I think you haven't been the same since… since that time. When we thought we'd lost you.'

'I'm all right.'

'Okay then.' Mum put on a smile. 'You'll be here for dinner, anyway? You're not going out… with any friends?'

'I'm in tonight. Stop worrying, Mum.'

Tiffany got the door closed. Peace at last. She glanced at her bed, but the dented pillow was empty save for a few hairs that weren't hers, being ginger. Now she was alone, she didn't want to be. She needed a cuddle, but not from any member of the human race. Reluctantly she returned downstairs.

'Where's Rufus?'

Dad slammed the dishwasher. 'Don't ask me. Your cat comes and goes as he pleases. Like someone else I know.'

Ignoring that jibe she opened the back door, to an unexpected blaze of sunshine. Rufus would be out choosing a warm wall. He wasn't on the rockery or monitoring the fishpond, so she went out front into Riversmead Drive. The poplar trees swirled light across the pavement with a shivery tambourine sound. She had an urge to scramble up among those yellowing leaves, leaping from branch to bough, never mind who saw. A quizzical head glanced down: a squirrel. Tiffany couldn't help smiling as the wind rinsed her hair. Of course, this was all she needed. Fresh air, warm sun. And a rest. Ben kept saying she was doing too much. She'd been driving herself too hard, and people had noticed. Soon, she promised, she would have a long break. If she could only get through next Saturday...

The daylight and the wind had done their work. She could live without that cuddle now. Nevertheless, she idly peered down the line of parked cars, to see if Rufus was curled up on a bonnet. She heard young voices and, without knowing why, walked towards them.

Children were straying into the road. None looked more than eight years old, and they seemed unaware that a car taking the corner would mow them all down. Tiffany quickened her stride.

'Stay on the path, you lot,' she called. 'Some of the drivers in this street, they're –'

Maniacs. A fair-haired girl turned round, and in moving revealed the thing that lay in the road. Tiffany ran towards it, every step seeming slower than the last, until she was sure she would be trying to reach the sprawled, still body of the cat forever.

He lay frozen in a twisted leap. His bared fangs and his eyes continued to blaze with snarl, as if, faced with his unavoidable fate, he had chosen at the end to turn and fight. He had lost. Rufus was dead.

'It was a man in a white car,' the little girl babbled. 'We saw it. He ran out. The car didn't stop.'

Another girl nodded fervently. 'It was horrible.'

Tiffany dropped to her knees.

'Do you know whose it is?' asked a boy.

'We should tell someone,' his friend agreed.

She touched his flank. The fur retained its soft heat, warm as a freshly baked ginger cake. She slid her hands beneath him and lifted and he came off the road crookedly, briefly held by a sticky patch.

It had been quick. That much was clear. She drew the cat close and pressed his cheek to hers. One of the kids made a *yuck* sound, shushed by an older boy.

After a time too long to measure, that same boy cleared his throat. 'You'd better come out of the road. There's a car.'

Stumbling with tears, Tiffany did as she was told. She was sobbing, still sobbing – she had no idea when this had begun. She only knew that it would never end, never never end as long as she drew breath. On the pavement she collapsed, cradling the limp body of her cat. A wail tore out the core of her.

'Are you all right?' asked the boy, hopelessly.

Tiffany blinked at the heaviness in her arms. Fresh spots of red speckled the ginger fur. Then more appeared. She sniffed, wiped her face and discovered that her nose was bleeding. She let it. The drops dripped from her chin to mingle with the drying patches of the cat's blood, until it was no longer possible to tell which was which.

2
THE SAND SHADOW

Some nights, he just wasn't in the mood for bounding over rooftops. Ben took the tube to London Bridge and walked. To avoid drawing attention on the train, he had left off his face-print and dressed in plain cargo trousers and a black hooded top, but he wore his pashki kit beneath as extra armour. Concrete grazes were an occupational hazard.

This curve of the riverbank was a labyrinth, all alleys, ancient brickwork and shadows cobbled together. A pub on the corner glowed like an old miner's lantern, the street lamps as rare as specks of panned gold. The cavernous rail bridge overhead echoed tipsy shouts and the clatter of too-high heels, as people streamed from the station in search of bright lights and fun. Ben walked the other way, into the dark.

At the waterline floated the ghostly apparition of the warship HMS Belfast, floodlit for tourists. Gurgling waters round its antique hull stirred cocktails of reflected colours from the neon signs of riverside bars. Ben walked on past the ship, following the Thames path and a map he had printed out. The place was right around here, supposedly. He drew upon the green catra, Mandira, and reached out with feline hearing.

'– doesn't matter. We can do it by ourselves.'

'Let's give him five more minutes.' Yusuf's voice.

'It's not up to us how long we give him! When the ship arrives, we move.'

'Then I hope it's late,' muttered Cecile.

Surely Tiffany hadn't forgotten that he could earwig on a conversation from half a street away.

'I said we don't need Ben. It'll be safer without him. He never listens to a word I say.'

'Hi.' Ben hopped up onto the canopy of the London Bridge City

Pier. The lurking Cat Kin sent up a cheer. Tiffany shushed them.

'For Pete's sake.' She crouched atop the angular roof, a sleek black silhouette with hair tied back, her forehead and cheekbones camouflaged in face-print.

'Sorry I'm late,' said Ben.

Cecile gave him her warmest smile. 'No sweat. Tube's always slower on Saturday nights.'

'Glad you made it before anyone had a hissy fit,' said Susie.

Ben was puzzled by a jingling sound as Tiffany stalked closer on all fours.

'Get down and take cover,' she said. 'The ship's due any time.'

'Yes boss.' Flattening onto his belly he caught Yusuf's eye, a wry moment. 'Where's Daniel? And Olly?'

Yusuf pointed towards HMS Belfast. 'On the gun turrets of that thing. Keeping lookout.'

More likely they had wanted to explore the warship. Ben wished he'd got here sooner.

'How long you been waiting?'

'An hour. Ish.' Yusuf shrugged. 'Tiffany didn't want to miss the boat.'

'And she's ready to wait till Sunday, right?'

'If we're caught because you're yakking –' Tiffany hissed.

'She'll skin you both,' Susie finished. Yusuf looked harassed. It must have been like this all evening.

Ben gnawed a fingernail. It was bad enough that he had abandoned his parents at Finsbury Park tube, after his first bust-up with them for months. For the life of them, they couldn't understand why he didn't want to come and see the show. Nor could Ben. He had ruined Mum's birthday, which made him total scum in his own opinion, and he deserved every yelling, chore and curfew he was sure to get tomorrow. But tonight it was Tiffany who was giving him the jitters.

She was really beginning to worry him. She had changed, and

he knew why. He had been there with Tiffany when Mrs Powell was killed, dying to save them both. Ben had not told any of his friends how often he thought of Felicity Powell. When he looked at Mum and Dad, when he saw himself in the mirror, when he opened his eyes each morning and found himself alive, his whole being breathed a silent thank-you to that snarky, cantankerous woman who had been his pashki teacher. It hurt him to remember how little he'd liked her, at first. But Tiffany… Tiffany had loved her. How did she feel? He shuddered to think.

This much was crystal clear. Tiffany was now a girl with a mission. Mrs Powell had spent her life protecting big cats, working on conservation projects across Asia, while secretly battling the poachers that the law couldn't touch. Kill a tiger, ran the rumours from Sri Lanka to Shanghai, and the Grey Cat will get you. Tiffany was only fourteen years old, so such global vigilantism remained out of reach for now, but Ben was dead wrong if he thought that would deter her. There was always London.

'She's pretty sure.' Yusuf was keeping his voice low. 'Her contact gave her the name of the ship and everything.'

'I suppose the info's kosher? Halal, I mean.'

Yusuf smirked. 'Ask her. I've never seen that forum she uses.'

Nor had Ben. That bothered him even more. Because Tiffany had been gleaning information from somewhere. Tip-offs about trades in leopard fur, reports of tiger parts smuggled into Chinatown for makers of traditional medicines. When pressed, she said her source was an online forum she had joined, called Vanished Harmony. How she had found this forum was a mystery in itself, for search engines never picked it up. As far as Ben could gather, it was a covert meeting space for eco-activists – exactly the sort of site that Mrs Powell might have frequented. Was that thought comforting, or not?

For a long time Tiffany had been frustrated, finding only patchy clues that led nowhere. But she wouldn't give up. She had prowled, she had sleuthed, she had fitted bits and pieces together until, to everyone's dismay, she told them it was game-on. The *Sand Shadow*, a light cargo vessel, was due into the Port of London on 27th September at 9:36pm, heading for a rendezvous at the London Bridge City Pier. And though its manifest listed only building materials, a source on Vanished Harmony claimed that the cargo was in fact tiger bones. Tiffany was hell-bent on intercepting it.

Ben huddled in a cleft of the pier roof, out of the wind. The city's lights blazed like a fairground above the waterline, shimmering in long icicles below it. If the night held any lingering summer warmth, the wide waters leeched it away.

Susie pulled her feet into a bored Mau-lotus position. 'Anyone bring snacks?'

'Olly did.' Cecile nodded towards the faraway HMS Belfast. Susie swore inventively. Tiffany turned to shush them and again Ben heard a tinkling, like the shake of tiny keys.

'What's that funny noise?'

'Dunno,' said Cecile, too quickly. After an awkward silence Tiffany shook her left wrist.

'It's this.' Jingle, jingle.

Girls, Ben thought – what were they like? 'You're wearing jewellery to a raid?'

'It's my cat's collar. I'm wearing it for him.'

Ben could have put his foot in his mouth (thanks to pashki, he really could). Her cat, of course. Tiffany's little brother, Stuart, had been thoughtful enough to phone and tell him the news, so that Ben could be ready and wouldn't say anything stupid, like just now.

He murmured to Yusuf, 'That's a bit silly, yeah? Wearing that thing on her wrist. People are going to –'

'– hear it?' said Tiffany, not even turning round. 'They might. If I let them.'

'Er,' said Ben.

11

'Rufus didn't let it ring.' Her voice was dreamy, yet heavy as lead. 'Not always. He was such a cat, he could move without his bell sounding. We put it on him so he wouldn't catch birds, but he still caught them. If he can do it, so will I. He'll be my teacher now.'

She returned to her vigil. Ben huddled with the other three to keep warm, peering down the river in both directions. It was worse than waiting for trains at Earl's Court.

'I think it's creepy-weird.' Susie had been quiet for as long as Susily possible. 'She hasn't even washed the bloodstains off that collar. You can see where –'

'But poor her,' Cecile cut in, as Tiffany's silhouette rose against the South Bank lights.

'There it is!'

The wind carried a shrill call, a slightly unconvincing caterwaul from Daniel and Olly's look-out post. A rumble echoed off the concrete riverbanks and Ben saw bright dots that were not reflections, moving against the water's sheen. Joining the dots made the outline of a boat.

'There's the name on the prow,' breathed Tiffany. '*Sand Shadow.*'

'And the plan is…?' Ben inquired.

'Wait for it to dock. Then see what happens. I'll know what to do.' She glanced at him, peevish. 'Where's your kit?'

'Under this stuff. It's chilly.'

'But you haven't put on your face-print. You're not taking this seriously!'

'I am!'

'He came, didn't he?' said Yusuf.

'Ben –' Tiffany seemed to bite back a sharper retort. 'Ben, it's only that the prints disguise us. If these people get a good look at you…'

'They won't.' He pulled his hood round the sides of his face. The ship's hull knifed through the oily water, and the hovering white bobs became lanterns at the tips of its twin masts. Except for a small cabin, which seemed to balance at the rear, the whole deck was a flatbed of tarpaulin, with any cargo hidden underneath.

Tiffany had told them in ghastly detail about the illegal trade in tiger parts. Shipments consisted mostly of bones, used in superstitious remedies for everything from arthritis to headaches. But no part of a dead tiger went to waste, it seemed. Claws could be powdered for insomnia cures, while tiger teeth were apparently as good as aspirins. Tiger fat was great if you happened to have leprosy (or rheumatism), and for bites and scratches you could apply the leather from a tiger's nose. Should you suffer from epilepsy, or malaria, a tiger's eyeball would see you right. Whiskers were for toothache. Finally, tiger brains could treat laziness and pimples. Yusuf had joked that they should give some to Olly, and Tiffany had gone berserk. 'It doesn't work, you idiot,' she had raged. '*None of it works*. That's what makes it even worse.'

Thut-thut-thut. The beat of the ship's motor thickened with its own echoes. On it came over the dark water, feeling its way with the whisker of light that was its bow wave.

'Tiffany?' said Ben.

'Ssh! What?'

'That boat isn't slowing down.'

She drew breath to argue. Yusuf cut in.

'It should have steered to port by now.'

'But it can't – !'

The ship was keeping to the middle of the river, its prow aimed at the central arch of London Bridge. Tiffany, frozen in dismay, watched it pass by.

'Guys!' Daniel came galumphing down the pier's gangway. 'That was the one, yeah? It was meant to stop here!'

'I never trusted that forum,' Yusuf began, breaking off as Tiffany hurtled past him.

'Come on!'

In one bound she was onto the Thames path, running after the ship, overtaking it. There was nothing to do but give chase. Now she was springing up the stone steps of the bridge. Ben struggled to get his stiff legs to move at cat speed. Daniel pointed in astonishment.

'Is she going to do what I think she's going to do?'

'Stop thinking,' Ben snapped, 'and catch her!'

He took a risk and shut his eyes for a full two seconds, still running. It worked. Like an indigo flame in the dark of his mind, his Ailur catra sputtered into life, pouring feline grace from his spine into his limbs. His feet found the rhythm of Eth walking and became an effortless wave, skimming over the concrete like the litter in the wind. Ben opened his eyes, darted ahead of Daniel and Yusuf and took the steps in three leaps.

A bus almost ran him over, whooshing past to fill his face with diesel. London Bridge was thick with traffic, black cabs, buses and bike rickshaws deploying to supply another night on the town. Through a gap between double-deckers Ben spotted Tiffany on the downriver side. He coughed out the fumes and ran across the road, forcing a taxi to brake. Tiffany was standing atop the bridge wall. Daniel had guessed right.

'Don't!' He sprang onto the wall himself and ran towards her. Far below he could see the cargo ship nosing out from under the bridge. 'Don't be an idiot –'

Tiffany spared him one glance. 'Ben. *Come on.*'

And jumped.

At first the darkness simply gulped her. Then Ben's cat vision kicked in, blinkering the glare of traffic and streetlights, in time to see her hit the flatbed deck of the ship, roll and slip under the tarpaulin.

She'd left him no choice. If this really was a criminal's vessel (and not a laughable mistake) then he had to go with her. As the ship fully birthed from the bridge he prepared to jump. It looked a ten metre fall – he'd need his best Pounce Drop and not a little luck. Unless he tried to leap and grab the rear mast instead. That might be safer. But the lamp at its tip was now ten feet away, fifteen… He gathered himself.

'Ben!'

It was a twenty-foot leap to the mast. Now or never.

'Ben, no!' A hand grabbed the hood of his top and yanked him backwards. He tumbled off the parapet to sprawl at Yusuf's feet.

'You prat!' He sprang up, his dignity bruised among other things. 'I could have made that jump…'

Yusuf shook his head. 'You'd have landed in the drink.'

'I could've swum and caught up…'

That was patently ridiculous. The rest of the Cat Kin came running, with a panting Olly last of all.

'What did I miss?' he gasped.

Ben pointed. The lights of the ship were dwindling to stars, too far away to catch before the next bridge. In vain he watched for some signal from Tiffany, while his guts churned with accusations. Why had he hung back like that? Why hadn't he followed? Mentally he replayed the moment of her leap, and realised that a curious sound, almost too fleeting to notice, must have been the *tink* of the cat bell on her wrist as she fell.

3

A SET OF TEETH

Barely a mile from this spot was an empty seat in the Adelphi Theatre, where he ought to have been sitting now, next to Mum and Dad, watching *Falling Star* build to its song-and-dance finale. It was pointless to think about it. Nothing mattered anymore except following that ship. The Thames path was being a pain, cutting behind buildings and generally frustrating his efforts to keep the vessel in sight. Ben pulled out his phone.

'Cecile! How far's it got?'

Traffic noise rattled in his ear. Cecile had stayed on the bridge for a vantage point.

'I… I dunno! I can't see it anymore. I think it turned its lights off.'

'Cat eyes!' he barked. 'Use Mandira!'

'I tried! Dark-seeing don't work so far away. At least, mine don't.'

Ben hung up and tried Tiffany's phone again. As before, it went into voicemail. He dialled Susie. She had climbed the dry-docked replica of the Golden Hind to be their second lookout. The rush of wind down the line sounded like the sea.

'Ahoy there!'

'Susie! Can you spot it?'

'I see no ships.'

He gritted his teeth. 'Just tell me where it is.'

'I told you. It went out of sight. But guess where I am, I'm in the crow's nest! It's amazing, Sir Francis Drake's lookout must have sighted the Spanish Armada from here. Only I don't really know why they call it a crow's nest, all I can see up here is seagull feathers and a very thick coating of pigeon –'

Ben cut her off, sprang up onto the river wall and gazed over the water. He saw only reflected city, with no boat lights at all.

'How can we lose a whole *ship?*'

'Well. It was only small,' offered Daniel.

Ben lost his temper. 'It's not a TV remote! It's forty foot long with two whacking great masts. And Tiffany's on it!'

Panicking was no way to solve this riddle. The ship hadn't sprouted wings, nor was it a submarine. Besides, wouldn't they have overtaken it by now…?

'Yoo-hoo.' Olly, trailing behind, called out. 'Come and see this.'

'What?'

'Think I found it.'

Ben ran back, sure that he hadn't. He found Olly lurking in an alley between waterfront buildings, an old wharf that had been concreted over. Crouched behind a no-cycling bollard, Olly nodded towards the river. There, moored at the bank, was the cargo boat.

'How did you…?' Ben actually rubbed his eyes. Olly shrugged. Yusuf appeared alongside them.

'Olly, my friend, you score ten.' Yusuf clapped them both on the shoulder. 'Me and Ben are this week's fools.'

'No,' Ben protested, 'we did not run past this. It wasn't here…'

'Of course it was, Ben. We missed it in the dark.'

'Dark? *Us?*'

'Never mind. We found it.' Yusuf crept closer on hands and knees and Ben followed. With its padlocked cabin and dark portholes, the ship could have been anchored there for days – only the tick of a cooling motor said otherwise. Ben crawled on board and lifted the tarpaulin. Cat vision revealed an empty hold.

'Tiffany?' Daniel whispered.

'She's not here.' Ben scanned the dock with his feline senses, trying to utter the imitation cat-call that Tiffany used as a signal. His broken voicebox was never up to it.

Daniel sniggered. 'What was that meant to be?'

'Ssh! I'm trying to –' Ben stopped, ears pricking. That faint miaow

17

had come from no cat. He crept back down the wharf towards a brick building several storeys high, with giant arched windows.

'What is this place?' murmured Yusuf.

'Warehouses,' said Olly.

'Not any more.' Daniel was a know-all in such matters. 'They turn these Victorian things into flats. My dad's done a few. These ones aren't finished.' He pointed out a sign for Mitchell & Lovatt, Estate Agents, promising luxury apartments at Clink Wharf by November.

'Flats,' Ben mused. 'Are you sure they don't still do a bit of warehousing on the side?'

A movement in a high window could have been a pigeon, or a waving hand. Again the fake miaow floated down. Ben located the furled ladder of the fire escape, ten feet off the ground, and with a Coilspring he jumped and swung himself up on to it, dangling upside down to answer the puzzled faces below.

'She's in there. You lot wait here.'

Yusuf said, 'What if you need backup?'

'We won't. I'm just fetching her out. This whole thing is stupid.'

'Er…' Olly waggled his phone. 'For your info, I have the police on speed-dial these days.'

Yusuf frowned through his cat paint. 'Maybe we should for once.'

'No.' Ben righted himself before the blood ran to his head. 'What can we report? Tiffany stowed away on a boat and now she's trespassing. Who are the police going to arrest?' He made a cat-ears hand sign. 'Keep alert.'

The fire escape zig-zagged up the building, crossing patterned brickwork that no modern builder would waste on a warehouse. A stealthy climb took him to a top-floor window grimed with plaster dust. He was trying to peer through it when a hand grabbed his shoulder.

'Don't you dare scream.' It was her. She was leaning out of the next window along, a frosted pane. 'In here. Quick.'

It proved a surprisingly tight squeeze, for he had grown and wasn't used to his new, burlier frame. He wriggled through into the kind of bathroom that his mum would swoon over, once the builders had finished tiling the walls and swept up all the mess from the marble floor.

'You took your sweet time.' Tiffany spoke scathingly, but the darkness couldn't hide her smile.

'Nice to see you too.' The bathroom door was shut. Through it came faint sounds. 'What's happening?'

'They're in this flat. The men from the boat.'

'You shouldn't have come in here by yourself.'

'*You* should have followed me.'

'Sorry. It happened so fast. I –' Ben didn't want make excuses. Already she was talking over him.

'They unloaded the cargo. It's in there. We've got 'em.' She unzipped her slim money-belt and drew out her phone. 'The battery's dead. *Horus!*'

Cursing in Ancient Egyptian was another of her worrying new habits.

'I've got mine.' Ben passed it over, expecting her to call their friends. But she switched it to camera mode. He blurted, 'No!'

'We need evidence.' In the screen's glow her face seemed ghostly. 'The scum who do this are never caught. No-one can prove anything. So it'll go on till there's no more tigers left. Or until we stop them.'

'We?'

'Who else is there? Governments, charities, they're all useless. The only thing that ever really scared them was Mrs Powell. And now she's gone.' Tiffany rubbed one eye, with a jingling sound. 'Ben. I don't want to be in this place any more than you do. Some of us would rather be at home, crying into our pillows. But I have to do this. Please help.'

'All right.' He forced a smile. 'It's not like I had any other plans tonight.'

She pressed her ear to the closed bathroom door.

'There's three people out there. No, four.' She fell silent and sniffed. 'All men. Not talking much. Must be waiting. To meet someone.'

'Maybe they're waiting for their buyers,' Ben said, and got her most withering glance: *Brilliant deduction, Sherlock.* Okay, he would shut up. Sometimes he didn't know why he bothered. He had wrecked Mum's special day to be here for Tiffany... but the self-pity would have to wait – what madness was she up to now?

'Don't open the door!'

'Just a crack.' Tiffany squinted round the door jamb, the camera phone ready. They spoke now in what she called kitten-whispers, a trick she had herself devised. In a kitten-whisper, you mouthed each word using no breath at all. It took feline hearing, and a lot of practice, to catch the shape of what was being said – effectively lip-reading without looking, so they could talk and not be overheard.

She sprang away from the door.

'Someone's coming!'

'Lock it.' Ben reached for the bolt. She stopped his hand.

'No! That'll give us away. Hide.'

'*Hide?*' Where, exactly? There was the shower corner, behind a clouded glass partition, but Tiffany reached it first and it wouldn't conceal two. With no other option, Ben slipped behind the opening door.

The man who entered turned on the light and made straight for the toilet. He urinated discreetly, checking over his shoulder, as if he didn't want anyone else knowing he had popped in here. Perhaps for the same reason, he didn't flush, but rinsed his hands under the cold tap and then, for want of a towel, dried them on his long dark coat. Though not a big man, his movements had an athletic grace, and his biceps thickened in his sleeve when he bent one arm to smooth his eyebrows in the mirror. These were black, like his short hair, strikingly black – so black that his pale, shaven cheeks had a blue tinge where stubble waited to grow through.

Now he was leaving. Ben almost relaxed. The man paused in the threshold. Ben, hidden by the door, couldn't see what had caught his attention. Surely not Tiffany – she had placed herself in a Siamese Stone freeze behind the shower screen, and would be less noticeable than the man's reflection. Ben glanced at the floor tiles, grimed with plaster dust, and there in two perfect trails were Tiffany's footprints and his own.

The man stepped back into the bathroom and closed the door. Ben stood against the wall, plain to see. But the man had turned away from him, pondering the footprints, visibly thinking: *Builders? No. These prints look too small. And they're trainers, not boots.* Then Ben's straining senses picked up Tiffany's kitten-whisper, at the outer limits of hearing.

Lion Jaw. Lion Jaw.

No. The girl was insane. Lion Jaw was a Ten Hooks combat move, the instructions for which she had dredged up from another near-invisible pashki website. It was highly effective, potentially deadly and yes, probably his only chance. Ben braced himself to leap. The man turned round and saw him.

Instead of calling out, the man smiled. It was not a nice smile. It suggested that he was happy to find kids here, because now he could have some fun. With a movement as casual as pulling out a pen, he drew from his coat something stubby and black. In the context of the bathroom it looked most like an electric razor. But as he advanced on Ben, pointing the object like a torch, a set of metal fangs at it's tip crackled with a spark.

Ben flung up his arms in a feeble shield, and when he looked again the man was reeling backwards, with someone's leg hooked round his neck in a Lion Jaw stranglehold. He uttered no sound as he folded to the floor, but his unseen attacker grunted with the impact. Ben unfroze himself and ran over. The attacker was Yusuf.

'Oh, no, we don't need backup. Yes, I'll bring her right out,' Yusuf grumbled. 'Big fat zero, Ben.'

He rose stiffly to his feet, rubbing his tailbone, and pulled the window closed again. The man lay out cold upon the tiles, his pale face making his hair seem blacker than ever. Tiffany stepped out from behind the shower screen.

'Well done, Yusuf. Nice Lion Jaw.' She stared at Ben. 'What is wrong with you?'

'What?' he kitten-whispered.

'If you hesitate like that once more, I'm doing it myself next time.'

Ben could hardly believe what he was not-quite-hearing.

'Go easy on him,' mouthed Yusuf. 'He had a stun gun in his face.'

'Is that what this thing is?' Tiffany picked up the weapon, which still looked like an electric razor. She pressed a trigger and a spark blazed between metal prongs.

'That'll be around half a million volts,' said Yusuf.

'Ouch. Fair enough.' She lifted the top off the toilet cistern and plopped the thing inside to drown.

Ben eyed the man on the floor. He was still breathing, in a snuffly way. 'Right. Let's get out of here.'

'Not yet,' said Tiffany. 'It's taken me months to get this far. We don't leave till I have what I came for.'

'They're gonna be in here any second!' Ben kitten-whispered while miming a furious yell. 'We just knocked one of them out!'

'*Yusuf* knocked him out. Anyway, they haven't missed him yet. Is there anything we can tie him up with? Take off his belt.'

Yusuf obeyed. Ben looked on aghast. The belt secured the man's wrists behind his back, while his shoelaces did for his ankles. Tiffany fastened both sets of bonds together.

'Now a gag,' she said. 'Toilet paper?'

'None here. Wait a sec.' Removing his trainer, Yusuf peeled off his sock. 'Stuff this in his mouth.'

'Sick-o!' Tiffany actually chuckled. 'What's that, one of your football socks? I can smell it from here.'

Yusuf teased the man's jaws apart and pushed the sock inside. Ben glared at Tiffany. 'What if he chokes on that?'

'He'll be fine. Yusuf will guard him. Let us know if he wakes up.'

'Okay,' said Yusuf, 'but… where are you two going?'

'Hunting.' Tiffany opened the bathroom door.

Maybe modern architects had strict instructions not to build any hiding places. Aside from the bathroom and bedroom, the whole flat was one open space, about the size of a squash court and nearly as bare. Scattered spotlights bleached a floor of unvarnished wooden boards, feathered with shadows where the men stood. A space destined to be a living room blended into a kitchen and dining area, with pipework exposed among cupboards where a fridge and washing machine might fit. The granite sideboard next to the sink was stacked with black plastic crates.

That was it – the room offered no nooks, crannies, alcoves, nor even any curtains, and not so much as a chair to duck behind. However, there was one thing it did have. This apartment had been built in the topmost section of the converted warehouse, to occupy what was effectively the loft. This meant that its roof was unusually high, and held up by a framework of wooden beams. It was these that made a handy forest among which to creep unseen.

Lying along one beam apiece, Ben and Tiffany peered down on the two men who stood by the crates, and a third who strolled restlessly about.

'There are principles, right?' The pacing man stopped to stare out of the window, at the Thames flowing black and bright as burning oil. He looked to be around forty but was dressed like a twenty-year old, his designer clothes a careful mix of crisp and rumpled. He also wore an odd pair of glasses, round frames that clung to his nose without ear stalks. Ben wondered if his face looked familiar, or if he was imagining it.

'Y'know. Creativity. Originality.' The man in the curious spectacles circled back to face the other two. 'I can't compromise. People believe in what I do. If I –'

'That is why we come to you.' The shorter of the duo was bald, or shaven-headed; a spotlight gleamed off his scalp. What he lacked in height he made up for in bulk. From a distance he might look fat but Ben wasn't fooled, it was mostly muscle, shrink-wrapped inside a smart business suit. His leaner, fair-haired companion stood as silent as a palace guard.

'It is your reputation, your influence, that we value most.' The bald man spoke with the same precise English as the Prime Minister. 'We would never ask you to compromise, Mister Bar–'

'No.' The interruption was quick as a gunslinger's. 'Don't use my name.'

The bald man looked amused. 'These apartments are empty. And my disciples keep secrets. Also my Lord, it goes without saying.' For a puzzling moment he glanced towards a far corner that was, as far as Ben could tell, unoccupied.

'Still. This is London. Home of the gutter press. You never know who might be snooping.' The man in the specs glanced up into the rafters. Ben locked his muscles in mid-movement, but only better-than-perfect eyesight could have seen him. The roof beams and their shadows made a useful camouflaging pattern, broken only by a square black patch that might have been a skylight.

'As you wish.' The bald man nodded graciously. 'But you are free to call me Mister Isidorus.'

Ben was aware of Tiffany climbing onto the beam above him, fiddling with the phone. His was a cheaper model than hers. She kitten-whispered, 'I want video! How do you make it video?'

'Just… select it!' Ben dared not even shrug. Tiffany stabbed buttons in frustration and her cat-bell jingled. Ben winced.

'Take that off. *Take it off!*'

Luckily, Specs had talked over the sound. 'Okey-dokey, Mister Isidorus. Let's see it.'

Tiffany shook her head – taking the collar off her wrist would only make more noise. Seeing her eyes, Ben's anger passed. She was scared, like he was. He sent up a comforting smile.

At a gesture from Mister Isidorus, his taller companion picked up a leather briefcase. In one flourish he snapped open the hasps and raised the lid. Tiffany leaned off her beam for a better view.

The contents of the case gleamed yellow. *Gold* was Ben's first thought, though he would change his mind. Light glinted off points like rows of teeth. Specs lifted intricate objects from beds of moulded foam, fingering a brass disc with teeth around its rim.

'With these you may assemble your scale model,' said Mister Isidorus. 'You will find it a useful cross-reference with the digital plans we supplied.'

Specs looked dubious. He picked two more discs at random and grated their teeth against each other. Cogs, they were brass cogs.

'And it needs to be ready in a month?'

'No delay,' said Mister Isidorus.

'That's tight.' Specs grimaced. 'But I can hire more engineers. Call in some favours at the foundry. I've had some thoughts about how I can develop your concept. Give it a bit more oomph.'

'No.' Mister Isidorus spoke sharply. 'No changes. No *oomph*. Exactly as you find it.'

'You know that's not how I work.'

'It is how you work for us.' Again Mister Isidorus sent his gaze across the room. When Ben had looked that way a moment ago, he was sure he had seen an empty corner. Now a rafter blocked his view.

Was somebody there after all? A fourth man? Specs looked over his shoulder but seemed to see no-one.

'I hear you.' He took off his glasses and gave them a wipe, suddenly ill at ease. 'The customer's always right.'

Mister Isidorus smiled. 'And now the customer will pay.'

Tiffany was filming away, panning Ben's phone between Specs, Mister Isidorus and the silent man with the briefcase. Ben could sense her impatience. Had they come here on a wild goose chase? Then the tall henchman lifted one of the crates from the sideboard and placed it on the floor. Mister Isidorus lifted the lid.

'Everything on your shopping list,' he said. 'With compliments.'

The crate brimmed with stuff that Ben couldn't at first identify, an assortment of colours and textures.

'Hoop-de-doo!' Specs delved with both hands, a child at a lucky dip. He pulled out a polythene bag and rattled the contents. 'Are these full sets, or…?'

'No. Each claw is of unique derivation. From a different animal.'

Specs clapped appreciatively. Tiffany exhaled a long, seething breath.

'Quiet,' Ben mouthed.

'The stock list.' Mister Isidorus received papers from his henchman. 'I summarise. Five kilos of claws. Three hundred sets of Siberian tiger teeth. Sixty kilos of bone from Indochinese tigers. Forty skulls of Sumatran tigers –'

Luckily Specs gasped even louder than Tiffany.

'You're yanking my chain! There's less than four hundred of those left.'

'Considerably fewer, now.' Mister Isidorus smiled serenely. 'And our *pièce de résistance*: eight skulls of the South China tiger.'

Specs frowned. 'That's already extinct.'

'In the wild, I believe.'

'I suppose you can prove…?'

'All in the documentation. You may seek a second opinion from a zoologist,' said Mister Isidorus, 'if you think they will survive the shock.'

Specs rooted through a second crate and pulled out two whole tiger skins.

'Rugs! Lovely. These soak up petrol like nobody's business. They can start the incinerator pile.'

Mister Isidorus blinked. 'Burn them? You will burn these?'

'Oh, yeah.' Specs glanced at the stack of unopened crates. 'You gave me everything I needed back in February. That's all done and dusted. This lot…' He made a sizzling sound and mimed smoke with waggly fingers.

'So, why…?'

'All I wanted was proof of death,' said Specs. 'Thanks ever so much.'

Tiffany made a choking noise and dropped the phone. It fell through the rafters. Ben saw his own right hand whip out and catch it. Tiffany froze in mid-gape. Ben turned the phone off and pocketed it. Specs looked up again, into the roof space, dismissing those faint noises with a headshake. Pigeons. He browsed a couple more crates.

'What does he mean?' Tiffany mouthed. 'Proof of death… I don't understand.'

Hopeless, Ben made the *shush* sign. The grisly stockpile disgusted him too, but more than anything he was confused. Who was buying what, and from whom? Mister Isidorus had called *himself* the customer. Yet he had given Specs that briefcase full of brass cogs and wheels, in addition to the crates of tiger parts, and Specs had given him nothing yet. Now the two were shaking hands.

'My men will help you move the goods to your vehicle,' said Mister Isidorus.

Specs chuckled and waved a travel card. 'Better not. I take the tube. Deliver it all to this address. It can't be traced to me.'

He scribbled on a scrap of paper. Mister Isidorus took the scrap as if it were a slug, anger twitching on his face. But he said, 'As you like. I don't suppose you'd care to help us reload it onto the ship?'

'No can do. Meeting chums for cocktails. I'm late as it is. Nice doing business with you.' Briefcase in hand, Specs did a little twirl out of the front door and was gone. Mister Isidorus and his henchman traded a look.

'I know, Kanif.' Mister Isidorus glared at the pile of crates. 'So long as he delivers. Call Sabu back from the ship to help.'

The taller man produced a phone and pressed a key.

'We should follow that scumbag –' Tiffany broke off as a sound floated through the apartment: a chime of three notes, repeating. Kanif looked bemused.

'Why is that – ?'

Ben worked out what the noise must be. It was a ringtone, and it was coming from the bathroom.

Mister Isidorus bellowed, 'Sabu!'

'Get out!' Ben hissed. The henchman ran to the bathroom and burst out again.

'Sabu is in there! Tied up. Someone got in. I saw them jump out of the window –'

'Quiet!' roared Mister Isidorus. 'Others are watching. My Lord feels them. Kanif, secure the windows. Lock the door. My Lord will find them.'

What did he mean? *Who* would find them? There was no-one else here.

A figure stepped from the corner of the room, the corner he had thought was empty. It was so tall that Ben could have reached down and touched its head – not that he wanted to, for this head was not human. A black snout curved down in a dragonish sneer, and from its crown rose twin black horns or ears. Glassy eyes shone black from a face like leather, with matted black hair tumbling behind.

A man. Ben tried to get ahead of his crazy thoughts. *Just a man in a mask.* Certainly the figure walked upright, like a man, and had a man's arms, muscular and ringed with bronze bands. Its sleeveless tunic shimmered like copper chain mail, above a white robe or kilt that bared sinewy calves and huge feet. In its right fist the figure bore a black staff, with a forked tip and a carved head that was a miniature of its own.

Tiffany gasped. 'Where did he come from?'

The apparition pointed up with its free hand.

'Above us!' Mister Isidorus flicked his wrist and a crescent-shape glinted between his thumb and finger. Some sort of knife? The henchman Kanif produced a stubby thing, another of those electric stun guns. The beast-headed figure drew itself up till its ears brushed the lowest rafters, and seemed to take aim with its staff.

'Tiffany!' Ben cried. She had gone like stone, staring down the length of the staff into the monster's black eyes. He sprang to an adjacent joist and seized her arm. 'Tiffany, move!'

'I can't…' Her speech was slurred. To Ben's horror, she began to topple sideways from her perch. He shook her and she jerked as if waking from a nightmare.

'Let's go!' he snapped. But there seemed to be nowhere they could go. In desperation he looked up. He had seen something earlier, out of the corner of his eye. A square of darkness in the sloping roof. A skylight.

'There!'

He leaped and Tiffany followed, as something whizzed between them. The bronze blade bounced off a rafter, knocking out splinters. Ben clambered to the highest beam, reached for the skylight and found no handle. It wasn't the kind that opened. It was simply a light well of reinforced glass, fixed in a square wooden frame. A dead end. He felt a thud through his feet as another blade lodged in the beam on which he balanced.

'Your phone!' Tiffany cried. 'Call the others. The police.'

Mister Isidorus shouted, 'Torch the apartment. They can burn with the cargo.'

Any help would come too late. Ben gathered himself. The golden catra blazed in the darkness of his mind, Parda for strength, every ounce he had. This would work first time, or not at all. In one explosive movement he flipped into a handstand, planting both hands squarely on the beam, and rammed upwards with both feet. With the force that could propel him over cars and between treetops, the soles of his trainers hit the skylight.

The whole cage of oaks beams juddered – his *bones* juddered – it felt as if he had broken his wrists. But the pane of wired glass tore out of its frame, flipped, and fell like a dropped plate. Down it clattered through the beams, breaking to scatter bits of itself onto the men below. Mister Isidorus had to dive out of its way and Kanif shielded his face. Ben did not see their monstrous accomplice.

Tiffany was out first. He scrambled up into the night air and ran after her across the rooftops, not slowing till they were hidden beneath the arches of the next railway bridge.

'You all right?' gasped Ben.

'Yeah. You?'

'Are you sure? You seemed a bit out of it, in there. For a sec.'

'What do you expect?' Tiffany scowled. 'It's… *evil*. What they're doing. All those tigers killed. All those bones.'

'Yeah. Sorry.' He had meant the moment when she locked eyes with the masked figure, and seemed to fall into a trance. Before he could ask her about that, she touched his shoulder.

'No. I'm sorry. That was brilliant.'

'Cheers. Any time.'

Her bell jingled as she mopped hair out of her eyes. A train trundled overhead.

'Tiffany?' said Ben, when it had passed.

'Mm?'
'Can we go home now?'

4
THERAPY

Someone had tried hard to make this place look nothing like a psychiatrist's office. It looked like a cosy living room. Perhaps it really was one – Tiffany couldn't be sure. She sat on a lilac sofa and was even allowed to put her sock feet on it. Purple orchids in china pots stood beside her glass of milk on the table, and atop the bookcase grew an ash tree that had shrunk in the wash – a miniature bonsai. Inspecting the bookcase during last week's 'visit', she had found mostly romance novels, travelogues and books about art, and not one on psychotherapy for mad children.

The blue armchair was where her counsellor always sat, at an angle so they weren't too much like chess players. The counsellor nibbled her usual custard cream biscuit.

'It's got so chilly lately. Do you find it chilly in here?'

What a good job it must be, to get two hundred pounds an hour for saying things like that. Mum and Dad had refused to tell her how much all this cost, as if Tiffany wasn't capable of googling "*Ellen Thornwill*"+ *counselling*. Indeed, her parents had approached the whole subject on tiptoe. It wasn't that their perfect daughter was broken and needed repairs. They weren't in despair over her falling grades, her truancy, her crying jags, her rages. No, Mum had put it most delicately: 'Would it help to talk about things with someone who isn't either of us?'

A month on, the answer appeared to be: not really.

Mrs Thornwill, or Ellen as she wanted to be called, was an aunt-ish sort of lady. She took obvious pride in her appearance without trying to look younger than her age. Her long, straight hair would be greying by now – in response, she had dyed the whole lot silver. Her hands were wrinkling, so she drew attention to them with such an armoury of rings that Tiffany wondered how she could bend her fingers. Standing up she was startlingly tall, and when walking she glided sedately, like a ship's mast.

Tiffany was surprised by what they didn't discuss. She knew that Mum and Dad blamed everything on her supposed abduction at thirteen, and that her behaviour now was the result, but so far the counsellor had barely raised the topic. All they seemed to do for their weekly hour was chat. Or rather, Mrs Thornwill chatted, and Tiffany mumbled.

'I see you like my bonsai.'

She had only been using the little tree as something to stare at.

'Hell to care for, to be honest,' said the counsellor. 'But it was a gift from my boyfriend. Am I allowed to say boyfriend at my age? Oh good. You have one, I bet.'

Clearly she didn't mean a bonsai tree.

'I have friends who are boys,' said Tiffany.

'Lucky you. I was at an all-girl's school. Scarred me for life! Is your school nice?'

'Suppose.'

'You know, don't you,' the counsellor slowed down, leaning back in her armchair, 'what your parents are most worried about.'

Me failing my exams, she thought. 'No. What?'

The counsellor smiled. 'Only what terrifies all good parents. The thought that their child might be taking drugs.'

Tiffany spurted laughter. 'Drugs!'

'No,' said the counsellor. 'I didn't think so. Forgive me for asking.'

Only now did Tiffany notice that any question had been asked. Mrs Thornwill brushed biscuit crumbs from her skirt. Her smile stayed warm, but Tiffany could see creases of desperation. She was beginning to look stumped. After four weeks and wads of Peter and Cathy Maine's cash, they were still stuck on square one.

'Fine. You're not on drugs. Anyone can see that.' The counsellor paused. 'And I see something else, too. If only I had a better way to put this. Your heart's broken, isn't it?'

It was the last thing Tiffany had expected. Her silence ballooned inside her, until she had to say it or burst.

'It's just that –'

'Yes?'

'It's just that everyone I care about always dies!'

'Who died?' asked the counsellor, softly.

Tiffany checked herself. The people she meant were Rufus and Mrs Powell. But the tale of Mrs Powell was too secret. And Rufus, well… Rufus was a cat. Only a cat. She groped for something else.

'Well,' she mumbled. 'There's my little brother.'

'Your brother? Stuart?' The counsellor blinked. 'He's not… He hasn't died?'

'No, no.' She regretted bringing this up. 'But… he will. I know he will. He's got…'

'Duchenne muscular dystrophy. Your mother told me.'

'So he'll die young. He'll die long before I do. Maybe even in his teens.'

'Or much later. I'm not any kind of doctor, but I made a point of looking this up. The outlook for children like him is much better these days. People with his condition are living into their forties. And it's all downhill from then on, whoever you are.' The counsellor pulled a wry face. 'The chances are, Tiffany, that Stuart will have many more years of life with you. What neither of you must do is waste those years in worrying. Make them happy years. Don't mourn for things you still have.'

Tiffany nodded, strangled by the lump in her throat. Sorrow conquered her embarrassment and it came out with a sob.

'And… my cat.'

She wept freely. The counsellor passed tissues but said nothing, not even to ask about the bell collar, jingling on Tiffany's wrist. At last, feeling like a terrible ninny, she was sniffing herself together when the doorbell rang. Dad was here to pick her up.

The counsellor rose from her chair. 'I'll tell him to wait a mo.' She went to use the hall speakerphone. On her return she nudged the plate of biscuits and Tiffany, suddenly ravenous, took two.

'It can be even harder with pets.' The counsellor revolved a ring on her thumb. 'We think we're not *allowed* to feel so bad. It's only a rabbit. It's only a cat. So we try and bear it alone. Put on a brave face. And that only makes it worse.'

'Yes.' Tiffany sat up. 'That's it, totally. Do you love cats too?'

'And worst of all,' said the counsellor, 'we can think it was our fault. That we should have looked after them better. We were their owners. They trusted us. We let them down.'

Tiffany hung her head.

'I wish...' She swallowed. 'That morning... Rufus went outside because of me. He wanted to get on my lap and I pushed him off. He wouldn't've got run over if I'd let him stay. And that also means the last thing I did, the last time he ever saw me, I was being horrible. He died thinking that I...'

'I don't suppose a cat thinks in quite that way,' said the counsellor. 'He would have forgotten why he came outside.'

'But he was outside because of me. He was there when the car came.'

'He had a cat flap?'

'Yes.'

The counsellor faced her squarely. 'Tiffany. Recently I read something. If you have a dog, and it digs up your neighbour's garden, then they can prosecute you. But if your cat does it, they can't.'

'Why?'

'Because you own a dog. You're responsible for it, by law. But the law knows that you can't control a cat. So although domestic cats are classified as tame, they're considered wild animals too. So you can't be held accountable for what your cat does.'

Tiffany lifted her head.

'Is that true?'

'As far as I know,' said Mrs Thornwill.

Tiffany felt a terrible weight lifting off her. She stroked a finger round her bloodstained leather bracelet. Of course, she'd always known it. You could put a collar and a bell on a cat, but that didn't make them yours. They'd still go off and do their own thing, getting fleas, getting abscesses, getting killed. Maybe she could have kept Rufus as an indoor cat, only letting him roam to the length of a tether. If he hadn't been given the run of the streets, Rufus would be alive today. But would he have been *as* alive?

'Actually,' said Tiffany, 'there's something else too.'

Her counsellor nodded. 'I noticed you did say *everyone*.'

'Not quite everyone.' Tiffany found a smile. 'But I had… a sort of friend. A woman. Quite an old one.'

'And she died? I see. Was she a relative?'

'No,' said Tiffany. 'She –'

The doorbell cut her off.

'Your Dad again. I recognise the impatient chime.' Mrs Thornwill looked genuinely sorry. 'You'd better hop to it. I have a feeling he's double-parked.'

Tiffany dawdled putting on her coat. In the doorway she turned round to look up at the much taller woman.

'Thank you, Mrs Thornwill.'

'Ellen!' her counsellor insisted. 'Enjoy your evening, Tiffany. See you next week.'

At school she sat up straighter in class, made proper notes and did her best to follow what the teachers said. During Maths, Ms Braby noticed her better mood and gave her encouraging looks.

She even forgave Dad for interrupting her session with Ellen. On reflection, it was lucky that he had. She had come within a whisker of talking about Mrs Powell, which of course she could not do, not even to a counsellor with a duty of confidentiality. Mrs Powell was one sorrow she really would have to bear alone.

Against all hope she had tracked down her pashki teacher, and Tiffany had known then that as well as a guide and mentor she had found a dear friend. With the other Cat Kin they had fought side by side, and when the polecats' leader, Martin Fisher, had fallen to his death from the tower block, Tiffany had dared to think that the horror was over. But her new-found joy had been shattered at once, as Felicity Powell, betrayed by the man who had once been her best friend, was buried with him in the ruins of the tower.

It might have been a comfort to leave flowers on her grave, but there was no grave she could visit. She learned that the police, upon digging both bodies out of the rubble, had assumed them to be a couple of homeless people, doomed by sheltering in the wrong building. A detective might have traced their anonymous resting places, but she couldn't. Besides, she shuddered at the thought of getting it wrong, and shedding tears on the headstone of Geoff White instead.

In the end, she had ventured back to Mrs Powell's old flat, abandoned since their dealings with John Stanford and Dr Cobb. Mrs Powell had always taped a spare front door key inside the cat flap. Tiffany had sat for a long time in the empty pashki studio, grieving where no-one could see her. Then, because it felt right, she'd tidied up a bit, vacuuming the carpets, clearing the cupboards and fridge of rotten foods, lighting a scented candle and watching it till it burned out. For safety's sake, she also unplugged every electrical appliance. Before she left, Tiffany found in the bedroom something to take and keep: a framed photo of Jim, Mrs Powell's beautiful silver cat. She often wondered what had become of him.

To everyone who helped to support this mission, thank-you. The Grey

Cat wishes me to tell you how grateful she is for so much mostly accurate information – Tiffany stopped typing to re-read the words onscreen.

'Get rid of that *mostly*,' Stuart suggested. She deleted it and continued.

The Grey Cat reported back to me that the raid was successful. There were loads of tiger bones and

'Loads?' Stuart rolled his eyes. 'You say *a significant haul*. The Grey Cat discovered a significant haul of illegal tiger parts.'

of illegal tiger prats, Tiffany typed, and corrected the mistake. 'Sort of right the first time.'

The cargo was shipped upriver and received by a single buyer, identity unknown. However, the Grey Cat shot video footage that is sure to put both the smugglers and the buyer in jail.

'*Convict them* sounds better,' said Stuart.

'Stop telling me what to put. I'm the one they tried to eviscerate.'

'What's that mean?'

'Gob shut or I'll show you.'

She typed: *I will post the pictures and clips here as soon as she gives them to me. Needless to say, there is still much to do. As long as these monsters remain at large, no rare animal is safe. If you have information that the Grey Cat can use, pass it on to her through me. Thanks again, everyone. Keep up the fight. – Tabby.*

She clicked the Post button. Her message appeared on the Vanished Harmony forum alongside her tabby cat avatar. Stuart pivoted his wheelchair to see the screen better.

'Why did you say you don't have the video clips yet?' he asked.

'Because…' She hesitated. 'The quality's rubbish. I had to film through the rafters. You can't see or hear very well. I don't think the police could use it.'

'Yes they could. It's brilliant. You've got nerves like titanium! I love the sea-sicky bit at the end where you drop the phone and Ben has to grab it.'

'Ssh. Not so loud.' She stiffened, tracking footsteps outside her bedroom door. Mum was watering the houseplants.

'You were saying, Alfred?'

Stuart beamed. He loved it when she called him Alfred – after Batman's butler. Opening the video file he skimmed through some highlights.

'They could get clear pictures of those men, easily,' he said. 'Except the one in the black mask. He made me choke on my apple when I saw him. Why is he wearing that thing?'

'Dunno. Disguise?'

'So wrong. You wear a false beard for that. Not a… wolf-aardvark carnival head. He sticks out a mile.'

Tiffany shifted uncomfortably. Yes, the masked man was impossible to miss, in the video clip. He appeared in snatches when the phone panned around, a shadowy figure standing motionless in the far corner. Yet both she and Ben had failed to see him at the time, until he stepped forward.

'I don't want to get distracted by him,' she said, truthfully.

'Distracted? But he's obviously the boss.'

'I said leave it.' Sudden fright made her snap. Seeing the dark shape freeze-framed on her laptop, she remembered staring down into its eyes, paralysed, as if it had reached up, grasped the cable of her brain, and *unplugged* her…

'Fine. Your funeral,' said Stuart. 'The other guys, then. You've got their faces. And some names.'

'Uh?'

'Names. You know. Mister Isidorus, Kanif, Sabu.'

'Oh…' Tiffany mopped her neck with a screen wipe she had thought was a tissue. The chill relaxed its grip on her. 'I think those names are fake. They looked more like Mikes and Nigels to me.'

'What about the man in the glasses? We've got his name.'

'We have?'

'Listen.' Stuart skipped the video back and clicked Play. Specs was interrupting the burly bald man.

We would never ask you to compromise, Mr Bar – No. Don't use my name.

'Mr Bar?' said Tiffany.

'It's Bar something, obviously,' said Stuart. 'Barrett. Barrow. Barrington-Stoke. Come on, it's better than nothing! And I'll tell you what else. I think he's a celebrity.'

'A *celebrity*? You pulled that idea out of where?'

Stuart did one of his effortful shrugs. 'It's a hunch. That thing about his name. He says stuff about the gutter press too. That means the newspapers.'

'I'm actually not dumb.' Exhausted, though. Tiffany shut her eyes. 'Still doesn't mean he's famous.'

'Post it on the forum,' Stuart insisted. 'Someone'll recognise him.'

'I might. Soon.'

'You know it can't be traced back to you. Is that what you're worried about?'

'No. Maybe.' He could read her too well. 'Yes.'

'Well, don't. It's impossible. Vanished Harmony is a darknet forum. All encrypted, no cookies. There's no way to see a member's real identity. You could be absolutely anyone.'

Tiffany considered her little brother. 'How do you know stuff like this?'

'I've always been the cleverest. And I don't get out much.'

Both were probably true. Seeing how he strained towards the screen, Tiffany felt guilty. She let him have her chair, giving him a cushion for extra support.

'Which reminds me,' he added. 'Why d'you tell them all that bobbins about the Grey Cat? You should take the credit yourself.'

'No. It's easier this way,' said Tiffany. 'When I joined, no-one knew who I was. But they'd heard of the Grey Cat. Mrs Powell was one of their senior moderators. The members of Vanished Harmony used to supply her with information. They're all conservationists and eco-warriors.'

'You mean they hug trees and sail in front of whaling ships?'

'Basically.' Tiffany clicked into her friends list. 'And some of them spy on poachers and smuggling rings. They can get in real danger, but they'll do anything to stop the trade.'

'And they pass the info to you, because they think you'll tell Mrs Powell?'

'Yes.' She smiled, sad. 'They don't know there isn't any Grey Cat anymore. Just me. And whichever of my friends aren't busy that evening.'

Stuart drew himself up in the chair, which for him was quite a feat, and gave her a look.

'What?' she asked.

'Ben was there for your raid,' he said. 'Why do you talk about him like that?'

'I didn't mean only him.' Yes she did. 'Look, he keeps missing pashki classes. And he doesn't seem to care about tigers going extinct.'

'I don't believe that. Anyway, he still helps.'

'Only after I've yelled at him. I don't know… he's not the same these days. It's all Mum-this and Dad-that, like he's six or something. I've fallen way down his list of priorities.'

'He'd do anything for you.'

'Pardon?' She frowned, then opted to laugh. Stuart knew nothing about it, he was only saying these things to cheer her up. But he meant well, of course he did.

She felt a fresh pang of tenderness for her brother, like a nudge on a knife that was already in her heart. It was true, what she had told her counsellor – the prospect of Stuart dying young was her greatest fear of all. That would be far, far worse than losing Rufus, worse than losing Mrs Powell. If she could have cut years off her own life and pasted them onto his, she would have reached for her mouse and done it, right now. But that piece of software didn't exist.

'You're staring at me. Stop it.' Stuart logged her out of Vanished Harmony and went browsing for games.

'Sorry.' An idea was stirring. She'd had ones like it before, but had always backed away from them.

'Your computer is as slow as a python poo,' Stuart grumbled. 'It's 'cos you save all your junk onto your desktop. I'm going to have to tidy this thing up for you.'

'Stuart.' She swivelled his chair towards herself. 'Look at me.'

'Okay. Looking. It's unpleasant, but I'm looking.'

'I'll help you down. Let's sit you on the floor.'

Stuart brushed her away – he was still strong enough to get off a chair, thank you very much.

'There we go. No, not like that. Kneel instead.' Tiffany helped to position his limbs. 'Kneel. Sit on your heels. Hands on the floor in front of you. Don't slouch. Good. From now on, this is what *sit* means.'

'What are we doing?' His eyes twinkled, guessing.

'Ssh. Concentrate. Balance.' She sat likewise, facing him. Where to begin? 'Tip your head down, like this. Bring your neck and shoulders up. Try to arch your spine.'

'It's hard for me…'

'I know. Try. Think of a cat. How a cat wakes up, and gets to its feet, and stretches… arching its back up. See it in your mind.'

'Hey!' Stuart grinned. 'That felt weird for a second. I didn't know my back could make that shape.'

'It didn't hurt?'

'No. The opposite. All tingly.'

'That's good.' Tiffany's heart beat faster. 'Now. Bring both hands up. Reach above your head. Imagine there's a tree trunk there, and you're a cat, and you're reaching up to scratch it.'

'I can't stretch well –'

'You're not Stuart. You're a cat. Copy.'

He didn't get very high, but it must have been higher than he expected, for he burst out laughing. 'That's cool!'

'You like it?'

'Yeah. Beats my physiotherapy any day.'

'Good. A couple more stretches. Then I'll show you the best way to rest…'

Tiffany knew it was a long shot. Perhaps a desperate one. And who could say if it would do any good? All that spurred her on was a memory of herself a few years ago, a weak and awkward girl, sitting out PE lessons on the sicky bench. Pashki had done so much for her. Was she foolish to hope for something more? Well then, she would be a fool.

5

GYM KITS

Standing guard at the gymnasium door, Daniel gave the all-clear signal. Ben let go of the top rung of the wall bars and let himself fall backwards, arms spread wide like a high diver, or a suicide. At first he simply fell. Then he flung his left arm up towards the ceiling and across his body, twisting his top half round to face the rapidly approaching floor, and did the same with his left leg, kicking it over the other to flip the rest of his body. In the last fraction of a second, before his nose could smack a dent in the floorboards, he whipped both feet under him and landed in a deep squat, with a thump that made the nearest windows rattle.

'Ow.' He stood, wincing, and hobbled to the bench in the corner. 'Not my best.'

'Yes, that was utter failure. *Nul points.*' Olly oozed sarcasm. Nearly everyone else had to practise their Falling Twist off a gym horse with crash mats around it. Only Tiffany could do it the way Ben did. She called across the gym.

'Rest in the Sitting Cat pose if you need a time-out. Don't plonk down on that bench.'

'Sorry. Didn't see the sign.' There wasn't a sign, of course.

'We wouldn't have seats in a real pashki studio. Or soft mats. Or any of this apparatus at all –' Tiffany broke off, as if even she was finding her annoying.

Ben bit his tongue and sat the way she wanted, his shin bones protesting like split planks. This place was no good, this place was *too* good – she had stopped making sense long ago.

As the Cat Kin's new club secretary, he'd had the job of finding them a better practice room than the old church hall. He had tramped all over Hackney before thinking of his own school gym. Mr Aguda, the head teacher, was very big on clubs run by pupils, and didn't care what went on in them so long as they were free of knives, drugs and permanent marker pens.

So on Fridays after classes, Ben would meet Daniel and Cecile in the gym, eat a packed tea and relax for half an hour, while the others made their way over from Tiffany's school, to be let in through the fire exit. Together they could enjoy a full hour of pashki with the use of mats, wall bars, ropes... it seemed perfect. But at first Tiffany had wrinkled her nose. He'd forgotten that she hated school sports. 'Are you mad?' she said. 'We can't meet here. It's got to be private!' And so it would be. Officially, the head of PE was meant to supervise their club, but Ben knew Mr Harman was a lazy skiver and they'd quickly reached an unspoken agreement: Harman wouldn't show up, and Ben wouldn't tell. It still didn't make Tiffany happy, but by then Ben had started to wonder if anything would.

Tiffany nailed her own Falling Twist, tumbling from ceiling height to touch down no louder than a basketball. She straightened, businesslike.

'Let's do a full sequence. The Bag, okay?'

Ben rose with a hasty calf stretch and found a space. A good pashki sequence could remind him why he loved doing this. Ancient sequences including the Moon Salutation and Flickers on Water, though Tiffany was fond of two that Mrs Powell herself had invented: Among The Pigeons, and Out Of The Bag.

Out Of The Bag began with the exercise they had been practising, the Falling Twist, but in slow motion and at ground level. Beginning in the Sun Arch, a stretch like a gymnastic bridge, they turned themselves over a limb at a time till they were face down on all fours, and then continued to finish back in the Sun Arch. It was a move that demanded absolute balance, and as he completed his twist Ben felt the refreshing blue wave wash through his mind.

Ptep is my head, the balancing blue sky.

For this was more than physical exercise. A pashki sequence also conditioned the Mau body, the feline inner self that Mrs Powell had taught them to awaken. Out Of The Bag was a sequence for stimulating all the catras in order. Falling Twist awoke Ptep, the head catra, which governed the cat's sense of equilibrium.

From his corner space, Olly hissed, 'Remind me what comes next.'

'Chasing The Bird,' said Daniel.

The twist flowed into something like a slow cartwheel, a handstand that became a sideways topple, then a stretch up with both hands to grasp at an invisible feather. Ben rolled into the second tumble, all his senses straining towards that imaginary bird, that momentary flash of green plumage.

Mandira is my green all-sensing eye.

From Chasing The Bird they slunk low into Shadowcatch, a forward creep as subtle as the movement of a clock's hands. A great move, this one, for sending calf muscles into spasm. As Ben's mind wrestled with the paradox of moving-yet-not-moving, he felt the simmering of copper energy, the catra humming in his throat zone.

Kelotaukhon, copper maw, my mystery.

Now he didn't need to think about what he was doing. He could have stepped aside to watch his body continue the sequence, even more graceful alone.

'Hunter Stretch,' Tiffany called out. 'Keep it going. Great so far.'

The Hunter worked the back, chest and legs while energising Parda, the golden catra and the core of strength. That stretch blended into the standard Arch On Guard, a shape that, like a lens, focused energy into the Oshtis catra in the belly. A Tailspin finished things off with a flourish, awakening Ailur at the base of the spine, and the whole sequence started over. Once more the six movements flowed together, and again, moving the Cat Kin onwards by a few strides each time, so that the seven of them slowly circled the gym. Then Yusuf and Susie strayed too close to each other, collided, and collapsed.

'Dizzy break!' cried Susie. Yusuf couldn't sit up for laughing. Tiffany stood, hands on hips, and gave them The Look.

'Trust the lovebirds to let the side down.' But she herself was grinning. 'That was awesome, everyone. Back to our best. Am I a brilliant teacher, or what?'

'A living legend!' said Cecile. She dabbed her face with a towel, trying not to smudge her tortoiseshell face-print. Olly pretended he was dying. Ben swigged from his water bottle and offered it to Tiffany.

'Yeah,' he said. 'Not too bad.'

'Really?'

'Of course really. She'd –' Ben worried about saying it, then did anyway. 'She'd be proud of you.'

'Thanks.' She took another gulp before addressing the group. 'Well done, you lot. We'll keep on like this, training and pushing ourselves, till we're better than we've ever been. Now we've got something to work towards.'

Daniel frowned. 'What something?'

'Don't tell us there are National Pashki Championships,' said Susie.

'You know what I mean,' said Tiffany. 'Our mission! The people who are killing the tigers. They're still out there.'

The warmth leaked out of the room.

'Thought we already dealt with that,' said Yusuf. 'Send your video clip to the cops.'

'Why is it a good idea when *you* say it?' asked Olly.

'It's not enough!' said Tiffany. 'A few blurry faces on Ben's rubbish phone won't catch anyone. I told you, that raid was only the beginning.'

'When did you tell us?' Susie inquired.

'And Mrs Powell said it herself, before me! This is a war. She had to wage a private war against people like this. That's why she needed us.'

Susie's smile was cold. 'I don't recall signing up for that.'

'She can't do it anymore!' Tiffany's voice cracked. 'Because – well, obviously, she can't. So I have to.' *And you lot do too.* Her unspoken words filled the silence. *Or else.*

Ben rubbed his aching legs. It was always like this, lately. Always when things were going so well.

'You're right,' he said.

Tiffany looked at him. 'Yeah?'

'My phone is rubbish.' He shrugged. 'I don't mind. Doesn't matter if it gets broken. Which it will, one of these days.'

She stared at him blankly.

'Look… Tiffany.' He felt bad saying this in front of the others. 'None of us have to do anything. That includes you. I don't know what Mrs Powell said to you, but…' he struggled to hold her gaze, 'I bet she wouldn't have asked you to take on those men at Clink Wharf. Not yet, anyway.'

'Because of course you knew her so much better than I did.'

'You think she'd have wanted us in there?' said Ben. 'With flying daggers and electric shocks? Be honest. Would Mrs Powell have sent you up against Monster Head?'

She laughed scornfully. 'It was a mask! We wear masks. Well, face paint. And as for the polecats… bandit masks all round!'

'I think that's his point,' said Yusuf.

'I don't know what tiger bone smugglers are meant to look like,' said Ben. 'But if Mister Isidorus and his mates are the normal kind, then I'm a…'

'Beagle,' said Olly, helpfully.

'All the more reason,' said Tiffany. 'Who's going to stop them if we won't?'

'Don't forget the ship.' The low voice was Cecile's. Tiffany looked irritated.

'Ship?'

'You know. Their cargo boat. It disappeared, didn't it?' Cecile narrowed her eyes. 'I was watching it on the water. Then I blinked and it wasn't there. I know you reckon it turned its lights off. But I'd've seen that, I'm sure I would've. It was… gone.'

Yusuf nodded. 'And we ran right past it.'

Tiffany chewed her lip. Then she said, 'So we train harder. Your dark-seeing needs sharpening. It let you down when it mattered most.'

Voices rose in protest. Ben cut them off.

'It might have been something else,' he said. 'You know what I'm talking about, Tiffany. The guy in the mask. He pulled the same trick. We didn't see him or hear him. Not till he moved. And we know if a mouse runs past! My phone's camera saw him but we didn't. Why not?'

She glanced away – she would bite that lip of hers raw if she wasn't careful. But when she turned back, her face was set.

'Maybe because there were joists in the way. Or because I had bigger things on my mind. People can't turn invisible. And nor can boats.' She glared at Cecile.

Ben ran his fingers inside the neck of his pashki kit, the sweat now horrid-smelling even to him. It was past time to get changed, to go home. He caught himself wondering if he might be ill for the next class. And how many others might come down with the same bug.

'We can.' Cecile spoke up, not cowed. 'We can turn invisible. Sort of. We can freeze, yeah? And move so hardly anyone sees us. What if this is something like that?'

Tiffany raised an eyebrow. 'A boat that does pashki?'

'She said something *like* that,' retorted Daniel.

'Look,' Ben sighed, 'please –'

'Yes?'

'Be careful. That's all.'

Tiffany gave him the eyes he was learning to recognise: *you have let me down again.*

'Careful. Oh yes. We must be careful, mustn't we? Always so careful.' Pivoting, she flicked the brake off the gym horse with one foot and dealt it a lashing roundhouse kick with the other. The horse scooted on its wheels across the polished floor and crashed into the wall. Tiffany spun back to face them, two spots of pink showing beneath her face print.

'Any scaredy-cat can think up reasons not to do anything,' she said. 'But I know this. Mrs Powell would have done it.'

Tiffany stalked back to her kit bag, almost managing to hide the fact that she was limping.

The new flat that he was glad to call home lay a short bus ride from the school. Yusuf was heading the same way, to join his dad for Friday evening prayers at the mosque. Early fireworks bloomed in the brown dark of the sky, giving them something nice to talk about as their bus crawled the congested roads towards Highbury. Ben rubbed at the traces of face-print that had seeped into his hair line, as he worked up his nerve to change the subject.

'Do your parents mind?' he asked. 'About you and Susie?'

Yusuf glanced at him, surprised and yet not.

'Nah. Why should they mind?'

'Well –' Ben felt awkward.

'Susie's not a Muslim, no. And last time I looked, we weren't getting married.' Yusuf laughed, easily. 'But, now that I mention it... even if we did, *maybe*, some day, years and years from now... I think my parents would be cool about it. For sure. It was like that for them too, sort of. You know, my dad's Iraqi but my mum's from New Jersey. After they met she converted –'

Ben nodded through the story, a version of which he had heard before. 'You've been going out with Susie, what, two years?'

'Only two? Feels longer.' Yusuf furrowed his brow in mock-horror.

'Still. You must be getting something right.'

'I guess.'

'I mean you... you know what you're doing.'

'Ben?' Yusuf's eyes were on him, searching, amused. 'You have girl problems!'

That had been easier than expected. So, only face-burning shame.

'Dunno really.'

'That sounds about right. Take it from me, my friend. When the topic is girls, Dunno is as good as it gets.'

Traffic halted their bus for the forty-eighth time. The bright sign of a kebab shop taunted Ben through the window. He missed his hot dinner on pashki days.

'Okay. Tell me the worst,' said Yusuf. 'Doctor Mansour, relationship counsellor, is sworn to secrecy.'

There was almost nothing to tell. That was the problem. Mumbling, Ben tried to get across the basic information that he liked Tiffany, liked her a lot, loved being friends with her… but how did you get beyond that? And should he even try? As feared, Yusuf burst out laughing.

'Never mind,' Ben snapped.

'Sorry. I'm not laughing at you.' Yusuf managed a straight face. 'I just always thought Tiffany was your girlfriend already. You telling me she isn't yet?'

That made Ben even more depressed.

'You're coming to *me* for advice?' Yusuf spread his empty hands. 'You've saved her life at least twice. And she's done it for you. Kissing should be a doddle after that.'

A doddle. It sounded funny when Yusuf said it, in the trace American accent he had never quite lost.

'Yeah,' said Ben. 'I keep missing my chance.'

'Next time, don't wait for the smoke to clear.' Yusuf looked up sharply. 'Uh-oh, there goes the minaret! Here's my stop.' He dinged the bell and the bus jerked to a halt. 'See you next week.'

'Wait.' Ben got up too and followed him out. He could walk home from here. Yusuf headed back up St Thomas Road and Ben tagged along, hoping the conversation wasn't over. It was the first time he'd shared this with anyone.

The mosque appeared sooner than he expected, nestling amid the terrace of houses, conspicuous only by its slender round tower. An old man passed with a younger companion and Yusuf followed them up the steps to the entrance. Ben felt abandoned. Then Yusuf turned and called down.

'Come in while I wash.' Anticipating Ben's reluctance, he added, 'No-one'll mind. Talk soft. And leave those there.' He indicated Ben's trainers, slipping off his own with a habitual flick of his heel. Shoes of every kind crowded the lobby, upon a magic carpet of cloths dyed in kaleidoscope colours. Ben pushed his trainers next to a pair of sandals, where he could easily snatch them up and run if necessary.

'Relax,' said Yusuf. 'You're allowed in.'

'Okay. I just feel a bit –'

Like a pork pie at a Jewish wedding, he almost said. But the feeling didn't last beyond the first few seconds. The mosque's entrance hall had a high, domed ceiling, as intricately patterned as the shoe mats, holding the silence like a cup. The noisy London street outside faded almost from memory, and a calm came over him. He struggled to recall why he'd followed Yusuf in here, so easy was it to stand and be still.

Beneath the gently glowing dome stood a hexagonal stone fountain, where men were lining up to splash water over their hands, arms, feet and faces. One small, white-haired gentleman appeared to be doing an unnecessarily thorough job of it, to judge by the shuffling, sighing queue behind him. Ben noticed a purple bruise in the centre of the man's forehead. Yusuf tapped his own brow and smiled.

'Praying too hard,' he murmured. 'So what's the plan? Will you ask her out on a date?'

'Might do.' Ben dreaded the prospect. He could imagine leaping Tower Bridge with Tiffany, but not sitting beside her in the cinema. 'What do I say? Anything I say… it'll be obvious. It'll be obvious what

I really mean.'

'Well, I'm not Casanova –' Yusuf broke off as the old man with the bruise passed close and gave them a warning glare. 'I'm no expert, but I don't think there's any trick to it. Forget about chat-up lines and clever stuff. If a girl likes you, she likes you. There's not a lot you can do about it. Either way.'

'So what do you think?'

'About Tiffany? Oh, she hates you.'

'But why?'

'Because you're a howling idiot, Ben. Of course she doesn't hate you! She likes you, of course she does. In fact I'd bet,' Yusuf lowered the volume, 'that it goes way, way beyond that.'

Ben smiled the joke away – because it was so obviously a joke – and tried to look casual.

'What about,' he suggested, 'the four of us go out somewhere? You and Susie, and me and her. Might be easier.'

'I see you have lost your mind. Once it's the four of us, it's not a date. It's Cat Kin. And the others will be pi– they'll be annoyed that they weren't invited. Come *on*, Ben. Fix up.' Yusuf looked to the dome as if requesting help from there. Apparently in answer, a chanting voice from hidden loudspeakers echoed through the hall.

'That's the second call.' At once Yusuf was brisk, serious. 'I have to get wudu'd and find my dad.'

The queue at the fountain dispersed. Men dried themselves and headed for double doors that led to a brighter room beyond. Yusuf whipped the socks off his feet and tried to pocket them. They wouldn't fit. Urgently he muttered, 'Look after these for me?'

'Um.' Ben drew back. 'I should be getting home. Can't you put 'em in your trainers?'

'I guess. Don't want them walking off, that's all. They're my last pair of footie socks. Mum bawled me out for losing my other pair.'

Ben followed him back to the shoe mat. 'People don't steal socks from here?'

'Of course not, dingbat. I used one sock as a gag, didn't I? Stuffed it in that crook's mouth. Obviously, I told Mum I lost it.'

Ben cut in. 'Your football sock? From the club you play in?'

'Yeah. Ben, look, I gotta go pray.'

'Yusuf.' His heart gave a sickly thud. 'Tell me that wasn't your actual team sock.'

'Not you too! Why? What's the big deal?'

Ben pulled one of Yusuf's socks from its trainer and unrolled it. Embroidered upon the hem was the crest of his local youth team – CLISSOLD STAGS – and on a label sewn inside it was his name.

6
TIME TO RELAX

People were fond of saying that cats had nine lives. Sometimes Tiffany felt like she was trying to live all nine at once.

Waking in the morning, or from a hasty nap, she had to stop and think about who she was meant to be. Was it a pile of homework calling for her attention, or a tiger-poaching cartel? Panic at breakfast – had she scrubbed off her face-print from her night of prowling? She would be changing for hockey at school and find her pashki kit in the locker. When she turned up late to see her counsellor, she blurted an apology for a late essay (her History teacher and Ellen were similar in the face). She forgot Dad's birthday; he pretended not to be hurt. Her biggest file of detective work went pooff when she saved a piece of Geography prep over it (Stuart, who had made a backup, got a kiss). She ricocheted between home and school, pashki classes and private investigations. Desperate for new clues, she staked out Chinatown alleys and riverside lockups, went sniffing around private boats in Docklands, before returning to bed in time for her wake-up cup of tea. Homework got botched in the car or during morning break. There was no time left, neither for her nor for anyone else. When Avril, once her very bestest friend, called up about some party, Tiffany breathed fire down the phone. Teen webzines had warned her that adolescence would be a stressful time. They had absolutely no pigging idea.

She was making an effort at school, she really was. Thanks to her counsellor, she could now concentrate for a spell on, say, the causes of the Russian Revolution. But then her mind would drift into thoughts of slaughtered tigers, or simply sink in exhaustion, turning the words before her into meaningless code.

Ben had stopped calling. She tried not to care. After she'd got home from last week's pashki class, her phone had lit up and serenaded her:

Ben calling. Taking a moment to check her hair (knowing it was absurd) she answered, 'Hi, Ben!' like a line she'd been rehearsing. But he seemed to have a different script. He started babbling instead about a sock, and Yusuf, and a terrible mistake. Too disappointed to listen, she'd stupidly hung up, and he hadn't been in touch since. One day she sat and watched her phone for an hour.

If she ever got a moment (but she never did; she was always telling Mum this, when she was asked to do some chore like emptying the dishwasher) – but if she ever *did* get a moment, she spent it with Stuart. Devising a programme of the gentlest pashki exercises, she held ten-minute sessions with him, the longest that his strength would allow. For these she saved all her patience. He was the most challenging pupil any pashki master could have, but then, she was not training him to thwart evildoers. His enemy was more sinister, and inside him. If pashki could empower her to leap twice her own height, then it ought to help Stuart at least climb the stairs. It might slow the wasting of his muscles and delay the worst that his illness kept in store. So she took him through half-sequences for strengthening limbs, back exercises to straighten his spine, and the meditations Omu and Pur, both of which speeded up healing. The leg stretches seemed to be doing the most good so far, counteracting the shrunken calf ligaments that had put his feet at a waddling angle.

Was it really helping? Certainly, on Sunday he had been a bundle of energy, although that was mainly thanks to the rides at Thorpe Park. Stuart lived for these fun days out, but Tiffany grumbled over losing half her weekend.

'You sourpuss,' said Stuart. 'A dose of rollercoasters is what you need. Take the laptop and do your detective work on the way.'

He did have some great ideas. They spent the whole car ride to Surrey logged into the Vanished Harmony forum, talking openly about how to catch tiger poachers, while Mum and Dad sat oblivious in the front, assuming they were playing a game. Tiffany caught up with the gossip from her contacts, whom she thought of as her private army – though in reality she knew very little about them as people. There was **ocelotspots**, a wildlife photographer; smoke_that_thunders, a pleasant but pushy conservationist campaigner, who at times could seem a bit too friendly; *chocolateeagle*, a hacker who targeted wildlife traffickers; and various other oddballs with names like **theirongiant** and **valkyrieraven88**.

She sent a private message to **happygolucky**, who of all her 'friends' was the closest she had to a real one. **Happygolucky** (who had once let slip her true name, Joy) was only sporadically online, being one of those young women who backpacked around the globe. Joy was too much a freewheeler to be useful as such, but Tiffany enjoyed chatting with her, shared her passion for big cats, and got a kick out of reading her traveller's tales. Perhaps surprisingly, Joy never showed interest in pashki or the Grey Cat, but Tiffany grew to like that, seizing her chance to have normal-ish conversations. Lately Joy had been hitch-hiking in India, and had sent Tiffany a file of leopard photos. One of these now served as her desktop wallpaper. Tiffany loved the way the leopard's honey eyes seemed to watch over her.

'How many gigabytes is this hideous picture?' Stuart sighed. 'That's what's slowing your computer down, I think.'

'Anything hideous is your reflection.' Tiffany finished her message to **happygolucky**, asking for more news and photos and fun. Dad turned off the M25 – they were nearly there. With waning enthusiasm, Tiffany re-opened her forum thread to post a fresh plea for information, while Stuart grumbled on about her cluttered computer.

'Your files aren't even password protected,' he said. 'If someone hacked your PC they could spy on you. Even steal your identity.'

'Steal my identity?' Tiffany sighed. 'Don't be silly, Stuart. Who on earth would want to be me?'

Her counsellor chuckled. 'Is that what you said to him?'

'Mm.'

'Good answer. But not really fair on yourself.' Ellen's face became gently serious. 'What's wrong with being Tiffany Maine?'

She shrugged. 'Dunno.'

'So it was a joke?'

'Erm. Yeah. Being me is quite cool, sometimes.' Tiffany let her mischievous hand grab the last biscuit with pink icing. She felt much happier now in these sessions, which could even make her look forward to Mondays.

'Did you and your brother have a good time?' asked Ellen. 'The rides at these parks, they scare the daylights out of me.'

They had scared the daylights out of Tiffany. By the end of that day her throat had been sore from squealing, her fingers numb with holding on. The family tradition was that she took care of Stuart during all the hurtling, spinning and plunging. In reality, he cackled gleefully from one hellish rollercoaster to the next, while making fun of her screams of terror.

'Yeah. It was great,' she said.

Ellen asked a few routine questions about school. Then the talk moved on to her friends, and Tiffany thought of Ben and felt guilty and cross and sad all at once. Her stumbling answer caused Ellen to probe a little. Perhaps she was being bullied? The idea was so ludicrous that Tiffany laughed. No, she was just too busy to see her friends much. The counsellor nodded sympathetically.

'Last week you mentioned a friend who died,' said Ellen. 'Do you still want to talk about her?'

Tiffany regretted that moment of weakness. She knew she could never talk about Mrs Powell.

'No. I'm over that now. I mean... I feel a lot better.'

'Good.' Ellen moved on. 'And Mum and Dad? You're getting along with them?'

'Er. Sometimes.'

'Sometimes meaning not much at all?'

Ellen could read her so well. Tiffany looked down. 'Right.'

'It isn't your fault. Nor theirs. Your parents aren't paying me to stop you disagreeing with them.'

'They're not?'

'Sure they would if they could, but…' Ellen was joking. 'Arguments can be healthy.'

'I don't *want* to fight,' said Tiffany. 'I say things to them… my dad especially. I wish I didn't.'

'You get angry?'

'I think sometimes… I'll make them hate me.'

'You lose your temper.'

Tiffany nodded, not trusting her voice.

'I'll teach you something.' Ellen wiggled the largest of her silver rings off her overcrowded thumb, and threaded it onto a thin gold chain. The ring dangled, scattering glints of light like water shaken off a dog.

Tiffany forced a laugh. 'You're not going to hypnotise me?'

'Hardly.' Ellen massaged the exposed band of flesh on her thumb. Her nineteen or so remaining rings clicked together. 'A simple relaxation technique. Once you've practised this a few times, you should find it easier to stay calm when you get stressed. Hold the end of the chain.'

Tiffany took the dangling ring.

'Okay. Rest your elbow on the table, like this.' Ellen positioned Tiffany's forearm, so that the ring and chain hung from her fingers like a fishing line. 'Keep your eyes on the ring as it moves. Breathe in… Slowly out. In through your nose, that's it… Out through the mouth.'

Tiffany watched the ring swing towards Ellen, towards herself.

'Let it hang free… Feel yourself relax. Now, imagine that it starts to swing clockwise.'

Soon enough, the ring began to travel in circles. Tiffany smiled. 'How'd you do that?'

'I didn't. That was you.' Ellen's voice was soft as a pillow. 'Now suppose it starts to swing the other way. Anti-clockwise.'

Though Tiffany was sure she did not move her hand, the ring obeyed her thought, flattening and then reversing its circle.

'Now it slows.' Ellen was somewhere close, but Tiffany's field of vision had shrunk to that oscillating glint of light. 'Ever more slowly, until it is barely moving. When it stops, you'll find you are completely relaxed, your mind open and refreshed… like a house on a sunny day… with all the windows and doors wide open…'

The chain slipped through her fingers. Ellen caught the falling ring before it could strike the table. She eased Tiffany back in her seat.

'There. Is that good?'

'Yes.' Tiffany blinked. The sofa beneath her felt like a floating bubble.

'All your cares, all your worries, drifting and disappearing.'

'Yes.' It was not like being drowsy, more the opposite. She was sharply aware of her surroundings, alert to every sound, the wheezes of the busy road outside, the gurgles of the fridge in the kitchen. Her wandering eyes picked up details she had never noticed before, like the tiny chip on the glass coffee table, and every title in the bookcase.

'Good, Tiffany. Breathe steadily in. Steadily out. We have a little more time to talk. How is your cat, by the way?'

'My cat?' Tiffany frowned. 'My cat died. He was hit by a car.' Tears rose, ready to spill.

'Never mind. It's okay now.'

'Okay.' Tiffany swallowed. She smiled. The tears sank down inside her. It was okay now.

'What was your favourite ride at Thorpe Park?' asked Ellen.

'I like the Rumba Rapids,' said Tiffany.

'They sound nice,' said Ellen. 'I heard a curious word lately. Pashki. Do you know what it means?'

'Yes.'

'How clever of you. Please tell me.'

'Sure!' It was nice to be asked easy questions. Tiffany told her counsellor what pashki was, and how much she enjoyed it. After a while, Ellen interrupted her.

'That's very interesting. I wonder who could have taught you such a thing. Was it Vanish Singh?'

'No. I've never heard of him.'

'Good. Then perhaps it was Geoffrey White?'

'No… yes… no, no!' Anguish seized her. She was sobbing, gasping for breath, flailing till she knocked a cushion off the sofa. Ellen touched her on her forehead.

'Ssh. It's all right. We won't talk of him. He's gone. He's no longer in the room.'

'Okay.' Tiffany felt her breathing steady. It was all right. She was calm. Had something happened to upset her, just then? She tried to think. No, she had always been calm.

'So, Tiffany.' Ellen's silver hair glimmered with the forward tilt of her head. 'Your pashki teacher. The woman you miss so much. What was her name?'

The doorbell sounded with Dad's usual drawn-out chime. Tiffany turned towards the noise.

'He's way early! Isn't he?'

Ellen checked her carriage clock. 'Goodness. No, he's punctual as ever. There's nothing like talk for making time fly.' She rose from the armchair to her impressive height. 'I'll let you dash. We don't want him getting another parking ticket.'

Putting on her coat, Tiffany tried to remember what they'd been talking about. Oh yes, her family day out at Thorpe Park. She wouldn't tell Dad how they'd frittered away the session. He might think he was wasting his money. She turned to say goodbye to Ellen.

'Oh. What happened to your ring?' Tiffany asked.

'My…?'

Tiffany pointed to the band of paler skin on Ellen's left thumb. 'It looks like you had another ring there. Did you lose one?'

'Oh!' Ellen creased her brow in consternation. 'Oh dear, you may be right. I expect the Hoover will find it. How funny that you noticed.'

Tiffany waved and hurried down to Dad's waiting car. She surprised him with a kiss on the ear and settled into the back seat, eager to get home, lie on her bed with a book, play her favourite new songs, and relax.

7
FEARFUL SYMMETRY

No sooner had Ben set foot inside the Tate Modern than Mum dashed to find the loo. Crossing the Thames on the footbridge she had complained of seasickness, and in the shadow of the vast art museum her face had turned a nauseous green. Ben waited with Dad outside the toilets, blowing on fingers turned red and numb by the river wind.

'Do you think she's okay?'

Dad hummed absently. 'What? Oh, course she is.'

'Hope it wasn't that fish.' Ben had helped to cook dinner last night.

'No.' Dad unbuttoned his parka. 'It's nothing. A tummy bug, I reckon. Ah, here she is. Okay, Lucy?'

Mum looked like death, but nodded. Dad put his arm round her. It was amazing that she'd wanted to go out at all. When her breakfast toast had come straight back up, Dad had tried to make her stay in bed, saying they didn't need a family outing every weekend. But Mum was stubborn, necking a couple of pills. 'Today's meant to be my treat, Ray,' she said. 'I'm not going to let this thing stop me doing stuff.' Ben thought she was being a bit silly there – after all, she'd be better in a day or two.

'Okay.' Mum clenched her jaw, determined. 'Art. Let's go and see some art.'

She led them through a doorway into an echoing space. Ben looked up, and up, and around, then the other way, and back again, absorbing the sheer size of this… you could hardly call it a room. At least three Olympic swimming pools could have fitted in here, with a ship floating on top. Mum, who had once come here often, explained. The Tate Modern had been a power station before they made it into an art museum, and this vast turbine hall was where they put the biggest, wildest exhibitions. Giant sculptures, an artificial sun, even disembodied sounds had all drawn crowds here in the past, and she recalled one artwork that was simply a giant crack in the floor – you could still see the scar of it, if you looked. But the new centrepiece had made national headlines, for within a month it had become the most popular ever.

Ben walked ahead of his parents towards the hall's most crowded end. Through the noise of hundreds of echoing voices, there broke a sharper sound.

CLICK CLUCK CLICK CLUCK CLICK CLUCK CLICK

He had to lift his head to see the whole thing. A clock face, mountainous, like Big Ben only bigger. And strange. The dial was smoky glass, ringed by symbols instead of numbers, but the angle of the giant silver hands said twenty-one minutes to eight. Ben checked his phone. The actual time was 12:10pm.

CLUCK CLICK CLUCK CLICK

The clock was running slow in more ways than one. Its tick was the laziest he'd ever heard, as slow as the breath of a deep sleeper. A gaggle of foreign schoolkids were trying to count in time with the ticks, laughing as they slipped out of sync, each tick more patient than their best efforts. A young man was using a phone app to measure the number of ticks per minute. Each fell like a heavy footstep, sending echoes up the long hall and back to merge in a muddy roar.

Dad appeared at his shoulder.

'Time's wrong,' he remarked.

'It's not there to tell you the time.' Mum was sucking a travel sweet to calm her stomach. 'It's a piece of installation art.'

Dad pretended to measure it with his arms.

'Won't fit on our bedroom wall,' he said. Mum stuck out her cherry-coloured tongue.

'Art isn't about looking nice, Ray. It's about… I don't know, making you think. Getting you to think in different ways.'

'I might not want to think in different ways,' said Dad.

'Oh – Give me strength,' said Mum. 'Appreciate it! Don't force me to explain it today. I'll puke.'

As her eyes danced over the structure, Ben felt an unexpected surge of love for her. She understood places like this. When he saw her admiring a piece of art, or at work on some craft of her own like a bathroom mosaic, she looked somehow different, a separate person from the woman who cooked his meals and ironed his shirts. Not Mum, but Lucy Gallagher, born Lucy Day, a fascinating almost-stranger.

Dad cast a few more dismissive glances at the clock. Ben moved closer to Mum and tried to see it through her eyes – Lucy's eyes. The clock's body was a colossal black structure, triangular, or rather a pyramid. To be even more precise, it was half a pyramid, sliced from top to bottom along the diagonal of the square base, with the dial set into the vertical face. Parts of the black carapace were laid open to expose the clockwork system inside. Ben marvelled at cogs the size of tractor tyres, apparently motionless, distantly connected to smaller components that revolved. A bronze globe like a moon swung on a steel hawser, in and out of view. Barrel-sized brass cylinders engaged with assemblies of cogs, like plates set to spin by performing waiters. Axles rotated, gear teeth meshed, the pendulum measured out its booming tick. A machine so familiar, yet extraordinary.

And yet, familiar.

'Do you suppose a giant cuckoo pops out of it?' Dad mused.

'Shut up, Dad,' murmured Ben. 'She's not feeling well.' He hugged Mum on impulse.

'This is brilliant,' he said. 'What does that booky-thing say?'

Mum had picked up a leaflet.

'It's called The Clock Is Set,' she said. 'Lucky we came when we did. Says here it's only running a while longer. It all ends just before Christmas.'

'Maybe they forgot to wind it,' said Dad, but he seemed interested now. 'Why?'

'Time for the next big exhibition, I suppose. They change over every few months.' Mum turned a page and read. '"The Clock Is Set invites us to reflect on the passing of ages. What is now will not always be. What was may come again. Is the future set for us like the past?"'

'Let's see.' Dad took the leaflet and read a different section. '"The unique clock mechanism inside this sculpture is the slowest ever constructed. It takes approximately two hours for the twenty-foot minute hand to advance by one minute, and an hour takes nearly five whole days."'

Now Ben knew what it reminded him of – the clocks at his school, of course, during double French. He was going to crack this joke when he noticed something odd about the people around them. Most had grown quieter, less inclined to wander about, and some had formed loose groups, gazing up at the clock face. Ben thought of rail travellers watching a departure board, awaiting their train. These people were definitely waiting – but for what?

CLUCK CLICK CLUCK CLICK

There came a pause longer than usual, one more half-second of silence. The onlookers held their breath.

KLUNK

The minute hand cranked onwards by one notch. It quivered and was still. The clock read twenty to eight. The watchers breathed again, phone cameras clicked, conversation returned. The crowds began to thin. Mum clapped.

'Oh, that's beautiful!'

'What is?' said Dad.

'The people. Didn't you notice? They like to see an actual minute pass. They gather and get ready, it's a special event. 'Cos it happens only about once every two hours.'

'I bet the hour's even better,' said Ben. 'Let's stay for that.'

Mum laughed. 'That's not for a couple of days yet! But I bet you there are ten times as many people here to watch the hour hand move. What a clever idea.' She had all her colour back now. 'That's the fun of these big artworks. The most interesting thing isn't always them. It's how people act around them. It's what they make you do.' She read again from the leaflet. 'Oh, yes. I'd love to be here for that.'

'Here for what?' Ben craned to see.

'It says the clock runs from midday to midnight, which will take it two months in total. And it'll stop dead on actual midnight on December the twenty-first, the winter solstice. Imagine that! Seeing those hands finally come together.'

'Won't be anyone here,' said Dad. 'Midnight. Place'll be closed.'

'It will be *open*,' said Mum. 'It's the Tate's event of the year. Music, lights, refreshments, everything. There'll be crowds as far back as the main doors. Don't let me leave without buying tickets.'

'Come on, Dad,' said Ben. 'Better than a carol service.'

'I like carols,' said Dad. But he had once been a boxer, and knew when he was beaten.

Properly fascinated now, Ben tried viewing from the side, with the hour hand pointing straight at him. At this angle it looked unnervingly sharp, a twelve-foot silver sword. The symbols around the dark crystal dial appeared to be Greek letters, embossed in some iridescent substance, perhaps opal. The topmost figure, the symbol for midnight, resembled a squiggly Z, or lightning.

'It's strange.' Mum pocketed the leaflet. 'I don't normally go for Miles Baron's art, but this one is really working on me.'

'Miles Baron? I've actually heard of him.' Dad was almost impressed. 'What does he usually do? Heaps of bricks? Unmade beds?'

'That sort of thing, I suppose. People say he's a genius, but he did this one piece, called TimeTide, which was a rusty nail through a square of tissue paper. And it sold for about a hundred thousand quid.'

'A hundred grand?' Dad laughed out loud. 'You're right. That is genius.'

The thought of so much cash, for so little, had stalled Ben's train of thought. His ears had pricked at something Mum had said, but he couldn't remember what.

'And some of his art,' Mum went on, 'is just creepy. Those sculptures he makes from dead animal parts. No thank you.'

Ben grabbed at Mum's coat sleeve.

'Dead animal parts?' No. This had to be wrong. 'Baron? His name's *Baron?*'

'Yes, cloth-ears. Miles Baron. He's only one of the country's most famous living artists. Oh, but then he's not a rap singer or an action movie star. No reason you should know him.'

'Can I – ?' Ben snatched the leaflet, found the photo on the back. The boyish but ageing features, the open-neck shirt. The peculiar eyeglasses without stalks.

It was Specs.

'Dandy, or what!' Dad chuckled.

'There's another Miles Baron exhibition on Level 3,' said Mum, encouraged by this apparent enthusiasm. 'That's the animal sculpture, though – Benjamin, what's the rush?'

Turning back, he clutched his stomach as convincingly as he could.

'Er. Got to find the loo. Think I'm coming down with your tummy bug.'

Ignoring Mum's puzzled shout – 'But you can't be!' – he ran, weaving against the flow of visitors, heading for the main stairs.

It looked almost grateful to have a visitor. Compared to the turbine hall, the upper floors were virtually deserted. Anyone interested in Miles Baron was downstairs gawping at the clock, for his hardcore fans had already seen this other gallery, and no-one else seemed to want to. The air in here had a stale, gluey smell, as if weary of being still for so long.

Ben stopped a pace away from the sculpture. The tiger was life-size, facing him eye to eye from its pedestal. In detail and poise it was also lifelike, which was ironic.

Ben had expected taxidermy, an animal stuffed or otherwise preserved. What he found was a bizarre jigsaw. Those eyes, so alive, were in fact nuggets of bone, polished and slitted with pupils apparently made of dried skin. Its stripy coat looked faintly wrong, and he realised that it was a patchwork of rags from many different tiger pelts, though it was hard to see the joins.

The tiger's coat only part-covered the model, exposing the artistry beneath. Its skinless, raised foreleg had a weird sheen, being moulded from many plastic packets, each full of dried tiger eyeballs. Its claws appeared to be tiger teeth, selected for size and curve. The pads of each paw looked real at first, but no – those were made from tiger noses. So it went on. A back leg was flayed bare to show how it was pieced together from tiger skulls. And the head was not a skull but a tessellation of claws. The tail was a train of toe bones. The tongue, a desiccated heart.

The information plaque nearby said that this was *Fearful Symmetry*, a sculpture by Miles Baron, created to draw attention to the threat of tiger extinction. The piece was assembled entirely from actual tiger parts that had been seized from smugglers (said the plaque) and legally authorised for use in this work. The website of a conservation charity was listed below. There was even a box for donations.

Ben was smoothing the fur on the tiger's neck when he heard a voice behind him.

'Please don't touch the exhibit.' A uniformed man moved into view. Ben jerked back, his flesh crawling.

'Don't worry.' The gallery attendant smiled kindly, mistaking his reaction. 'Just taking care nobody damages it.'

'Okay.' Ben fumbled with his phone, snapped one photo, and fled.

As he had expected, Tiffany arrived in a foul mood.

'Ben, what is this? I told you we were never meeting here again. If you lot think you can outvote me…'

'We don't.' Ben shut his eyes. 'It's one time.'

The Cat Kin had gathered in the ruined chapel in Abney Park cemetery. Sleet spat through bare branches, pattered on the evergreens and blew in through the chapel's glassless windows. Steeple-high boughs draped ivy almost to the ground, baffling both sound and the weakening daylight. Inside, it was almost like night. This had never been the cheeriest of buildings, and now it might as well have been cursed. The chapel had been Geoff White's choice of lair, which was why Tiffany loathed it so. But for that very reason, it seemed the right place to tell her what he knew.

She took it better than he had feared.

'Miles Baron. *Miles Baron*. I'm going to kill him.'

Tiffany picked up a stone from a crumbling arch and with demented strength hurled it at the wall. It chipped the brick of the window jamb, bounced and almost took Ben's head off.

'Don't do that!' he yelped. Susie and Cecile moved in, together steering Tiffany towards the chapel's driest corner, their gentle voices coaxing her to sit. She was gasping, asthmatic with rage. Cecile hugged her and summoned a purr. The soothing rumble rang through the chilly walls and Tiffany grew calmer.

Olly sat on a ruined pew, shaking his head.

'I can't believe it. Not Miles Baron. Not *the* Miles Baron.'

'Why not?' asked Daniel.

'Because!' Olly boggled at Daniel. 'I mean… he's an artist! One of the biggest names in the business. I admit, I don't much like his stuff, but my art teacher says…'

'That he's a genius,' Ben finished for him. 'Right.'

'Miles *Baron?*' Olly said again. Tiffany raised her head.

'You didn't recognise him?' she demanded. 'You of all people? You must have seen the video ten times. Olly never spotted the famous artist? Good luck with getting into art college!'

'I didn't think.' Olly looked wretched. 'He did remind me of someone… but I thought, no way! And remember,' he added, craftily, 'it was on Ben's phone. Bad picture.'

Ben sighed.

'Isidorus calling him Mr Bar– ?' Tiffany shook her cat-bell at Olly. 'Remind me, what is the point of you?'

Olly's face twitched in anger, and for a moment Ben thought he might storm out.

'Easy.' Yusuf spread his hands as if smoothing out a bed sheet. 'Maybe Olly missed a trick. But so did we. None of us recognised him.'

'My brother guessed,' Tiffany said softly. 'My little brother. He thought that guy might be famous. I didn't listen.'

'But aren't you missing something else now?' said Yusuf.

'Like what?'

'Like, we've got him!' Yusuf grinned. 'We nailed the sucker. We know who he is.'

Ben kicked himself for not seeing it first. He beamed at Tiffany, suddenly full of pride.

'Hey. You did it!'

'You mean you had *doubts*?' Yusuf slipped him a knowing wink. 'All those nights she spent detecting… it was bound to pay off. And it has. First thing tomorrow, we'll take that video to the police, and they'll drag Miles Baron out of his four-poster bed. And Tiffany gets a medal!'

'What about us?' said Susie. 'We helped.'

'There might be a cash reward,' said Daniel. 'We could share that. Half for Tiffany, a third for Ben, and a third for the rest of us – no, wait…'

They were all trying to high-five Tiffany or pat her on the back. She edged away.

'Not yet,' she said. 'No police.'

'*What?*' Olly howled it at the roof.

'Baron's a multi-millionaire,' she said. 'And famous. People like him always wriggle out of things. Don't they, Ben?'

Ben scuffed his foot in the dust, remembering. 'Yeah. Some do. But they arrested John Stanford in the end. And they'll get Baron too.'

'And he'll get released on bail, and do a runner.' Tiffany clenched her fists. 'No.'

'There's nothing else we can do,' said Yusuf.

'There is. We pay Baron a visit.'

'Not me,' said Susie. Olly and Daniel made their feelings plain too. Cecile looked torn.

'I think it's a really bad idea,' she murmured.

'Why?' Yusuf asked Tiffany. 'Give us a reason!'

'That's exactly what I'm going to ask him,' said Tiffany. 'I want him to explain why he's killing the tigers. He's made a work of art about them going extinct – but he *wants* it to happen. He's *making* it happen. And people think he's wonderful.'

Ben wished he'd never gone to that stupid art gallery.

'You're not Mrs Powell,' he said. 'Show the police the video.'

'I'm going after Miles Baron. Alone, if I have to.' But she looked and sounded less sure.

'He's right, Tiffs,' said Yusuf. 'You know how I feel. I've been mad on big cats since I was tiny. One day I'm going to run my own sanctuary. Inshallah.' His face darkened. 'And I'd like to throw Miles Baron to the tigers. But it's not about what we'd like. There's a right way and a wrong way…'

'Spare me the holier-than-thou stuff.' Tiffany waved him silent. 'Of course I'm not going to kill anyone. But I will make Baron confess, on camera, so there's no chance he can weasel out of it. I'll put him in jail, and I'll ruin him, and no-one will buy a Miles Baron masterpiece again.'

Yusuf backed off, leaving her sitting alone.

'It's not for us to do,' he said. 'You know we can't, Tiffany. You know that.'

She looked too weary to argue any more. Ben stepped out of the chapel for some fresher air. With any luck, this was the end of it. Grey dusk had dissolved all but the cemetery treetops. The sleet fell faster, weeping down the steeple.

There were more exhibition rooms than he remembered. He wandered from one to the next. Where had that tiger sculpture gone? His footsteps rang very loud and slow, but no, that sound was the tick, tick, tick from the turbine hall.

Here was the right gallery. He crossed a hardwood floor like a vast empty plain, till he stood before *Fearful Symmetry*. It looked different. The macabre sculpture stood upright on two legs, and instead of a tiger's face it had a face-print, out of which stared helpless brown eyes, and he realised that the sound he had mistaken for the clock was actually her fingers, scratching at the pedestal as she tried in vain to free herself –

He woke to his own shout. It was dark, London dark, which meant orange. He groped for his pillow and duvet, making sure that he was Ben, and this his bedroom. The nightmare was melting away when the sound came again. *Scratch… scratch… tap*.

On went his bedside light. At his window he saw the shadow. Heard the jingle.

'Tiffany?'

He rolled out of bed and undid the window latch. She jumped down onto his carpet.

'Brrr! Horus, it's cold out there.' She wore double layers, a hooded tracksuit over her pashki kit. Finding his radiator, she sighed in disappointment. The heating was off.

For a sleepy moment, Ben's imagination went haywire. What was

Tiffany doing here, in his bedroom, at night? The depressing answer filtered through to him.

'Tiffany, no!'

'What?'

'I'm not going with you. And neither are you.' He paused, aware that something was wrong with that sentence. 'You can't go raiding Miles Baron's house!'

'You can't stop me.' She smiled coquettishly. 'But I thought I'd give you the chance to keep me company. You know, protect me. The usual. Don't you want me to be safe?'

'Of course I do, but…'

'Come on, then. Wait. Better change out of those pyjamas first. Don't worry,' she winked, 'I promise not to look.'

Tiffany turned her back. Ben stayed where he was, his pyjama top buttoned to the neck.

'No!' he said. 'Tiffany, I'm telling you, *no*. Go take a flying leap.'

8

BARON MANOR

'You're gorgeous,' said Tiffany.

Ben said nothing. He knew she didn't mean him. They had ridden a chain of night buses to be here, mostly on their roofs, and he was numb, weary, and unable to work out why he was no longer at home in bed.

'You gorgeousness.' Tiffany stroked the red fox that lay in her arms. 'I shall name you Jethro.'

On the other hand, perhaps this was simply a weird dream.

'Well, Ben?' Tiffany deigned to notice him again. 'What will you call yours?'

'I dunno. Rabies?' said Ben.

'Never mind.'

'I'll mind if it bites me. It's already given me fleas. I can feel – Whoa, no you don't!' Ben gripped his fox as it writhed and gave a foul-smelling bark.

'You're holding him wrong.' Tiffany caressed her own fox behind its ears.

'Okay, swap,' said Ben. 'I'll have Jethro and you can have Psycho.'

'You said his name was Rabies.'

'I'm saying that you picked a lucky fox!'

They both got the giggles then. Not very silently, they crept through the leafy thickets that grew close to the fence.

'Right,' said Tiffany. 'Let's fox his security.'

'Oh, ha ha ha.'

Finding Miles Baron's address had been easy. His blog bragged about his Georgian mansion beside Greenwich Park, where from his studio he could see across the meadows to the Royal Observatory, and watch the joggers and dog walkers. The lives of ordinary Londoners were his inspiration, he said, provided (Ben presumed) that they stayed well outside his spiked eight-foot railings. To get near the front door you had to pass security gates, cameras and motion detectors, and if you weren't invited all hell would break loose.

In a nearby street Tiffany had found foxes scavenging from bins. With Eth-walking and a silent Dash Pounce, it was easy as catching giant mice. The fox that Tiffany scooped up had been too surprised to struggle. Ben's still trying to eat his fingers.

Hiding in the rhododendron bushes that buffered the main gates, Tiffany wriggled out of her hooded top and wrapped it round her fox to make a sort of sling, which she tied to her back using the sleeves. Then she held Ben's fox so that he could do the same, with more difficulty and snarling. When his wriggling knapsack was secure, the pair of them eyed the high, spear-like railings. Ben's catras awoke, pulsing indigo and gold, and with a familiar shiver his joints and ligaments found their perfect alignment.

'Ready?' said Tiffany.

They went at the fence in a Scramble Leap, a vertical hop-step-and-jump too nimble for gravity to notice. Ben grabbed two railing spikes and somersaulted himself over them, dropping lightly to the turf on the other side.

'Woo…!' Touching down beside him, Tiffany smiled. 'Quicker than me, that time.'

The windows of the house caught the city glow, shaping its darkness. In places the walls and eaves looked scruffy, and Ben heard wind ruffling through a cladding of ivy. Tiffany unhooked her sling.

'Off you go, Agent Jethro. For Queen and country!'

'Don't look at me.' Ben unwrapped his fox and flung the struggling beast out of biting range. 'I have no idea what she's on about.'

Agents Rabies and Jethro fled towards the house. The foxes weren't halfway across the lawn when a floodlight flicked on, casting a pale cone across the grass like a leftover slice of day. The manor house sprang into colour, a sprawling red brick edifice, its roof crested with slender chimneys as numerous as organ pipes. A second light blazed forth and a wall-mounted camera swivelled to track the scampering shadows.

'Perfect,' said Tiffany. 'Let's go.'

They skirted the edges of the floodlit zones, as low and swift as the running foxes. When their patch went dark they lay flat. Ben watched Rabies and Jethro dashing in dazzled circles, trying to melt into a night that kept melting around them. Whenever a fox triggered a light and a camera followed the movement, Tiffany was off again with Ben at her heels, crossing the blind beams of motion detectors that had already been tripped. And so, not invisible but unnoticeable, they zig-zagged closer to the house.

'I can't decide,' said Ben, as they hid behind a bird bath, 'whether you're brilliant or stupid.'

'Funny.' Tiffany re-tied her shoelace. 'That's cats all over. Rufus, you know, he learned to work our kitchen tap to get himself a drink. Then he fell in the washing-up bowl.' Trailing off wistfully, she peered around the stone basin. 'Whoops. They're moving again.'

No sooner had they broken cover than she dived belly down onto the patio. Ben dropped beside her. A door had opened in the mansion's nearest wing. Out swept a torch beam – Ben was sure it touched them. He put all his will into seeming part of the stonework.

A man's voice muttered, 'Foxes. Thought I poisoned you.'

Shining the torch, a coated figure descended porch steps to the garden, striding after the pale gleams of fox eyes. 'Go on! Geddout of it.'

'Now,' said Tiffany.

They made it to the open porch. A doorway just inside it led into an office full of video screens, showing the gardens and the gates from many angles. The man was a security guard. At the sound of his returning footsteps they ran on past the office to a closed door at the end of the hall way. This led into a chilly, dungeon-dark room, with a flagstone floor and shapes like medieval weapons hanging from the walls – they were pots and pans, and this was a huge kitchen. Ben heard the distant grumbles of the night watchman as he pulled off his boots in the office.

'Maybe –' He hated to raise this, but... 'Could you take off your bell? Just while we're breaking into this mansion.'

She touched the collar on her wrist.

'No need. Listen!' On tiptoe she bounded to an Aga cooking range. He heard only the faintest rustling, as good as silence to an untrained ear. 'Remember I was practising? I can do it now! I can move without it sounding.' She gave herself a clap and the bell jingled. 'Well. When I concentrate!'

'Okay then. Concentrate.'

Stone stairs led up from the kitchen, a flight so narrow that it might have been designed to torment the butlers and maids who had worked here in generations past. Yet at the top of it Ben felt he was passing into a different house altogether. The space he entered looked like the penthouse of a Hollywood director. Sofas, tables, plants and pillars were the only obstacles dividing a sweep of wooden floor, smooth as an ice rink yet warm underfoot. One corner housed a full-size drinks bar; another appeared to be a home cinema. Free-standing plinths bore elegant sculptures. A little bridge spanned an indoor brook, the waters tumbling over glass boulders. Ben whistled.

'Not bad.'

'No,' said Tiffany. 'Bad. Really bad.'

With a final envious glance around his dream living room, Ben followed her up a translucent staircase that rose through the ceiling with no obvious means of support.

'Do you know where you're going?' he inquired.

'He'll be in bed. Bedroom means upstairs.'

Her voice stayed alarmingly calm. Was it too late to stop her, to end this craziness? He wished he'd locked her in his wardrobe when he'd had the chance. All he could do now was make a vow to himself that Tiffany would get home safe tonight, if it killed him.

The first floor retained some English heritage character, though the corniced walls and wainscoting were interrupted with modern touches. Bookshelves seemed to float on the walls, and an abstract stained-glass window scattered moonlight onto maple floorboards. Along the landing hung pictures, mostly pen-and-ink drawings, things that looked half-real, half-dreamed: a face that was also a Swiss cheese, riddled with holes; a piano that turned into prison bars; an eye that seemed to follow them. Ben noted the artist's signature on each.

'These are pretty good.' Miles Baron could certainly draw, when he wasn't messing around with rusty nails or dead tigers. Tiffany shook her head, refusing to look. The landing bottlenecked into a corridor, where the drawings gave way to photographs.

'The guy's divorced,' said Ben.

'Huh? How come you know so much?'

'The pictures.' Two children kept cropping up in the photos, a girl of about eight and a boy maybe half that. 'There aren't any kids that age living here,' said Ben, 'or there'd be toys and things under our feet. And if their mum was dead, there'd still be pictures of her, but there aren't. So mum's off somewhere else, with both kids. See?'

'Fascinating,' said Tiffany. 'You're mistaking me for someone who gives a – Ssh! What was that?'

A murmur of voices. She signalled: back to the landing. They crept to the top of the staircase, its glassy treads now traced in light from below. Ben got ready to grab Tiffany and leap at the nearest window if necessary.

'What the hell have you done to your hair?' The louder of the two voices spoke up, immediately familiar. Ben craned his neck below the landing to get a better view. He saw a pair of feet in black slippers, and the hem of a dark red dressing gown.

'Hair?' The second voice was female, and nervous. Ben peered lower till he was almost hanging in the stairwell like a bat. Near the bridge over the indoor brook he saw a young woman in a creased maid's uniform. She touched her sleep-mussed black hair. 'Very sorry Mister Baron. I brush.'

She spoke thickly, partly due to her limited English and partly, Ben guessed, from having been woken at three in the morning.

'Never mind the hair.' The man in the gown and slippers trudged to the nearest sofa. He could only be Miles Baron, though without those peculiar stalkless spectacles his face was strangely bland, with a weak chin and not much expression. The leather sofa sighed as Baron sank into it, turning on a reading light.

'I can't sleep, April. Bring me a tray of my remedy.'

The maid smiled pleasantly. 'Yes sir. Lemon tea. You like it here or in bedroom?'

Her accent was a sweet, slow chant – Miles Baron should have asked her to read him a bedtime story, if he wanted to relax. But he snapped at her.

'No, April! Not lemon tea. My *remedy*, I said.'

'Yes?' Confusion crossed the maid's face. 'Lemon tea, I think. Remedy is lemon tea?'

'*Mint* tea!' Miles Baron clapped his forehead with both hands, as if this fact was known to every English schoolchild. 'My remedy is mint tea! Mint tea to help me sleep!'

The maid turned to go.

'And cognac!' Baron burst out. 'Remedy is mint tea and cognac. On a tray. Don't mix them yourself! Mint tea in a pot, with a strainer. The cognac in a decanter. Make sure you pour it from the right bottle! The Delamain Reserve 1951. Cup and saucer, brandy glass. Teaspoon. Napkin.' With his hands, he mimed where he wanted each of these on the tray. 'Got that?'

'Yes, Mister Baron,' she lisped.

'I'll take it in the first floor drawing room,' said Baron.

Her face puckered in alarm.

'The – ?'

'Bring it to me in the drawing room,' Baron repeated. Wearily he rose and plodded towards the staircase, turning on two more lights in passing. The whole living space was now bright as day. Ben nudged Tiffany to make sure she was ready to move.

'Drawing – ?' The maid's frown deepened. 'Studio?'

'Not to studio!' snapped Baron. 'To the drawing room!'

April's mouth hung open in despair.

'The lounge!' Miles Baron exploded. 'Drawing room is lounge! Lounge is drawing room! Bring my remedy on a tray to the upstairs drawing room!'

'Sir.' April smoothed her uniform, curtsied and departed.

'Wait.' Miles Baron called her back. From the pocket of his dressing gown he drew the funny stalkless spectacles and perched them on his nose. 'Not there. I've changed my mind. Bring it to the pool room. Better light in there.'

April curtsied again, though she seemed to repress a shudder. Perhaps she had visions of Baron playing pool by himself all night, and waking her to bring refreshments between frames. Miles Baron headed for a leather-padded door that looked like a relic from the original manor house.

Tiffany said, 'That poor girl.'

'Guess she hasn't worked here long,' said Ben. 'Don't suppose many do.'

'What a monster. Imagine being dragged from your bed in the middle of the night to have some megalomaniac order you about!'

'Yeah, imagine.' Ben gave a hollow laugh, which luckily she didn't pick up on. She was already springing down the stairs.

'After him!'

In the hallway beyond the leather door they had to shade their eyes. Baron had switched on every light, the wall-mounted candle lamps, the ceiling spotlights and two immense crystal chandeliers. The glare split their shadows into leaves as they ran down the corridor, and Ben expected at any moment to be stopped by a shout. At the far end another staircase climbed into more electric light.

'Up there,' said Tiffany.

Ben held her back. Stalking their quarry through floodlit corridors didn't seem like such a wizard plan. There was something weird going on here. Baron surely did not need so much light to find his way around his own house. He was acting like a child who was scared of bogeymen.

'Let's find another way up,' said Ben.

He found himself leading the way, following the hall around two more corners till it ended in a big, solid-looking door. Tiffany tried the handle. Half a dozen steel bolts released from sockets around the frame, and when she tried to push it open she grunted.

'Whoa. This is heavy. Little help?'

Ben had to shove with his shoulder, for the door was held shut by sprung hinges as well as its own considerable weight. He wondered if this might be a strong-room, or a soundproof studio where the artist could work undisturbed. When the door was open a foot, Tiffany kitten-whispered, 'Smell anyone?'

Something smelled, that was for sure – something damp and rank and slimy. Ben peered inside.

'Woah.' Amazement overcame caution. He heaved his way past the door and stood inhaling the humid air. 'Now that's flash.'

Tiffany shrugged. 'It's a fish pond.'

'A fifty-foot indoor fish pond. With an island. And a statue. And look up there.' Ben pointed to a balcony shaded with potted palm trees, venus fly traps and other exotic plants. Sun lamps mimicked a tropical evening.

'Still not impressed. Remember how he pays for all this.'

The pond filled the room, leaving only walkways around the edges – this feature was meant to be enjoyed from the clear-walled balcony above. The bottle-green waters lay flat as a mirror, stirred only by bubbles from aerators at either end. Out of the middle rose a long, plant-fringed island, a plinth for that large bronze statue of a crocodile. This sculpture was so lifelike that Ben had to look at it twice, before assuring himself that the greenish tint of crocodile skin was just algae growing on its metal scales. It was also unrealistically big.

Tiffany hissed impatiently. 'Wrong turning. He's gone upstairs.'

'We could head him off from here. Climb up to that balcony.' But a walk around the poolside changed his mind. The balcony overhung the water on all sides, so there was no good place from which to jump. Also it looked too high – any leap to grab that balcony rail would be a personal best for either of them. Ben returned.

'You win. Back the way we came.'

Tiffany was sneering at the water.

'For a fancy indoor fish pond,' she said, 'he's seriously lacking any fish.'

Ben thought, *No fish?* and a sound pulled his head up. Footsteps echoed in the viewing gallery. Tiffany, distracted, let go of the heavy door and it swung shut with a clunk of bolts. Ben lunged for the metal doorknob and twisted it, uselessly. This handle wasn't even connected to any mechanism.

'Can I help you?'

Miles Baron stood on the balcony, cup and saucer in hand and a smile on his bland face.

The pool room, Ben thought, kicking himself. Now they were snookered.

9
THE POOL ROOM

If the door was locked, if they were trapped in here – well, she wouldn't care about that. Whenever Rufus had collided with a locked cat flap, he had shaken his head and simply walked away, pretending he hadn't meant to go out at all. Tiffany turned coolly around.

Common sense told her that she ought to be afraid. But the man in the red bathrobe, peering down through those ridiculous pince-nez spectacles, filled her only with loathing.

'Yes, you can help me.' Her voice rang off the tiles. 'You can tell me why you've been slaughtering tigers.'

'Ah.' Miles Baron leaned on the balcony rail, his cup and saucer precariously balanced. 'That's a new one. No-one asked me that question before. They ask me, what does it mean, Miles? Where do you get your ideas? Or they ask me, why do you stick together piles of trash and call it art? Why don't you learn to draw? Yes. I get asked many questions. But never that one. Are you an art critic, Miss – ?'

'You've been killing tigers,' Tiffany repeated. 'Buying their bones, to make your sick sculpture. You bought them from Mister Isidorus. That's right – ' she saw his grimace, 'I know about him. I was there. I filmed you.'

'Thanks for telling him that,' Ben murmured.

Miles Baron's cup rattled.

'You're Cat Kin, aren't you?' he said.

That caught her by surprise.

'They warned me I might run into you.' Baron tightened the scarlet cord of his robe, despite the hothouse atmosphere. 'So you've come.'

'Who's *they?*' Ben demanded.

'Yes, we have,' said Tiffany, twice as loud. Baron appeared to be scared of them – that was good enough for her. She gave him a cat stare, as if she were the one looking down upon him, and not the one trapped below. 'We've come to stop you.'

'Stop me?' Baron uttered a wild laugh. 'Stop me sleeping? No need, believe me.'

'She means tigers,' Ben shouted, and even Tiffany was startled, for he sounded genuinely enraged.

'Now there's the question.' Miles Baron smiled. 'Are you sure you're not art critics? You could write my next review.'

Ben merely glared until Baron spoke again.

'You saw my sculpture? Fearful Symmetry?'

Ben nodded.

'My masterpiece,' said Miles Baron. 'People are saying it's the other thing… but they don't understand. Fearful Symmetry is my magnum opus. When you understand it. That model I built from tiger parts, that's only the frame. The real art, the real *masterpiece*…' His bland face suddenly animated. 'No-one has ever done it before. Made an animal extinct *on purpose*. Oh, we've caused it lots of times, the dodo, the thylacine, but only by accident. But my Fearful Symmetry is unique. When it's completed, there won't be a tiger alive in the world. Not *anywhere*. There will only be my sculpture. The greatest work of art ever conceived.'

She would have screamed at him then, but she needed breath for that. All she could grasp was that Miles Baron had been exterminating tigers, not for medicines, not for profit, nor even for sport. He had been doing it, quite literally, for nothing.

'My mum's a better artist than you,' said Ben.

The cheapest shot, but it cleared Tiffany's head like pure oxygen. Baron scowled.

'Oh, yes. And I'm supposed to care what a pair of zitty vandals think? I'll remind you that this is private property. When I call the police your next stop will be… wherever they send juvenile offenders these days.'

'And yours will be Pentonville prison,' said Tiffany. 'Do you want to call, or shall I?'

'Help me,' said Miles Baron.

The words were so quiet, and so inexplicable, that at first Tiffany assumed her feline hearing had picked up a television from another part of the house.

'*What?*' she hissed.

'You have to help me,' said Miles Baron. His eyes behind their lenses grew wet and staring. 'Help me and I'll let you out. Is that a deal?'

'Don't talk to me!' she snarled, but Ben touched her arm.

'Help you why?' he demanded. 'And how?'

'They told me you'd come.' Now Baron was talking more to himself. 'The Cat Kin are out there, he said. Watch out for the Cat Kin.'

'Who said that?' said Ben. 'Mister Isidorus?'

Miles Baron looked round sharply, as if someone might be lurking behind him.

'Quiet,' he breathed. 'The Set can hear. They get inside you. That's how they work. His voice, in my head. When the lights are out. And her. And the dreadful one.'

He sounded barking mad. But these ravings were starting to ring unpleasant bells in Tiffany's brain.

'What do you mean, set? Set of what?' Then she somehow registered the capital S. It was a name. The Set. He was talking about some organisation, no doubt the people he'd been working with. She tried to think. The word was stirring other memories too.

'Can you protect me?' Baron clutched at his bedtime drink, grinding the cup against the saucer. 'Tell me you can!'

Tiffany mustered all her defiance, only for Ben to butt in.

'Yes, we can,' he said. 'Unlock the door and we'll talk.'

Thank Ra he was here – she would never have thought of saying that. For a moment Baron wilted with gratitude. Then, gripping the rail, he peered down like a vulture.

'But hold on a sec,' he said. 'They told me you'd be cunning. That you'd try to trick me. I might be better off keeping you there. Yes. They'd thank me for capturing you.'

'No!' said Tiffany.

'You can't trust them,' said Ben.

'Exactly,' Tiffany chimed in. 'They lied to you!'

She had the hang of this now – say any random nonsense that Baron might want to hear. Baron's gaze wandered across the pool, lingering on the island, where the sun lamps glistened on the scales of the enormous statue of a crocodile. Suddenly he gave a bellow.

'*You have to save me!*'

'We will,' stammered Tiffany. Fear had found her at last.

'No!' Miles Baron shouted – but not, it seemed, at them. He squeezed his head in his hands. 'I'm not! I'm not a grass. I never met the Cat Kin. Leave me alone!'

'Who's he talking to?' Ben hissed. Tiffany shuddered, watching Baron rant and whimper at some inner voice.

'I made it for you,' he wailed. 'I did what you wanted. Please...'

'We've got to get up there.' Ben ran around the pool's edge. 'Find something we can climb!'

Again Tiffany scanned the length of the pool room, and drew a blank. Their Mau claws couldn't scale such smooth walls, the balcony was too high to reach with a jump, and the overhang made any such leap impossible.

'Let us out!' she shouted. 'I promise we'll help!'

As suddenly as he had gone to pieces, Baron appeared to recover. He lowered his hands, releasing fistfuls of hair, and smiled from a face glistening with sweat.

'Help me?' he said. 'But you hate me. Remember? No, I'm not falling for that. You can stay there.'

'But we can protect you from Isidorus!' said Ben. 'It's him, isn't it?'

'You can't fight the Set.' Baron's smile widened like a gash. 'I'll tell them they can collect you here. What's left of you.' He turned away, casually knocking his cup and saucer off the balcony rail. 'See you later.'

With a swish of robe, he was gone. The saucer and cup dropped, splish-splash, into the pool. The crocodile statue on the island turned its head towards the sound.

Tiffany knew it must be an illusion, a waking dream. That was the trouble with so many sleepless nights –

'You come back here!' Ben yelled up at the balcony.

'Ben!' Tiffany gasped. 'Ben – what is that... Look!'

The crocodile head swung back again, dismissing the splashes as not interesting, and swivelled instead towards Tiffany and Ben. Its jaws parted to reveal wood-saws of teeth.

'Uh –' Ben, looking like he'd been punched in the stomach, stepped backwards and collided with the locked door. 'Oh. Get. *Stuffed.*'

'I don't think it is,' said Tiffany.

It was like a conjuring trick. She saw the crocodile flop off the island, pour itself under the water and disappear. She had barely begun to think that they might soon be in serious trouble, when the pool's smooth skin burst beside her. If she had wasted time screaming, she would have died with the echo. Instead she flung herself headlong as the crocodile smashed from water to air and snapped the space where she had been standing.

She reached the pool's opposite corner. Now she screamed. Across the greenish water, which was slopping now in swimming-pool waves, the crocodile ambled along the narrow walkway, dragging a wet trail like a slug's. From snout to tail tip it almost spanned the pool's short side, along which two cars could have parked. At a slithery trot it reached the wall, turned the corner with improbable rubberiness, and was suddenly on her side of the room again, accelerating towards her.

She flailed as something grabbed her arm.

'Move, Tiffany!' Ben hauled her away from the charging reptile. Her fastest would never be enough, she was sure, but she ran to put off death for a few more seconds. When presently she found all four of her limbs still intact, she looked back. To her surprise, the crocodile was now some distance behind, though still gamely dry-swimming towards them along the walkway. The creature wasn't actually that quick on its feet. Her terror had made it seem as fast as a motorbike.

'Stay out of its reach.' Ben was panting. 'That's all we have to do. Remember, crocs are cold-blooded. Cold-blooded animals get tired quicker.'

'Are they? Do they?' She would have struggled to remember her name at this moment.

'Yeah... I'm pretty sure.'

At a fast backwards walk they completed their first lap of the room. All the way round, she noticed, Ben kept himself between her and the crocodile. Then the beast charged with a rippling gallop and they had to run. The tiles underfoot were now flooded, and she needed her best Eth walk to keep from slipping. At the next corner Ben skidded to a stop.

'See?' he said. 'We're too fast for it. Just wait till it gives up.'

'But we'll still be locked in,' she said. 'Unless... What was the name of that girl? Baron's maid?'

'Um. Something foreign.'

'No, it wasn't. April, that was it. *April!*' she yelled. 'April, we're trapped in the pool room!'

Ben shouted too, and rattled the locked door when they passed it again. Pausing to listen for an answer, Tiffany realised something wasn't right. She stared up and down the empty pool sides.

'Where's it gone?'

Water erupted, drenching them both. The crocodile surged ashore.

Tiffany dived out of reach but Ben was hemmed in the corner. He slashed an uppercut into its gaping lower jaw, then again, his Mau claws singing. The crocodile seemed hardly to notice, merely snapping at Ben's blurred hands.

'Get away!' she shrieked. With a sideways roll Ben eluded its bite and ran round the pool to join her.

'Phew. That thing's armoured like…' He shook his head. 'Claws can't touch it. Unless I go for its eyes…'

'Don't even think about it. Uh-oh –' The crocodile had slipped back into the pool. This reptile wasn't stupid. 'Split up!' she cried. 'It can only chase one of us. Watch the water with your dark-seeing. And use your cat hearing. You can hear the beat of its tail in the lowest range.'

'This is all stuff I know!' Ben yelled, and had to double back as a crocodile fountain intercepted him. He stumbled towards her, almost laughing from the shock.

'Something else,' he gasped. 'Saw it on TV. You can hold a crocodile's mouth closed with a rubber band.'

Tiffany heard this as gibberish. 'Do you have a rubber band? I don't have a rubber band!'

'Forget the rubber band!' Ben split from her again as the crocodile dived. 'What I'm saying is, it doesn't take much strength. Nothing can stop a croc's mouth closing, but it's meant to be really easy to hold it shut.'

'I'm calling the maid again,' said Tiffany. She aimed her shouts – *April! April!* – towards the balconies, hoping the sound might carry beyond. It was maddening to stare up at that viewing gallery, so close, yet just too high and awkward to reach. There *had* to be a way to get up there.

Ben yelled from the adjacent walkway, 'Tiff – !' and the rest was lost in a roar. In shouting she hadn't heard its underwater approach. Stunned blind, with a searing pain in her left side, she thought *This is how it feels to be eaten.* In truth, she had expected worse. It hurt only slightly more than her worst ever bruises –

Coldness revived her, and she was on the streaming stone floor. What she'd mistaken for blood was water pouring back into the pond. She rolled and saw the crocodile squirming above her.

And there was Ben.

He was clinging astride the crocodile's neck, hugging its closed mouth in a variation on the Ten Hooks Vermin Choke. The beast's head alone was as long as Ben's torso, his arms seeming punier than string even though they were, unbelievably, binding those enormous jaws together.

Her hip throbbed with pain. She touched the area, terrified her hand would come back red, but her prowl-suit wasn't even torn. Not a bite, then – a glancing blow, as Ben leapt on the beast to wrestle it away.

A scrabbling claw scratched her calf and she rolled clear. Still dazed, she had a dreamy moment. Ben was fighting a crocodile for her. In a very strange way, this was the best day of her life.

The crocodile bucked and tossed Ben into the pool. The splash made a hole that slapped shut over him. Tiffany choked on his name.

For a moment two froggy eyes considered her. Then a cloudy third eyelid blinked across each one, and the crocodile jack-knifed into the water. She shrieked her throat raw. Ben burst to the surface, striking out with fast crawl towards the island, but Tiffany saw the shadow underneath him, chasing with lazy, unmatchable speed.

It was faster than reflex. She simply moved. In a Felasticon leap she soared over the pond, twisting mid-air to face the water as Ben clawed himself gasping onto the island. The crocodile shot itself out of the pool and lunged for him, just as Tiffany touched down.

PTAH

She hit it with the pashki stun-gun – *ptah*, the cat-spit of sound that could stop foes in their tracks. The crocodile swerved by the tiniest of angles, enough to send its teeth crunching into rock instead of Ben's leg. It sank and rebounded like a monstrous cork, whereupon Tiffany kicked its jaw as hard as she could.

'Get off him!'

She dragged Ben to higher ground, where he sicked up mouthfuls of water.

'No!' She smacked him round the head. '*Get up!* I need you –'

The crocodile beached itself upon the island, its tail churning white water behind it. Tiffany fired off another *ptah*, and a cobble stone flew past her to bounce off the monster's forehead. Back it slithered into the water. She looked round at Ben – *Nice shot*. Still coughing, he searched among the ornamental plants.

'Find loose stones,' he croaked. 'Can you throw?'

'Of course I can!' But this was the place for honesty. 'Maybe not that well.'

'Okay. Chuck 'em to me. Or wait till it's really close.'

'I will *not* wait till it's really close!'

The crocodile glided past beneath the surface, a weirdly beautiful shimmer of gold and grey like some magical watery train. Again it streamed by, circling the shoreline, choosing its next landing ground. How small the island suddenly seemed. And she had thought this could not get any worse.

'If it climbs out we're dead! There's nowhere to run to. Ben, we have to jump back over! Can you make it to the side?'

He eyed the water. 'Maybe.'

'*Maybe* isn't good enough!'

Ben hefted another stone. 'I mean, yeah. You did it.'

'But I can jump farther than you.'

'Uh? Since when?'

'Since… Look, I train harder! You've been slacking. All you do in class is faff around…'

A spray of water, a V of jaws. Ben flung his rock and winged a foreleg. The claws lost purchase and the beast resumed circling.

'Whatever.' He groped for more stones. Most were cemented in place. 'Gotta risk it. I'm not spending all night on croc island.'

'I'll jump first,' said Tiffany. 'I can catch your hand if you fall short.'

'As if!' He tried for a confident grin, but his eyes betrayed him. One dip had been more than enough. She could see how terrified he was of ending up back in that water.

Tiffany gathered herself for the return jump. Then she found she was staring up at the viewing gallery. She'd not seen it from this angle before. The balcony's overhang made it unreachable from the walkway – but from where they were now, marooned in the centre of the pond, it was a straight diagonal leap to the safety railing. Yes, it still looked very, very high. But at her very best...

Maybe.

Ben seemed to read her mind.

'You're not – !'

'I can do it.' She swallowed. 'I can.'

'Jump up there from here?'

'I have to,' she said. 'Got no choice. If we jump back to the side, that thing'll just chase us till we drop. This is the only way out. When I'm up, I'll come down the stairs and open the door. Then you jump across.'

Ben turned on the spot, watching the water, his last stone raised ready to throw. 'You'd better be sure. If you're not sure...'

'I am.' Tiffany gritted her teeth. She remembered how they used to squabble, vying with each other to be the best in the class. That urge to show off in front of him still lingered, pushing her, daring her. 'Watch and learn, kitten.'

No longer did she have to think about which catras to call. Her Mau body knew what it needed to ignite. Blue and indigo fused in the darkness of her mind, forming a lens to focus the golden rays of Parda, and every sinew in her body trembled, primed for simultaneous detonation.

She nailed her gaze to the balcony rail, and hit the switch.

Perhaps she grew in height by an inch or more as her spine became a spring. Everything vanished in the ecstasy of flight. Then, through the gaps in her outstretched fingers, she saw the rail of the balcony above her, and knew in one missed heartbeat that she would not make it. The leap was easily a record for her, more than ten feet straight up and nearly as much across. But it wasn't enough to reach the rail.

Her palms smacked into the balcony's clear safety barrier and slid down it. She scrabbled at the plastic till her fingers snagged the only handhold available, the lip of floor that jutted underneath the barrier. She dangled. The last air left her lungs in the strangest noise, part groan of frustration, part wail of fear.

'*Tiffany! Hold on!*'

Unnecessary advice from Ben there. Even so, she wasn't sure she could follow it. Already the tendons in her wrists were on fire. Hanging from her fingertips she strained for a chin-up, excruciating and pointless, for the rail was too high to grab. Her legs kicked below her, trying to climb upon thin air.

'Ben. Help.'

Don't look down, she thought, as she looked down. Below her, the waters ruptured. From here it looked like a grotesque flower growing, opening two giant petals rimmed with teeth. Launched upon its thrashing tail, the crocodile reared its front end out of the water to snap at her flailing feet. Her ankles felt the wind of its jaws and it plunged back down, leaving the sole of her left trainer flapping in tatters.

Her fingers slipped. She had no strength for Mau claws.

'*Ben…*'

In the corner of her eye she saw him, crouched on the island's shore. There was nothing either of them could do. The crocodile's snout broke the surface again and it climbed into the air to get her.

Ben moved. He rose like a sprinter as if to run across the surface of the water. And then… then he *did*.

At the splash of his second stride, she realised. He was running up the crocodile's back. As it reared upon its tail, as high as a man, Ben reached the nape of its neck, bounded up onto its opening jaws, and from that rising springboard he launched himself aloft to vault onto the balcony rail.

'*Grab hold!*'

She seized the hand that he thrust down to her. Then she was over the rail and lying on the gallery, limp as a landed fish. Ben sank beside her, his clothes squidging out water. Niagara-sized splashes echoed off the ceiling as the crocodile went mental far below.

'Nice,' she paused for breath, 'one.' Her heartbeat slowed till it was merely racing. 'Why can't you do stuff like that in pashki class?'

He laughed weakly, laid flat on the floor. Tiffany found only shreds of her left trainer.

'Damn! That lizard ate one of my Pumas.'

She shucked off the remaining trainer and tossed it over the rail, plop.

'More pocket money down the drain.'

'Add shoes to your Christmas list.' Ben smoothed his bedraggled hair. 'A new pair of Crocs.'

'Oh shut up.'

With moody silences, Ben was making it clear that he wanted to go home. But tonight Tiffany had traipsed halfway across London and almost fallen down a crocodile's throat, and now she had to walk around in damp socks. To cap it all, in the confusion of getting locked in the pool room, she had forgotten to video Baron's confession. She could not leave empty-handed.

They followed the trail of bright lights from one wing of the mansion to the other, without finding the artist himself. Occasionally a footfall thumped on a floor above or below, and Baron's scent glowed from banisters and doorknobs, laced with a tang that Tiffany recognised as fear.

Then she opened a door and found darkness. The faint echo of the latch was enough to tell her that the room was big, uncarpeted and sparsely furnished. Mismatched objects littered the floor: a trumpet, a bowling ball, an ancient reel-to-reel tape recorder, a road atlas... Two easels stood against the wall, one paint-splattered, one clean, beside a modest shelf of art materials.

'His studio,' said Ben.

In a cupboard beneath a drawing desk, she found it.

'Gotcha.' Tiffany pulled out a black leather briefcase. Inside was a panel of foam lining, with holes of various shapes and sizes, all empty. She glanced at Ben for confirmation. 'So. Why did Mister Isidorus give him *this?*'

'Those brass cogs and stuff...' Ben spoke under his breath. 'Isidorus said they were for a scale model.'

Their eyes met. The clock, of course.

'His biggest ever exhibition,' Ben murmured, 'but he didn't design it himself. Someone else did. What's that about...?' Rummaging in the apparently empty foam compartments, he fished something out, the size of a keyring fob. 'Hey. A flash drive. There might be files on here.'

'Give.' Tiffany took it. This briefcase might help, but it wasn't enough. She needed solid proof, something tiger-related.

'Wait.' Ben caught his breath. 'That's it.'

'What is?'

'His exhibition. The title of it. Tiffany, it's called The Clock Is Set.'

'Set?' she echoed. 'You mean, like – ?'

Before she could fathom this new riddle, a sound made her spin, jingling her bell. Ben rose into Arch on Guard.

'Listen.'

A sob, Tiffany was sure. A grown man, crying.

'Hide!' hissed Ben.

'It's Baron who has to hide from me.' She strode to the door. Outside was a corridor, and silence, as if the weeping had simply switched off. She was entertaining thoughts about haunted mansions when the silence broke with an extraordinary series of noises: a thud, a judder of wood, then several loud slams. Ben ran past her and she gave chase, wondering why she'd picked up this splinter of terror.

They reached a landing above an elegant staircase. Hanging from the other side of the handrail was a taut and shivering scarlet cord. The floor of the landing obscured Tiffany's view, but her mind filled in the blanks. That cord was from Miles Baron's bathrobe, and the weight twitching on the end of it must be Miles Baron. He had knotted it round his neck, tied the other end to the banisters and thrown himself over the handrail. Out of the stairwell came the *slam* of his bare feet kicking the wall.

Ben dived on his belly and swiped at the cord. It parted with a twang at the touch of his Mau claws. A second of silence ended with a complicated thud.

'What – ?' Tiffany couldn't move. 'What did you do?'

'Quick.' Ben sprang down the stairs. Twenty feet below, Miles Baron lay on the lobby floor, the knotted cord trailing from his neck. Ben tugged at the noose to loosen it.

'He's breathing. Help me get him into the recovery position.'

Her world was still in slow-mo. 'Ben… you cut him down!'

'Yeah. He was trying to hang himself. Didn't you see?' Ben bent one of Miles Baron's legs and used it as a lever to roll him over. He had obviously learned first aid.

'But…'

'But what?' Ben's stare was piercing.

She thought, *But he deserved it. Baron deserves to die.* Then she had a vision of watching him actually do it. She imagined another version of tonight, in which Ben wasn't here, in which she stood upon this

97

landing, not cutting the cord, watching it twist and jerk. What would she have thought as she walked out of the house, perhaps passing under the dangling dead body? That there was a good night's work?

She ran down the stairs to Ben.

'Thanks,' she said.

'Trust me. It's better he's alive,' said Ben. 'People won't stop hunting tigers just because he's dead.'

Tiffany had to sit down. How close she had come, how horribly close, to being Baron's executioner.

'But – suicide,' she said. 'Why?'

Baron gurgled a groan as Ben moved a leg that looked very broken.

'Them,' he muttered. 'Must be. Isidorus and his set. He tried to tell us, didn't he? He said they get inside you. That's how they work.'

'Get inside? How?'

'Search me. But he was acting pretty mad before. We've seen that gang pull off some weird stuff, right? Vanishing boats and so on. Might be a sort of hypnosis. Maybe they fixed it so that he'd kill himself before he could turn them in.'

Tiffany tried to silence faint alarm bells that had started to ring inside her head.

'Hypnosis can't do that.'

'Maybe theirs can,' said Ben.

From the hall came hurrying footsteps.

'Who…' April the maid stopped in a doorway, her hair wilder than ever. She backed away, uttering cries that might have been her own language, or pure panic.

'It's okay…' Tiffany broke off. She reflected that the maid could see two dripping wet intruders standing over her twisted, half-strangled employer. *Okay* didn't quite cover it. She needed another word.

'Run?' she said to Ben.

He agreed.

10

 STRINGS AND TANGLES

Soon it was all too clear how badly Tiffany's plan had backfired. The third item on Monday's evening news reported that Miles Baron, the UK's most controversial artist, had been taken to hospital following an accident. In Tuesday's news the story had leapfrogged to the top: controversial artist Miles Baron was in intensive care, his injuries confirmed as the result of a break-in at his Greenwich home. By Wednesday, they were no longer bothering to call him 'the controversial artist', and on Friday the Tate Modern had to introduce a new queuing system to cope with the crowds. The artist's mysterious brush with death had sent his fame skyrocketing, and the whole world wanted to see 'The Clock Is Set'. Ben turned off the TV, imagining Tiffany throwing things at hers.

Ben went Christmas shopping, but it couldn't distract him for long. Between a hamburger stand and a market stall selling Buddha incense burners, assailed by wildly differing smells from either side, he pulled his mewing phone from his pocket.

'What is it, Tiffany?'

He had to plug the other ear to hear her. Spitalfields Market could make a Turkish bazaar seem a bit flat. In here, you didn't choose where to walk, you just joined a bit of crowd that was surging in the right direction. Ben anchored himself to a pillar that held up the roof of the market, near to where Daniel stood browsing a rack of designer sweatbands.

So far, today had gone okay. After breakfast Dad had slipped him twenty quid to get a present for Mum, and when he checked his jacket pockets at the bus stop he found a note from Mum and twenty pounds to buy something for Dad. Ben had got Dad a DVD about Muhammad Ali, and Mum's gifts were a tub of organic moisturiser, an assortment of herb seeds for her window boxes, a CD of yoga chants and a brick of butterscotch chocolate. Adding the change to the tenner he had managed to save up, he was left with sixteen pounds and only one remaining problem: what to buy for Tiffany.

Shopping with Daniel made it that much trickier to browse stalls of necklaces, girly scarves and perfumes. Luckily Daniel was the last person to notice, obsessed as he was with finding jewellery for himself. He had recently achieved his ambition of mustering his own street dance crew, and the next step was getting suitably kitted out, only he didn't really have any money right now, but maybe he could pay Ben back…? On reflection, the phone call was a welcome interruption.

'I've found him.' Tiffany rarely bothered with stuff like 'hello'. 'Ben, the masked man… I know who he is.'

'What?' Ben sought shelter from the crowd noise inside a grotto of hanging rugs. The man running the stall eyed him suspiciously. 'Did you say mask?'

'You know. Monster Head. The man in the black mask. At the Clink Wharf apartments. With Mister Isidorus.'

'Okay. Slow down.' He stuck his head between rolled carpets so as to hear her better. She had uploaded the flash drive, she said. It contained instructions.

'Instructions for what?'

'Building that clock in the Tate, of course. Everything's here, the full-scale dimensions… there's even an animation of the finished mechanism.'

Ben's stomach did a flip. 'It's a time bomb?'

'No. It's a clock.'

'But –'

'That's all it is, so far as we can tell. A giant clock. Stuart says it's got far too many gears, but those might just be to make it run so slowly.'

Ben saw the stallholder staring, alerted by the word *bomb*. He said, louder, 'So it's only a work of art after all?'

'Maybe,' said Tiffany. 'I thought it must be some con-trick at first. Now I'm not sure… Anyway, that's not why I called you.'

She trailed off and coughed. Her throat sounded raw from all that screaming the other night. Ben waited.

'Listen,' Tiffany continued. 'That guy with the monster head. Me and Stuart went through the files on the memory stick. There's stuff there about… about the thing Baron said. The Set.'

'Yeah, what is that?'

'Hard to describe it. A gang. Or a criminal network. Or a religious cult. It looks really old.'

She paused. Ben knew she wanted him to ask.

'How old?'

'As old as pashki.' Static muffled her words. 'They're from the same place, Ben. The Set began in Ancient Egypt.'

The carpet seller was looking at Ben as if he were a dog with a cocked leg. Ben squeezed out past a young couple who had stopped to stroke a rug's rich nap, and found a new quiet spot behind Daniel's bling stall. Tiffany was still talking.

'Set or Seth is the name of an Egyptian god. There are pictures of him in the documents on the drive. And hieroglyphs. The Set must be a cult that still follows the god Set. Like the Cat Kin worship the cat goddess.'

'Do we?'

'Ben, be serious!'

'Let me guess. Set wasn't one of the nice cuddly gods.'

'No,' said Tiffany. 'Not unless you like storms, darkness, earthquakes, and being hacked into little pieces.'

'Oh. He did a lot of that?'

'Look him up. To worship a god like that, you'd have to be…'

Like those men at the flat, Ben thought. He chinned his phone to pass his shopping bag to the other hand. 'You said something about the guy in the mask.'

'That was him.' A click on the line might have been Tiffany swallowing. 'The pictures of Set in the files. They're the same.'

Ben started to say something – he wasn't sure what. Tiffany spoke first, almost too fast to follow.

'In the ancient tomb paintings, Set is shown as a huge man with a beast head. A long snout and pointy ears or horns, like a cross between a goat and a jackal. No-one has ever worked out what the Set animal is meant to be. But that was him. The thing we saw.'

'Tiffany – ' Ben cut in. 'He was a man, not a thing. You don't get Egyptian gods in London.'

'No. Of course not.' She seemed gladdened by his response. 'I mean, he was *dressed* as Set. Playing the part. Which might make him a high priest or something…' Her husky voice petered out, betraying a great weariness. 'Ben. I thought this would be over by now.'

'Me too.'

'I thought all I had to do was get Miles Baron.'

'Wasn't it?'

Ben heard the rasp of her fingernails against her phone.

'We messed up,' she said. 'I can't go to the police now. All that evidence I got, months of investigating –' She blew a loud raspberry.

'It's enough,' he insisted. 'We could put him in jail.'

'Who? Us?' She laughed bitterly. 'Wake up. We're the bungling intruders. We'd get locked up for longer than him. All we've done is make him more famous!'

'We can send your evidence to the police. Y'know, anonymously.' He took a deep breath. 'I'll send it, if you want.'

'*No*, Ben. I mean, thanks,' she added. 'Thanks for the offer. But we've only got one option now.'

Ben nodded to himself, watching the tide of Christmas shoppers, happy to be lost among them. Tiffany was right. The only sensible choice for them was to lie low and wait until this trouble had blown over.

'We have to go after the Set,' said Tiffany.

'*What?*'

'The Set killed the tigers, Ben.' She was audibly gritting her teeth. 'That's how they paid Miles Baron. They're the ones behind it all.'

'That's no reason to risk our necks by… And what do you mean? Go after them *how?*'

She ignored that question. 'What would be stupid is doing nothing. Are you hoping they won't notice us? They already have.'

Ben's phone grew slippery in his grip. 'Baron said a lot of weird stuff.'

'And some of it made sense. Ben, the Set know about the Cat Kin. We've got to get them before –'

She didn't finish. *Before they get us.*

'Okay.' His bag of Christmas shopping felt like it was full of bricks. 'What job have you got lined up for me?'

'You can start by telling the others,' said Tiffany. She coughed. 'I'm losing my voice.'

Ben hid his face in the leaping bubbles of his Coke, drinking to avoid having to make smalltalk. Yusuf's mum Jane had shown him into the house with gushing, un-English delight, while her husband Gabir cracked silly jokes to put him at ease, and Yusuf had opened his bedroom door in the usual friendly manner, but still Ben had a feeling that he wasn't entirely welcome.

Susie, fidgeting on the chair by the desk, cast a tight smile his way. She beckoned Yusuf close and murmured something. Ben chose not to overhear. A knock at the door made Susie jump.

'You guys want snacks?' Even after years of living in London, Jane Mansour sounded American. She breezed right on in, cleared Yusuf's desk and set down a tray bearing a dish of stuffed olives and three bags of crisps. Yusuf shooed her from the room with smiles and thank-you-moms and barely concealed impatience.

Ben was tempted to leave too. Turning up without calling ahead, he hadn't thought that Susie might be here, and that she and Yusuf might not want more company. He'd been a twit. But Yusuf had made him sit down and chill out, and Susie didn't look peed off at him, exactly, just miserable. She was sniffing and wiping her delicate almond eyes. Ben wondered in alarm what on earth he had interrupted, till Yusuf told him.

Susie had been suspended from school. No, he hadn't misheard. She'd been suspended for cheating in last summer's exams. Ben could only shake his head. It was so obviously a mistake. Susie was top of her class in most subjects, and wouldn't need to cheat. But to his amazement she nodded, bitterly.

'I did. Sort of. In Maths. I'm not so good at Maths.'

Meaning she didn't always get more than eighty percent marks. Ben listened as she explained. She'd had doubts about a couple of questions in the Maths paper, and as her mind wandered, her cat hearing had awakened. On the far side of the hall she heard two fellow pupils cheating, whispering about those very questions. Their approach sounded right, so she filled in her answers accordingly. Both were wrong.

Three sets of identical mistakes, one from a candidate seated many rows apart, caught the eyes of the teachers who did the marking. Before long they were investigating all of Susie's exam papers for similarities with others.

'They're mad!' Yusuf burst out. 'Why do they think you'd crib? One of the biggest swats in the whole year…'

'Exactly.' Susie crumpled in despair. 'They don't think I copied. It's worse than that. They think there's a big cheating scam and I'm the ringleader. Of course people would pay me to give them the answers. It all makes perfect, perfect sense!'

Yusuf murmured helpless words of comfort, stopping short of putting his arm round her. Once more Ben wished he wasn't here.

Through her tears, Susie continued. The headteacher wanted the names of everyone to whom she had given help. Of course, there were no names to tell. So she was suspended until she had a change of heart, or until someone else coughed up the information. She supposed there must really be some sort of cheating racket going on, to make the teachers so sure. But of course, she knew nothing about it.

'I'm going to be expelled,' she wailed. 'I know I'll be expelled.' And she was sure no other good school would take her after that. She could kiss goodbye to her future. Her parents were practically in shock. For the Liu family, doing well at school was life itself. Susie appeared genuinely afraid that if she didn't grade in the top one per cent they might abandon her to starve on a hillside.

'It's gonna be okay.' Yusuf stroked her hair. 'Trust me.'

'Dad would go mental at me just for coming here.'

Yusuf frowned. 'Why? Because I'm – ?'

'No.' Susie sighed. 'Because you're a boy, that's all. Boyfriends lower grades. What else matters except *grades*?'

She sought out the plate of olives and set to eating them one by one. Yusuf stared from his window, as if the answer to his girlfriend's problems might be projected on the grey clouds covering London.

'Ben?' He frowned. 'Did you say you had stuff to tell us?'

'Er…'

'I know,' Yusuf smiled. 'Tell us more about your fun with the croc the other night. That'll cheer us up.'

Susie was now savaging a bag of crisps with her teeth to get it open. Ben put aside his empty glass.

'Never mind,' he said. 'It wasn't that important. We can talk about it later. At pashki.'

He mumbled something bland and supportive and got out of there.

Neither Susie nor Yusuf came to the next pashki class. Nor did Daniel, who was really sorry, but tonight was the only night this week that his dance crew could practice. Also missing, for the first time ever, was Tiffany. She explained in a blisteringly long text message that her sore throat had got so bad, her parents had imprisoned her in bed, to be force-fed hot lemon and honey. She finished by reminding Ben, in capital letters, to pass on her warnings about the Set.

But with only Cecile and Olly there to tell, it wasn't quite the council of war he had anticipated. Ever the loyal disciple, Cecile assured him that of course she'd be there for anything the Cat Kin had to do, and Olly said it was fine by him, so long as no exotic reptiles were involved. Then, almost in the same breath, Olly suggested an end-of-term Cat Kin party, an evening of sausage rolls, mince pies and video games at his house. Cecile was far more enthused about that, and at once got busy helping Olly to plan it. Ben had the uncomfortable impression that she didn't get asked to many parties. This was puzzling, for no-one could be nicer than Cecile, and at school she had no shortage of friends. But Ben knew that she lived in a tiny, messy, overcrowded flat in the worst sink estate in the borough. Cecile, groomed and tidy herself to the point of obsession, made no secret that she loathed the place and was ashamed to bring anyone home. That might explain why she herself got left off guest lists.

The possibility of a full-blown Christmas party, at Olly's enormous house of all places, was obviously such a dizzying prospect that Ben hated to interrupt. With all the talk of which games to play and what music and food they should have, they managed perhaps five minutes of actual pashki, and then it was time to leave. Ben, feeling guilty, repeated Tiffany's urgent message, and both of them promised to be ready if called. On the way home he left voicemails for the absentees, and eventually got back similar promises by text. But Susie's was just *Yeah whatever* and the others were hardly more sincere. He would have to tell them all again, he knew. He went to bed wondering how.

At breakfast there was something in the air.

Both Mum and Dad seemed in good moods, even more so than usual, chirping around the kitchen while he sat munching Sugar Puffs. Yet he could feel a tension too, as if behind their bright smiles they were worried.

Mum piled her plate with four slices of toast, thickly buttered them and started eating. It looked like she had her appetite back, after her bout of sickness. In fact she might even have put on weight.

Ben heard Dad clear his throat, saw him glance across the table. Mum put a spoonful of sugar in her tea. She didn't normally take sugar. Her other hand she placed lightly on her stomach.

'Ben,' she said. 'We've got some news.'

Alone in his room, he thought, *Okay*.

Okay, fine.

I can live with that.

Resting his elbows on the window sill he gazed down Gillespie Drive, to the distant green of Highbury Fields, sliced by the misty rays of the morning sun.

Okay.

What was so bad about that? Nothing. He couldn't understand why Mum and Dad had seemed afraid to tell him. A new baby on the way? That was fine by him. No, it was more than fine. It was great. It was fantastic.

A bit of a surprise, but fantastic.

Clearly Mum had mistaken his first dumbstruck look for horror, for she had stumbled into what sounded almost like an apology. She and Ray had always meant to have another kid – 'give you a little sister or brother' – only things had got in the way. It was obvious what she meant by 'things', but she passed over those seven years of separation with just a small sigh. Now she was – well, she would be forty-one next year, and soon it would be too late. Did Ben understand?

All he'd been able to do was nod and say 'Okay' a lot. Then he had to leave them both looking worried, to go to his room for a think. There he decided that he was, actually, thrilled. This was more than he had dared to hope. Ever since Mum and Dad had got back together, he had been living on his nerves, waiting for something to go wrong. It was all too perfect to be real. But a baby on the way! That was real. That clinched it.

He returned to the kitchen, gave Mum a hug, cheekily congratulated Dad, and told them both exactly what he thought of it. They looked unimaginably relieved.

'But if you think I'm changing any nappies,' he said, 'forget it.'

'Never mind, I'll manage. No –' Mum jabbed a finger towards Dad, '*you* don't get out of it this time.'

As Ben poured another bowl of cereal to celebrate, he was surprised to see Mum's anxious face return.

'There's one more thing,' she said.

'Mm?'

'We've only been in this flat a few months, I know, but,' she bit her lip. 'I don't think it'll be big enough for four.'

'Not big enough?' He held his hands apart. 'Babies are only that long.'

Dad laughed. 'Ben, you've been getting smaller by the year. When you started out you had more stuff than I did. Cots and buggies and toys and clothes… it's like bringing home an elephant.'

Ben cottoned on. 'You mean we'll have to move again?'

'Soon,' said Mum. 'I'm not sure when. Before it comes, or could be after. The sooner the better, I think. It's not long till your big exams, and I don't want you trying to study in a tiny flat with a screaming baby. We might afford a house if we look outside of London. You'll have more space to yourself there.'

Ben felt their eyes upon him. They were waiting for the inevitable teenage tantrum, for him to shout and refuse to go along with this. After all, Mum had been here before. When she'd moved out of

London last year she had wanted to take Ben, but he had dug in his heels and stayed with Dad. How she must have been dreading this.

Finishing his second breakfast, he looked up at their nervous smiles and saw that, for the first time, they needed his permission. They wanted him on their side, but they couldn't force him to be. He had to choose.

'I'd want a bigger bedroom,' he said.

'Definitely,' said Dad.

'Could I still play loud music?'

Mum's face turned rosy. 'You don't mind?'

He shook his head.

Of course, he minded. Inside, his thoughts were churning like Lottery balls – but he could predict how they would come out. He would grow used to the idea of a new town and a new school. Because this time it was different. When Mum had wanted him to move before, that had been for bad reasons. This reason was good. And too important for him to mess up.

So he kept telling himself, as he lay awake that night. What did it matter if they lived a few miles out of London? He could carry on seeing Tiffany, he'd only have to hop on a train, or she could come and visit him, if she wanted to. Would she? His thoughts spun for a moment on that point. But moving house, that was no problem. New school, not a problem.

Sleep would not come. He lay first on one side, then the other. It was very late indeed when he sat up in bed and buried his face in his hands.

He was thrilled about the baby. He was fine about moving house. He was happy. That was the truth. And that was the trouble.

Through the noise of his mind he heard Tiffany's warning.

Are you hoping they won't notice us? They already have. The Set know about the Cat Kin.

He had never been so happy.

He had never had so much to lose.
Why did this have to happen *now?*

11

THE WATCHING EYES

When Ellen opened the door, Tiffany's brave face slipped, and it was hard not to fall into her counsellor's arms. Ellen was startled.

'Tiffany! Your appointment's not today?'

'Mrs Thornwill.'

'Ellen, please. Come in, Tiffany. What's wrong?'

'Ellen –' Tiffany held back a sob. 'I've done… something terrible.'

The counsellor looked her up and down, from her muddy trainers to her rain-flattened hair.

'You came here by yourself? On the bus?'

Tiffany sank into the sofa, wishing it might swallow her. Ellen fetched her some water.

'Wait till you're ready, Tiffany. My next appointment cancelled, luckily, so we've got time. Are things bad again? You've been doing so well.'

'It's not to do with any of that.' She couldn't bear Ellen's kind words. 'My brother. Stuart. I think –'

'Yes?'

'I think I might have killed him.'

Ellen was amazing. Her face betrayed not a flicker of alarm. She merely nodded and sat in the blue armchair, as if Tiffany had remarked on the weather. Her eyes invited Tiffany to go on.

Well. It was like this. She and Stuart had been doing something on her computer. Playing online games, she told Ellen, because obviously the truth wouldn't do. In reality they had been studying the files from the stolen flash drive.

They had found a letter to Miles Baron, signed simply 'Isidorus', an inventory of the smuggled tiger parts (which Tiffany could not bear to read), and – by far the largest file – the plans for the installation artwork, The Clock Is Set. They had plodded through mazes of diagrams, some of them animated, describing gear trains and cog assemblies, far more complex than in any normal clock. Throughout the instructions were images like Egyptian tomb paintings: ankh symbols, chimeric beasts, and the now-familiar portrait of Set, his one visible eye peering from the screen.

'Set was the chaos god, wasn't he?' Stuart opened a fresh browser tab to show her a mythology website he had bookmarked. 'The god of darkness. Look what it says here: for the Ancient Greeks, Set became Typhon, the storm monster who nearly destroyed the Olympian gods. And see this. Another name for him was Setan.'

'Like… Satan?'

''xactly. The devil.' Stuart half-coughed it. He sounded wheezy today, but that was nothing new. His muscular dystrophy kept him from breathing as deeply as he ought to, so phlegm built up in his lungs. By contrast, Tiffany had shaken off her own sore throat in less than two days. She didn't have time to be ill.

'And just like our devil, he started out a good guy.' Stuart tapped the keyboard impatiently. 'Oh, come on! Your laptop is so slow. There, got it.'

Tiffany read the new page. It narrated the Ancient Egyptian myth of the sun god Ra, who sailed his barge through the sky every day, and then every night through the underworld. In that perilous abyss, a serpent would attack the barge, but Ra's great minion Set would fend it off with his spear, to ensure the sun would rise again the next day.

'So Set was Ra's right-hand man?' said Tiffany. 'Why'd he turn evil?'

'Dunno. People always do in myths, don't they? The person you trust to watch your back tries to stab it.'

'Not just in myths.' Unwelcome thoughts of Geoff White clouded her mind. Then a memory stirred. Hadn't Geoff said that word, once? *Set.* Yes, he had. More than that – he had screamed it in murderous rage, as if it were the worst curse on earth. And then Tiffany heard, like an echo, the voice of Mrs Powell, talking to her as the rising sun lit the moors.

Do I pray to Isis? Do I shun the evil Set?

'That's what she meant,' Tiffany said softly. Of course, Mrs Powell might have been speaking figuratively, referring only to the Ancient Egyptian god. But had she also been hinting at something more? Had she known that an organisation called the Set was still out there? Maybe that was one of the reasons she had trained the Cat Kin in the first place.

'Another thing.' Stuart wheezed his words. She noticed with a start how pale he was, how he wilted in his chair. 'I don't think Set would like cats.'

'Doesn't sound as if he likes anyone much.'

'No, but… some of the myths say that after Set turned evil, the cat goddess took over the defence of the barge, chasing off the serpent each night.'

'That makes sense,' said Tiffany. 'Pasht is sometimes called the Eye of Ra.'

'Poor old Set, though.' Stuart tried to smile. 'Losing your job's bad enough, but then being replaced by a cat…'

Tiffany laughed dutifully. Going downstairs to make their lunch, however, she found his joke niggling at her. Set and Ra were just myths, of course they were… but others might not see it that way. Some people – crazy, fanatical people – might take that tale very seriously. If the cat goddess had indeed replaced Set as the sun-god's favourite, then Set was going to be mightily hacked off at her. It would be safe to say that he wasn't a cat person.

The Set had paid Miles Baron in dead cats.

She opened a tin of tuna, mashed it with mayonnaise, cut slices of the white loaf and spread them with the mixture. Finding half a cucumber in the fridge, she used the potato peeler to make wafer-thin slices, the only way she liked it, and layered these into the sandwiches. Now the kettle was boiling, she'd put it on without noticing, of course to make Stuart some warm lemon for his chest. He really ought to be resting today, not sitting up at his computer… she started guiltily, remembering whose computer it was. Her brother shouldn't be doing her donkey work, however much he begged to help. He would tire himself out.

She grated ginger root into lemon juice, spooned in honey and half-filled the mug from the kettle. Popping in one of Stuart's hot-drink straws, she carried the mug and their sandwiches upstairs.

'Be careful with this.' She entered his bedroom sideways. 'Let it cool a bit before you sip.'

For some reason she had to finish the sentence, even while she took in the shape of him crumpled upon the floor.

'Stuart!'

Things became blurry after that. She remembered rolling him over, and the gurgling whistle in his throat as he started breathing again, and the tremble of the bedroom floor as both Mum and Dad came pounding up the stairs in answer to her scream. She remembered the paramedics arriving almost on Dad's heels, an impossibility, so she must have blanked out the time they spent waiting for the ambulance. But one other detail did stay with her. The moment before Mum burst into the room, Tiffany had looked up to see the face of Set, magnified on the computer screen at 400 per cent zoom, his goat-wolf head turned askance to fix her with one bone white eye.

Stuart had choked on phlegm and passed out. The paramedics gave him oxygen and his eyelids fluttered. Mum rode with him in the ambulance and Dad stayed behind. Dad was great at first, congratulating Tiffany on her quick response. Then she must have said a wrong thing. His mood changed.

'What were you thinking of, hanging around in his room? You've got a cold, you know you have to stay away from him!'

'Sorry, I… forgot.'

'You don't forget that! You know what happens when he gets a chest infection!'

'He'll be all right though,' Tiffany pleaded.

Dad blew up.

'*I don't know!* And if he is, it'll be no thanks to you. You stupid, *stupid* girl!'

Tiffany fled the house. Her first impulse was to go and see Ben and weep onto his shoulder. Instead she somehow ended up in Highgate, at her counsellor's private surgery.

Her sore eyes had got stuck staring at Ellen's bonsai tree. Its branches were half bare and tiny leaves littered the bookcase. Ellen had mentioned how hard these trees were to look after.

'Stuart's really ill. And it's my fault.'

Ellen wrinkled her brow in amusement. 'Because you breathed on him?'

'I had a cold. If I'm ill I always steer clear of him, it's like… house rules. Only this time I didn't, because it was so important…' Tiffany realised she had slipped up, 'I mean, because… he had this new game, and he wanted me to… to play it.'

Ellen made a dismissive gesture; she didn't have to know every detail.

'People catch colds,' she said. 'You can't be held accountable for your germs. Your dad was upset. When people are scared they over-react. He doesn't blame you. More likely he blames himself.'

Tiffany nodded, miserable, uncomforted.

'Do you think Stuart will be all right?'

'Do you?' asked Ellen.

'They've taken him back to Great Ormond Street.'

'Hmm. They're famous for being good, aren't they?'

Tiffany shrugged, admitting, 'Yes.'

'One of the best, I hear.'

Tiffany smiled through tears. No, there was no need to panic. Scares like this were practically routine for Stuart, and as usual he would be home in a few days' time. She was glad she'd come here. Ellen was fantastic. Somehow she always managed to make it better. Tiffany reached for her glass of water, but her hand still shook. The weight of worry came back down on her, crushing.

'Are you ready to go home?' asked Ellen.

Tiffany shook her head.

'Afraid to face your dad?'

Tiffany nodded.

'See if this helps.' Ellen pulled the largest silver ring from her right thumb. 'Did I ever teach you a little relaxation technique?'

Tiffany frowned. Something about that ring was familiar, but… 'No. No, you never did.'

Ellen unfastened her thin golden neck chain and threaded it through the ring. She placed the chain in Tiffany's hand. The ring swung like a pendulum, glittering.

'That's pretty,' said Tiffany. Watching it travel in circles made her realise how tired she was. How worn out, drowsy, ready to unwind. Already it felt as if she had been following the ring, this steady swing back and forth, back and forth, for minutes. Her speech slurred. 'That's a pretty ring.'

'Do you like it?' Ellen smiled, baring her white teeth. 'It belongs to a set. Now, Tiffany, my poor, foolish little tabby cat. Where did we get to?'

She and Dad kissed and made up. He said sorry for losing his temper, told her three times that nothing was her fault, and called her by his pet name for her, Truffle, until she had to ask him to stop. It was only the pair of them in the house, so he cooked dinner for two, a seafood risotto, and let her have half a glass of white wine. Dessert was a delicious redcurrant cheesecake from some very fine supermarket.

Full up and pleasantly squiffy, Tiffany relaxed on her bed. Unable to decide what music to put on, she found herself listening instead to the silence in the empty bedroom next door. Although she always felt calmer after seeing her counsellor, lately she had come home from each visit feeling oddly tired as well. Sort of… drained, and wrung out. It was similar to the way she felt after taking hard exams, the sort that sucked her brain dry.

She wandered into thoughts of Mrs Powell. Many memories were bobbing unexpectedly close to the surface, as if she had only recently been sharing them with someone. How she wished she could really do that. Have a proper chin-wag about Felicity Powell. She doubted that even Ben would understand. To him and the other Cat Kin, Mrs Powell had been a guide and guardian, but to Tiffany she had been a friend. A difficult friend, yes, prickly and maddening and yet, in spite of all that, a joy to be with.

Her phone rang. The name on the screen made her snatch it up.

'Mum? How is he?'

A pause.

'I'm okay.' The words trailed into a wet rattle. Not Mum.

'Stuart? You should be resting.'

'Mum's gone to the canteen for some dinner.' He stopped again. It sounded like he was having to haul his every breath up a gravelly slope. 'She left her phone on my bedside,' another breath, 'cabinet. I have to…'

'Stuart, don't! You'll wear yourself out.'

'…talk to you.'

It made her sick, how weak he sounded.

'Stuart, you lie down and rest. That's an order. I'm going to hang up now.'

'Shut up and let me talk, you silly cow.'

She was startled into silence. The line went windy as Stuart recovered from the effort.

'I found out,' he gasped. 'Before I fainted.'

'Found out what?'

'Why your laptop is so slow.'

At first she couldn't believe he was phoning from his hospital bed to discuss an I.T. problem. Then she began to piece together his breathless sentences. While she was downstairs making lunch, he said, he had tried to sort out the computer by running a virus check. The security software had flashed a red alert. There were no actual viruses, but Tiffany's laptop was riddled with spyware. Programs that allowed someone out there to read anything on her hard drive.

She gripped the phone. 'Did you get rid of it?'

'I was trying to. When I…'

'Sorry. Stupid question. How did it get there? From the memory stick?'

No, it had been there for ages, he reckoned. It had almost certainly come from an attachment. She must have opened an emailed file which had then installed the spyware.

'I don't open files from strangers,' she protested.

'Might not be from a stranger. Might be someone you think you know. Off that forum?'

Tiffany thought hard. There were some odd sorts on the Vanished Harmony forum, no doubt about it. She was careful about which ones she contacted. But none of them had ever sent her an attachment, had they? Oh, but there had been one, just one. From **happygolucky**, the backpacker. Every so often, Joy sent emails from her travels, politely enquiring how Tiffany was getting on, telling her about the beach market in Mumbai, or complaining of a smog in Beijing… Joy had emailed her that zip file of leopard photos. Including the leopard that was now her desktop wallpaper, with the eyes that always seemed to be watching her.

No, it was impossible. Joy was definitely her friend. She would never have sent spyware. Tiffany squirmed with doubts. It dawned on her that she had no solid proof that the forum member called **happygolucky** was the person she claimed to be. That fuzzy picture of a young blonde woman could have been anyone. Joy's stories of travelling in Asia could be entirely made-up. She might not even be a she. She might be Mister Isidorus himself. But if that was the case... The thought made Tiffany dizzy.

'This is serious,' wheezed Stuart. 'Whoever sent that spyware, they know all about you now. Everything on your PC.'

Tiffany bit her knuckle, thinking: *our home address!* Was that stored on her computer? She tried to recall if she had written her address in any documents, or ordered something online. But no. It was Mum's computer they used for internet shopping, and she never wrote paper letters. That was a tiny relief. But the spy would still have learned about pashki, and the Cat Kin, and the fact that she had uploaded a flash drive of secret files belonging to the Set.

Stuart had talked too much. His voice dissolved in coughs.

'Rest now,' said Tiffany. 'Thanks for the warning. You're a hero, you know.'

'I'm –' Cough.

'Yes you are. Nothing stops you. I'm amazed you can even *lift* that phone. Now put it down,' ordered Tiffany, 'and put your oxygen mask back on.'

'I'm off the oxygen now, Tiffany,' Stuart panted, 'I'm scared.'

'Don't be scared.' She shut her eyes. 'You're going to be fine.'

'Not me. You. You...' he cleared his throat, 'always say you want to follow Mrs Powell. But I don't want you to... follow her too far.'

'Too far?' Tiffany sat up straighter. The bell tinkled on her wrist.

'If something happened to you,' Stuart wheezed. 'You know what I mean.'

She went cold all over.

'That would stop me,' said Stuart.

'Cut it out,' she said. 'I'll be fine. You'll be fine. Stuart, listen. No-one is going to die. Do you hear me? *No-one is going to die.*'

12

MIRRORS AND MESSAGES

Crouching almost in the gutter of the roof, Ben fixed his gaze upon the street light as the wind shook it. Before another gust could blow him off course, he leaped into the glare like a moth.

The post shuddered as he grabbed the lamp housing, remembering too late how hot it would be. He dangled from the crossbar, dazzled blind, managing by a whisker not to fall on Dad's van. Sliding a little way down the post, he gripped with his heels and let his baked hands and face cool in the wind. When his eyes at last cleared of dancing purple, he summoned his Mandira catra and looked back through his open bedroom window.

On his bedside chest of drawers stood the mirror in which he brushed his hair. Ben slid a centimetre or two further down till he was staring into its dead centre. Yes. This was the point, right… here. He plucked the marker pen from his pocket and made an X on the lamp post. Then, clinging on with both feet and one hand, he reached into his knapsack and pulled out a car's rear-view mirror.

It was his last one.

The mirror went between his teeth, like a pirate's knife, while he rooted in another pocket for his nearly-empty tube of Super Glue. He squeezed the last few dribbles onto the X and pressed the stalk of the rear-view mirror firmly in place, while the wind swayed the lamp post and his extremities turned numb with cold. He hoped no-one was awake and looking out of their window at him, lit up like a Christmas decoration.

When the glue had bonded he adjusted the mirror's angle, tilting it till it reflected the mirror in his bedroom. Then he tweaked it till he could see two more: one attached to the TV aerial, and another stuck to a satellite dish. He did a final check: bedroom mirror – roof mirror

– dish mirror. At last, the angles were perfect.

Ben slid down to the pavement and let himself back into the block. On the stairs he checked a fourth mirror that he'd wedged inside a ventilation fan. Satisfied, he tiptoed into the flat and flopped onto his bed. Job done. It had only taken him half the night.

Lacking the cash to buy a network of security cameras, this was the best he could manage. Ben knew Hamish's Car Dump like an old playground, from when he and the lads from the arcade used to sneak into the Dalston breaker's yard in search of junk and danger. Yesterday evening's visit had been his first for years, clambering from wreck to wreck, snapping off as many rear-view mirrors as he could find. Now eight of those mirrors adorned the outside of the flat, angled on their adjustable stalks to bounce light between them.

Every possible entrance to the flat – door, window or balcony – had a mirror in line of sight. All directed their reflections towards four more mirrors attached to nearby trees and the lamp post, which in turn relayed the images to his bedroom mirror. In theory, if anyone so much as approached his home, he would be able to glance up from his bed or his desk and see them coming.

Fighting off sleep, he got up to test his new system. He had to lean in close to his bedside mirror until his breath misted the glass, for the images that reached him were vanishingly small, like objects seen through a backward telescope. His cat-like eyesight might be able to catch a movement, but recognising a face would be beyond him. He'd have no way of telling between a Set assassin and the postman. For a moment he sagged, dejected at his wasted efforts. Still, a glimpse was a glimpse. And he felt sure that, even as a faraway speck, the sight of a Set agent would make his inner cat's fur stand on end.

The pull of his duvet grew too strong to resist. Ben let himself melt into its warmth, his eyelids falling, and at once saw the flaw in his plan. That net of mirrors would only work while he was here, and awake. Tomorrow he'd have to improve it… find a way of adding noises to alert him. Could he slip tinfoil under the hall carpets? Persuade Dad to install alarms? And how would he protect his family when he wasn't around? He drifted into dreams of buying Mum a pepper spray, of Dad carrying a knuckle-duster, of a newborn baby in an armoured buggy...

A cat mewed in the darkness. He sat up.

His phone. Not the long, miaowing ringtone, but the softer mew that meant a text message. Ben found the thing under his bed. He did not feel tired; he felt like he'd been run over by a steamroller.

The screen glowed. The message was from Yusuf.

All Set for some fun? Come to mine now.

Ben rubbed his eyes. Now? What did Yusuf mean, now? It was the very pit of night. He supposed it was a mistake, an old message that had got delayed. Then he noticed that capital S. Of course. Yusuf was telling him, in cryptic fashion, that this was urgent.

Ben hunted for his clothes, realised he was still in them. Rather than waste time texting back, he stuffed his bed with pillows, the usual precaution. Then, not without a shiver of reluctance, he opened his window for the umpteenth time that night. There were no suitable buses to surf at this godforsaken hour. It would have to be the rooftops.

Luck was with him. At the last chimney in his street he heard a rumble, a freight train on the overground line that ran through Seven Sisters, creeping softly past the sleeping houses. In sprints and leaps Ben chased the sound, bounding to a bridge with seconds to spare before the train's rearmost truck rolled underneath. He dropped onto the roof.

Now he could have his lie down. Hot from his dash, he stared up at silver winter stars. The train trundled on, the vibrations massaging his sore shoulders. A smell of fumes laced the frosty air, as if a diesel had recently passed this way.

A mosque's illuminated turret peered above a housing terrace, signalling his stop. Ben hit the tracks running and scrambled up the embankment, noticing the spiked fence at the top when he was already safely over it. Steering by the minaret he found a side road that led (he was pretty sure) to Yusuf's street.

It was as silent as London ever could be. Walking along the pavement now, like a normal person, Ben could hear the squeak of his trainers, the sighs of steam from houses whose central heating had switched on early. The streetlights shone for nobody's benefit. He could saunter up the middle of the car-less road. The smell he had noticed on the railway still lingered, no longer so much like diesel. Someone might have had a late fireworks party.

Rounding a bend, he heard voices. The T-junction was a paintbox of lights, yellow windows, the red tails of vehicles, and blue light, pulsing over the asphalt and brickwork in a complicated rhythm.

A car accident, he thought. T'was the season for drunk drivers. Ben approached, hoping they hadn't closed the road, not fancying another rooftop shortcut. A thin crowd had formed along a tape barrier, here and there revealing, from beneath thick overcoats, the hems of dressing gowns or pyjama trousers, blowing around bare ankles.

He reached the barrier. POLICE LINE. DO NOT CROSS. That paper shop, over there, he knew was right near Yusuf's house. Turning to get his bearings, he was dazzled by blue: a police car, two ambulances, fire engines. Through the flicker-light moved what seemed to be a party of skeletons, the reflective stripes on their uniforms showing in the darkness like bones.

Ben ducked under the tape and ran towards the vehicles, using pashki to seem like one more swirling shadow. The uniformed men and women had better things to do than notice a passing breeze, and he evaded them all, slipped between the fire engines and saw the house.

That's not Yusuf's house, was his first, relieved thought.

Then he blinked and it was.

It did not match the house in his memory because it had no door, no glass in the windows and hardly any roof. The tiles had caved in like a sunken cake, exposing joists blackened and snapped like spent matches. A solitary fireman stood aiming a hose into what had been the lounge, patiently, as if filling a swimming pool. Any flames had long since died, leaving only smoky tendrils that squirmed around the water jet. A worm of unused hose trailed in the road, where the gutters ran black with foul, stinking streams. The smell caught in Ben's throat and nausea forced him down on one knee. Crouched in the filthy dregs behind the fire engine, he heard a man shouting.

'Why them? Tell me that. What harm did they do?'

Half the neighbourhood had been roused out of bed and now stood gathered along the police tape. Ben saw young couples, men with dark or greying beards, and boys around his own age. Nearly everyone was of either Middle Eastern or Asian appearance. Women in headscarves huddled together in the cold, noisily weeping. A little way apart stood three men, a father and his grown-up sons, Ben guessed. At the father's feet was a reel of garden hose and one of the young men clutched a kitchen fire extinguisher. Again the voice broke through the general murmur.

'How did this happen? We want an answer!'

A paunchy man with thinning hair and fierce eyes yelled into the face of a policeman. He made wild gestures, like a desperate market seller.

'This family, this family –' The man narrowly avoided knocking off the policeman's helmet. 'Gabir Mansour is my friend, my good friend. I know his house like my own. He is cautious man. Everywhere, he has the smoke alarms, the sprinklers. The little hammers for breaking double glazing. How is it he does not get out? How is it he and his family do not wake up? Eh? You tell me this!'

The officer said something calming, but it had the opposite effect.

'Accident? You are blind?' The arms flew up. 'This is no accident. This is hatred. Listen to me! You investigate!'

A female officer joined her colleague, trying to pacify the man with nods and gentle words. Then Ben heard the tinkling bell and spun round. Tiffany almost ran into him.

'Ben! Where's Yusuf? Where is he?'

'I – I don't…' He stared at her, helpless.

'You got his text?' she panted. 'He… he must have been calling us for help. In code. Are his Mum and Dad okay?'

He had no answer. She pushed past, saw the gutted house and made a tiny whimpering sound.

'I don't think –' Ben began to say, but the big man in the crowd was protesting again, almost fighting the two police officers.

'I want to make statement… Take me to your police station… A man and his wife and son are dead!'

Tiffany rounded on Ben as if he'd said it.

'*Where is Yusuf?*' Her scream echoed off the houses. Two paramedics and a fireman noticed them.

'Hey,' shouted the fireman. 'Stay back. It's unsafe.'

Figures in luminous jackets closed in. Tiffany ran towards the ambulances, but a paramedic intercepted her as she wilted in shock. About to give chase, Ben felt a firm but not unfriendly grip on his shoulder, steering him back towards the tape.

'Better not, eh?' The policeman's face softened. 'Come on. The best place now is back to bed.'

Ben could only stare at the two ambulances, their doors now closed. One after the other they moved off, in no apparent hurry, their lights whirling but their sirens silent.

'Sorry,' said the policeman.

'Did –' Ben made a mighty effort. 'Did anyone get out?'

But he was now behind the barrier, and the policeman was walking away.

He found Tiffany shivering in a bus shelter. He sat beside her. No vehicles or people passed and neither of them spoke. From the sky Ben heard sirens, the usual night-time serenade, the police cars across town on their nightly calls, nothing to do with what had happened here. A plane's landing lights splashed glowing footprints through the cloud shrouding the city. He hardly noticed the chilly damp of the plastic seat. It felt as if he had banged a nerve, the ultimate funny bone, that deadened every fibre of his being.

A bird twittered in a roadside tree. Tiffany wiped her eyes.

'He's dead, isn't he?' she said.

Ben said nothing.

'Yusuf's dead,' said Tiffany. 'So's his family. They burned his house down.' She wept freely.

Ben tugged at her sleeve.

'Let's go. It's nearly morning.'

No response. She might have ended up frosted to the bench, if her phone had not uttered a miaow. She fumbled it out.

'Ben. Look.' The glowing screen read **Yusuf calling**.

'It's him,' she gasped. 'He's not dead. He's calling me, he's calling –' Her thumb found the answer button. 'Hello? Yusuf? Where are you?'

Moments passed. She frowned.

'There's no-one there.'

The phone lit up again. A mew: a text message.

'Yusuf again!'

'No!' Ben snatched it from her. 'Don't you see? That's not Yusuf. It's whoever's got his mobile.'

He had to steady the phone with both hands to read the message. It said: **You should not have upset me**

Tiffany let out a low wail.

'Ben. Did we do this? Is it our fault? Is Yusuf dead because of us?'

13
BATTLE OF THE CATS

It didn't feel real, it couldn't be real, couldn't *really* be real. Yusuf had been murdered. No. He'd seen Yusuf just the other day. He could not be dead. This was a mistake, a misunderstanding. Ben had sat there on Yusuf's bed, talking to him and Susie –

Oh no, he thought. *Susie.*

He'd forgotten about Susie.

She would find out. Well, of course she'd find out. Yusuf was dead. Yes he was, he was dead. You couldn't keep that secret. Crazily, Ben was tempted to try. If Susie found out, it would break her heart. He had to hide this from her. Cover it up so she'd never know, never, ever suspect what had happened. How could he do that, how, how?

How?

Susie would know within hours. A day at the most. She would know her boyfriend was dead.

Her heart would break.

Trodden cigarette butts littered the pavement, twitching in the wind like repulsive half-killed creatures. They became the only inhabitants of his world. He could not turn to look at Tiffany, nor raise his hands to wipe his eyes.

Yusuf, he thought. Only that. *Yusuf.* He chased after sparks of hope, remembering how Mrs Powell had once survived being shot, and how many times he himself had cheated death. Surely a mere house fire could never kill one of the Cat Kin. Yusuf would have woken up, if intruders had broken in. He would have escaped any fire, after first rescuing his mother and father, of course…

His mother and father, who were dead. Like him. Because he hadn't woken up. People had made sure of that.

'I tried to warn him,' Ben murmured. 'Like you told me to. But…'

it wasn't a good time. Susie was there, she's got some problem at school…'

Susie again. He shut his eyes. Shutting his eyes didn't help.

Tiffany said, in a flat voice, 'It wasn't a good time.'

He looked away. Tiffany's phone mewed again. She raised it jerkily. Even when she had it turned round the right way, she seemed to have trouble reading the screen.

'Ben,' she moaned. 'Ben, what does this say?'

He peered at the new text message. It said:

Now I set fire to yours.

'It's them again,' Ben blurted, stupid with shock and grief. He reread the message and his wits returned. 'Tiffany! They mean your house. We have to – we have to…'

She was on her feet.

'My mum and dad! They – Oh, they can't, they *can't!* Ben, *come on!*'

She was running, running as fast as he had ever seen her move, wildly running in an instinctive beeline towards her home, almost two miles away. Ben gave chase as she cut through a row of detached houses, crossing railings tipped with iron vine leaves, a diamond patterned patio, a bike shed, a flower bed and the yard wall at the back.

'Faster, come on!' she gasped.

'Don't, Tiffany. It's too far –' If they kept on at this pace they would melt into puddles of exhaustion. Even pashki had its limits. It could make you faster and more agile, but it couldn't give you energy you didn't have. She ignored him – her family might be trapped by flames at this moment, she would claw her way through concrete to reach them. Still running, Ben held his breath, trying to *listen*. For some moments, the dimmest of noises had been nagging at him, a rumble thinly spread in all directions, a sound so familiar it was like nothing at all. It was the silence of London. It was –

'Buses!'

Scrambling to the crest of a roof, he caught at Tiffany's arm. This was the hour. The day's first kick of life, when the city's earliest risers, the cleaners, the caterers, the hospital porters, the train drivers and the meat merchants, would be struggling out of bed, and all across London the fleets of buses were stirring in readiness. High on the rooftop Ben turned his head, trawling the skyline for just the right sound, picking up a rev and a roar to the east, and another over that way, on the fringe of Finsbury Park.

'This way!'

At the corner of Green Lanes they climbed the tallest tree, in time for the double-decker 341 that turned into the junction. Tiffany dropped ahead of him through the boughs and then they were clinging to the bus's roof. Through near-empty streets they whizzed towards Stoke Newington, a mist-rain blowing in their faces.

Tiffany squeezed his arm in thanks. He gave his bravest smile, though doubt gnawed his insides. Was there even a chance that they would be in time? Wouldn't the text have been sent, like the other, deliberately too late?

'I'm glad Stuart got ill.' Tiffany leaned sharply as the bus cornered. 'He'll be safe, he's still in hospital. But Mum and Dad were both sleeping at home last night… oh, why can't this stupid driver go any faster?'

Ben flipped through bus routes in his mind.

'We'll need to change rides,' he shouted, over the roar of engine and wind. 'What numbers pass near your house?'

Her teeth were chattering. 'I c-can't remem-ember! My dad drives me everywhere.'

It didn't matter – he'd already seen their next move. Here it came, blinking through the trees towards the crossroads ahead, a good old number 73. He crawled with Tiffany to the edge of the slippery roof and prepared to leap. Switching buses heading in different directions was always tricky, requiring an ice-dancer's timing and balance. But as their bus crossed the traffic lights Ben's concentration wavered, assailed by another pang of grief. *Yusuf. Why Yusuf?*

And then it was a thought. Why Yusuf?

Tiffany braced for the jump. He grabbed her hair. She yelled as he tugged her back from the edge.

'Stop,' he gasped.

'What did you do that for?' She flailed at him, forcing him to shield his face. Their bus rolled on through the crossroads into the next street, now moving farther away from Tiffany's home.

'Stop,' he repeated. 'Listen to me.'

She didn't stop, she didn't listen. She vaulted off the speeding vehicle onto a parked van, slithered down its bonnet to the pavement and went tearing off in the direction they had come from. Ben swore and went after her.

'Stay there,' he yelled. 'Don't take another step.'

She turned and continued walking, backwards, past the shuttered shops on the corner of Newington Green. Her face was a snarl of disbelief.

'Ben, are you mad? I have to save my family. I don't care how dangerous it is.'

'What if you wouldn't be saving them?' He moved out of the light of an advertising billboard and lowered his voice. 'What if this is a way to kill them?'

Her snarl weakened. 'Explain. *Fast.*'

'The sock,' said Ben. 'Yusuf's sock.'

He couldn't blame her for gawping. Taking a deep breath he talked as quickly as he could.

'He used his sock as a gag, remember? On that guy at Clink Wharf. He left it behind and the Set must have taken it. That was his *football* sock, Tiffany. It had his name sewn inside, and the crest of his football club. That'd be enough to find out his address. It's how they tracked him down.'

Tiffany stopped moving. 'So?'

'That's why they went for Yusuf,' said Ben. 'He was the only one of us they knew how to find.'

She frowned a question. Ben stepped closer.

'Tiffany, think! Why would they send you a warning? Because they want you to go rushing home. And lead them there.'

Her eyes filled with a terrible doubt.

'Lead them?'

'They could be following us –' Ben reflected on that; it seemed unlikely. 'Or tracking us. Watching from buildings. They could have spies all over. I think… this is a trick to get to the rest of us. Because they don't know where we live. They don't even know our names.'

Tiffany's frantic look returned.

'Yes they do! They texted me!'

'The first text –' Ben forced himself to think. 'Maybe they sent it to Yusuf's whole phone book. To see who came.' A new idea struck him. 'Did you reply? Text back?'

'I… I said I was on my way.'

Another piece fitted into place. Tiffany had replied; he hadn't.

'That's it!' he hissed. 'That's why they've texted you now and not me. They know your name and number. But that's *all* they know. They don't know where you *live*, Tiffany. Not yet.' He held her wrist – she was trying even now to edge away. 'Don't go home. We have to –'

She wrenched free of him.

'You're guessing! What if you're wrong?'

'I'm –' Hesitation was fatal. 'It's the only thing that makes sense. This is how they work, Tiffany! Don't listen to them. It's a trap.'

She seemed to stare through him, backing away as if from a devil whispering temptations.

'My parents could be burning to death and you're… you're… *why are you trying to stop me?*'

Tiffany bolted. Ben made a desperate grab that unbalanced her, and she collided with a litter bin.

'Wait.' Ben spun her round. She punched him in the face.

It surprised him more than it hurt. And it hurt a lot. At first he was sure it had been a brick thrown from a passing car. Finding himself sitting inexplicably upon the pavement, he lifted his dazed head to see Tiffany turning to run. Reflex took over and he swept a leg round, tripping her.

'Please stop! I'm trying to help –'

'*Let me go!*'

Now the kick came. He guessed that, if it connected, he might not be getting up any time soon. The only possible dodge was to roll on the asphalt, scraping his already aching face and tasting grit and who-knew-what else. There was nothing for it – she was mad with fear, beyond reason, about to make a fatal mistake. Unable to think of anything better, he lashed out with a kick of his own. It struck Tiffany under the ribcage and folded her in half.

'Sorry.' He got to his feet as she crumpled in the gutter, winded. 'Are you okay? I didn't mean to…' *Great*, he thought bitterly. *Brilliant work, Ben.* Shaking with the shock of what had happened, disgusted at what he had done, he circled to her other side so she wouldn't be able to run again.

'Tiffany. I'm so sorry.' He reached out a tentative hand. 'Please. Think. Is there *any* other way they could know where you live? Any way at all? No. There isn't –'

She unfolded and struck, almost too fast for him to flinch. Wild slashes of her hooked fingers forced him back against the shop fronts. He did his best to dodge, to fend her off, stammering pleas that went unheeded. She was like a wounded animal, gone berserk. One blow got through his Cross-Pads block, rocking his head back into something hard that cracked, and then he was twisting desperately aside as the shop window behind him became a breaking wave of glass. Frightened, he began to counter-strike, all the while begging her to stop, to calm down. His glancing Sun-Motes jab made her stagger, and he seized his chance to pin her arms by her sides, confident that he must be far stronger. Tiffany jackknifed and flung him into the roadside railings, terror lending her a strength that knocked all hope out of him, along with his breath. He fell to his knees. This was ridiculous – Tiffany was beating him up.

'*Stop!*' He managed to catch her swiping hand, forcing it upwards, showing it to her. 'Look. Please. Look at this.'

Tiffany froze, blinking stupidly, as if she'd woken too soon from a strange dream. She noticed her bloodied fingers.

'Am I cut?' She frowned at him, the question eerily calm. 'Was it the broken glass?'

'No.' Ben sniffed and wiped his sleeve across his face. 'I think that's from my nose.'

Tiffany's eyelids fluttered, like lights flickering back on. Ben found a used tissue in his pocket and tried to stem his streaming nosebleed, pinching gingerly at nostrils that were grazed from the pavement. Tiffany sat heavily beside him, in the road.

'Oh,' she gasped. 'Ben. What am I doing?'

She was pale and shaking, her hand not quite daring to brush his face.

'Are you all right?' she pleaded. 'I'm sorry. I'm so sorry.'

'I'm okay,' Ben lied.

'But… how could I do that? I can't believe it.'

'S'alright. You were scared, that's all.'

He got up, wincing all the way.

'Why?' She wiped her eyes. 'I'd never hurt you.'

'Forget it.'

Experience had taught him to carry a first aid kit.

Neither of them knew where they were walking now. So long as the road or footpath didn't lead towards Tiffany's home, they took it. The borders of Hackney blurred into Haringey, or Islington, Ben couldn't be sure. He had never felt more shattered, nor so lost. Though the sky continued dark, signs of day were springing up all around, in trickles of morning traffic and budding queues at bus stops. Ben probed his swollen lip with the tip of his tongue, tasting the zincy smear of antiseptic cream. Tiffany took out her phone.

'I'll check,' she said.

'Don't use that thing.'

'One quick call. I won't speak.'

'No,' said Ben. 'The Set got to us by using our phones. So…' He turned his own mobile off, pointedly. She sighed and did the same.

'Ben… you are sure? One hundred and twenty per cent sure?'

'Yes.' He made himself believe it. The Set's message was a bluff. He could not bear to think anything else.

'It was to find out where you live,' he repeated. 'There's no other way they could know. Is there?'

'No,' said Tiffany, after an agonising silence. 'Unless… No.'

'Positive?'

She frowned. 'Stuart did find spyware on my laptop. I guess that's from the Set too. But I don't keep my house address on my computer.' After another pause she shook her head, as if dismissing an unspoken thought. 'You must be right. They don't know where we live. All they had was his football sock…'

A terrible silence followed them all the way to the end of the street. When they had to stop at the crossing, Tiffany murmured, 'Thanks.'

'No problem.'

'I'm sorry I… you know.'

'Me too.' Ben winced at the memory of kicking her. How the Set would have loved to see that. Maybe they had. Maybe they had watched, laughing with delight, as he and Tiffany tore lumps out of each other. Had they *meant* it to happen? His flesh crawled. Even now they might be walking into a trap. Had the bluff been a double-bluff? It would be safest to check. Secretly he palmed his phone, turned it on – then gritted his teeth, prised out the battery and dropped it down a drain.

The Set get inside your head.

'I don't think anyone's following us,' Tiffany murmured. Her tone was carefully neutral, but Ben could tell she was still grappling with doubts.

'I told you. They can't match us on foot. They must have spies posted all over.' He looked up at the luxury flats on the corner, the glass façade catching the first grey light from the sky. Was that a movement in the top window? Two slats of a Venetian blind had flicked together, as if a person peering out had stepped hurriedly back.

They passed the chained gates of a primary school. A motorcycle courier with a blacked-out visor was puttering along the kerbside, apparently searching for an address. The faceless helmet glanced at them and the bike turned down a side road, with a snarl of motor that rose, then deepened. No parcel had been delivered.

At a bus top stood a woman in a brown coat. As they drew near, Ben felt hairs prickle over his neck, and a crimson pulse from his Oshtis catra. Tiffany caught her breath, as if feeling it too. At the corner Ben looked back. The woman wasn't staring after them, but she held a phone as if sending a message.

They hurried down the next road, into the shadow of a tower block undergoing renovation. Builders glanced down from scaffolding. A road sweeper picked at the gutter. A teenaged paper-girl lugged a fluorescent bag door to door, passing a drunk who sprawled on a bench. Ben looked in despair from one to another. A taxi seemed to slow down for no reason, and he thought he saw keen eyes gazing out of the back seat.

'No,' said Tiffany, when he mentioned it. 'That taxi's light was on, it didn't have a passenger. And the paper girl couldn't have been one of them. They're not everywhere, Ben. They can't be.'

The traffic thickened, streaming south towards the heart of the city. A new day. It was somehow shocking, that time had not stopped, that the world carried merrily on. For one brief, blessed moment Ben was sure: he had only dreamed that Yusuf had been killed. Then he stumbled and felt cold and sick. No, *that* had been the dream. He was dozing as he walked.

Tiffany yawned. 'What day is it?'

'Monday. I think.'

'School?' Tiffany went a shade greyer.

'You're never square enough to go today!' Ben almost laughed. 'Throw a sicky. No-one cares in the last week of term.'

'At my school they do...' She stopped walking. 'Ben, what are we thinking? We can't go home. If we're with our families, we put them in danger. You said so.'

Yes, he had. But he had only been thinking of tonight, not of tomorrow, nor the days after that. Only now did the full horror of it begin to sink in.

'Right.' Feebly he tried to joke about it. 'Know any comfortable park benches?'

Her eyes narrowed. 'There is somewhere. A place I'm sure they don't know about. Oh, but... they'd only follow us there.'

They had stopped at the end of Blackstock Road, chock-a-block with buses queuing nose to tail, waiting their turn to deposit passengers at Finsbury Park station. Ben had come to hate the red and white logo of the London Underground, for it awakened too many memories of his time at the Hermitage. But now it gave him an idea.

'I'd like to see them try,' he said.

14
FLATMATES

The key was where she'd left it. Working by touch, Tiffany unpicked the tape securing it to the inside of the door and drew it out through the catflap.

'*Voila.*'

Losing their shadowy pursuers had been easy in the end. Slipping into Finsbury Park tube station, they had slunk along the tunnels, in between the passing trains, until they reached the forgotten Hermitage station, as dark and silent as an abandoned mine now that the polecats had fled. Ben knew his way up to the secret exit, a manhole in the Hermitage Road business park, and they'd emerged into the frosty dawn light, at last certain that no-one could be tailing them anymore. Tiffany had wavered then – surely it was safe to go home now? But she knew in her gut that it wouldn't be, not as long as the Set were at large.

She unlocked the door of Mrs Powell's flat and stepped inside.

'It still smells of her.' Tiffany closed her eyes and breathed in, at once a torment and a joy. Her nostrils filled with dust, stale air, and the disinfectant someone had splashed on the common stairwell, yet underneath it all there lingered that unmistakable blend of pear blossom soap, tea caddy, and cat. It stayed only as long as the echo of a voice, or the mist-print of a hand upon a window, and with one more sniff it was lost.

Ben clicked the light switch but the hall stayed dark. The fluorescent tubes in the kitchen wouldn't work either.

'Power's cut off.' He flopped onto the nearest dining chair. 'No-one around to pay the bills. Great. No lights and no heating. In the middle of winter.'

'Wait a sec.' Tiffany rummaged in the odds-and-ends drawer, where Mrs Powell had kept her scented candles and sticky tape. The plastic card was not quite where she remembered – it had somehow tucked itself inside a sheet of instructions for the gas boiler. She took the card to the linen cupboard in the hall and found the power meter at the back. The card fitted the slot and the meter's display lit up: £6.40.

Tiffany switched on the hall light.

'Abracadabra!' She clapped. 'We've got electricity and we've got gas.'

'She was on a card meter?' Ben grinned in relief.

'Yep. But we haven't got much credit left. Better save it.' She turned the light back off. Ben was looking at her curiously.

'Do you come here a lot, then?' he asked.

'Only a couple of times. While she was away. And then once after she…' *Say it*, she told herself, 'after she died. I cleared out the cupboards and tidied up.'

'Why?'

'Because…' Tiffany shrugged. She would rather not get into this. 'She was always so clean and tidy. And I needed to – Anyway,' she interrupted herself, 'good thing I did. We've got a place to stay. The Set will never find us here.'

Leaving Ben drinking from the kitchen tap, she went through the bead curtain into the pashki studio. The bare wooden floor lay under a film of dust. Full of memories, Tiffany danced across it in a quick Eth walk, then stopped – she was too weary, her heart too heavy. The studio looked smaller than her memory of it, in the way of all former classrooms. It was only two years but how long ago it felt, when she had first sat here as one of seven confused children, while a strange old woman studied them inscrutably. There was that old poster, its corners curling a little more, explaining the system of catras: six coloured eyes superimposed on the image of the cat, and the human. Beside it, the empty cork noticeboard, never more to display another Pashki Sequence of the Week.

With the studio taking up most of the flat, the other rooms were like afterthoughts: a poky lounge that squeezed in a sofa, coffee table and TV, a no-frills bathroom, and Mrs Powell's tiny bedroom with its single bed stripped to the mattress. When she saw this, Tiffany swayed on her feet. She would have to lie down soon, or drop.

Turning back into the hallway, she met a vivid memory of Mrs Powell pouncing on her from the shadows, on the night when she'd come here alone, in desperate need of help.

Tiffany! What in the name of Anubis are you doing here?

What indeed.

The studio was the only part of the flat where she didn't feel like an intruder. Aimlessly she walked its floor, her near-silent footsteps sounding impossibly loud. There, right there, upon that knot in the grain of the wood, was where her teacher had habitually stood, leading the group in catra exercises. The plaster walls seemed to preserve her voice.

Who leads the Cat Kin now? You do, Tiffany. Or else no-one does.

'But I don't know,' she murmured. 'I don't know what to do anymore.'

Back came the reply out of her memory, sharp as a scratch.

Do not sit forever at my feet.

Mrs Powell had tried to tell her. To warn her.

Use pashki as a way to keep fit. Or give it up. Or else follow it to whatever dangerous place it leads you.

She could have stayed at home, safe and warm and well-fed. But she hadn't and here she was. She had let pashki lead her to that dangerous place.

A noise made her start. Ben stood propped in the studio doorway. She had almost forgotten he was with her.

'Um.' He coughed and looked awkward. 'I'm gonna grab some sleep.'

'Yeah. Me too,' said Tiffany. 'There's pillows and stuff in the cupboard.'

'Thanks. Er…' Ben appeared to struggle with a difficult question. 'Thing is, I've had a look around, and… Did Mrs Powell have any other bedrooms?'

Ben got the sofa. Tiffany made up Mrs Powell's bed. Though the unaired sheets had a dank smell and felt chilly as earth to the touch, the moment she was tucked under them she sank into the deepest sleep of her life. If she had dreams, they stayed buried, beyond recall. When she woke she was lying on the same side, with not the faintest idea of what time it was, nor even what day.

She stretched. Ow, but she ached. Her ribs in particular felt as if someone had kicked them. Gradually, memory returned.

'Ben?'

Dragon-breath left her mouth. This room was *cold*. With an effort of will she rolled out of bed and quickly dressed in the tracksuit she'd worn over her pashki kit last night. It was grubby and sweat-stained, and she grimaced to put it back on.

In the tiny lounge she found Ben, dead to the world upon the sofa. She watched him for a while, amused by his slack-jawed sleep face, marvelling at snores as loud as passing motorbikes, which nonetheless failed to wake him. Tiring of this entertainment, she lowered a strand of her hair to tickle his nose, till he sneezed.

'Ungh!' He awoke with flapping arms. 'Tiffany! What…?'

It struck her then that she was leaning over him, her face (her lips!) inches from his own as he lay there. In a spasm of embarrassment she pulled away and almost fell over the coffee table. Ben sat up, bleary-eyed, fortunately too groggy to notice what had happened. Not that anything *had* happened.

'Time to get up,' she said briskly.

While he was groping for his bearings, she nabbed the bathroom first. After gulping water in palmfuls out of the basin, she let herself drift away in the bliss of a hot shower. There was even a sliver of pear-blossom soap. Towelling her hair, she had to sit down on the damp floor, faint with hunger. She badly needed some breakfast, or lunch, or… what time exactly *was* it? Back at the bedroom window she studied the gloom, decided it was darker than before. Not morning, then, but late afternoon, merging into dusk. They had slept through the whole day.

In the kitchen Ben was inspecting cupboards.

'There's no food,' she told him. 'I threw it out when I cleaned up.'

'Even the tins?'

Wistfully, she remembered. 'I took those home. Typical! Come on, Ben, leave it –' he was stubbornly opening every cupboard and drawer, 'listen to me, for a change.'

'Ha!' With a victorious cry, Ben retrieved half a packet of Rich Tea biscuits from a high shelf. 'Wrong, as ever.'

'Are you mad? Throw those away. Weevils, weevils!'

Ben took out a biscuit and bit it. There was, to Tiffany's very great surprise, a crunch.

'Thought you said you tidied up in here.' Ben offered the packet.

'So I missed one cupboard,' said Tiffany. 'Cleaning lady is not my job. Make a note of that, please.'

She fingered the top biscuit with the utmost suspicion. It had gone only slightly soft. The edge she nibbled tasted okay, so she ate the rest. Ben took three more. A minute later the packet lay dead between them.

'Now what?' said Ben. 'We starve?'

'No. We shop.' Tiffany pulled her bank card from her money belt.

The weather was mercifully dry, clear enough to show Venus bright against a darkening blue sky, and cold enough to reawaken all Tiffany's aches and pains and made her yearn for her furry coat and winter boots. From the end of the road she looked back at Theobald Mansions. Twilight showed the apartment block at its grimmest, a lump of rust-coloured brick which obscene graffiti could scarcely make worse. Lower and first-floor windows were cracked or boarded up, others covered with chicken wire, for a reason she understood when she saw the unprotected ones, caked in pigeon filth. The so-called balconies of the upper flats were little more than windows with railings, providing the bare minimum outside space to drape laundry or to cram a broken bicycle. Tiffany had never had to wonder why Mrs Powell's flat stayed empty, why it hadn't been taken over by new tenants or repossessed. It was obvious that no-one wanted it. People didn't move into Theobald Mansions unless they had no other choice.

She found a cash machine and drew out twenty pounds. In Stoke Newington High Street, a grocer's shop offered a miniscule range of unappealing foods at astronomical prices. Tiffany piled a basket with tins of what must have been caviar, though the labels said baked beans, and got cereal and milk and bread and spread. She topped up the energy card with a few extra pounds of credit, and was bemused to leave the shop with only two coins in change.

Back at the flat they sat down to beans on toast. Neither of them spoke till they had polished off a whole tin each, plus half a loaf of bread. At last Ben shunted back his chair and burped behind his hand.

'Good thing we have separate rooms,' he murmured.

Tiffany laughed and put the kettle on. A box of tea bags had also come to light, at the back of the same cupboard where Ben had found the biscuits. She was glad, if surprised, that she'd missed both of those during her clear-out.

It was nice to be no longer cold and hungry and exhausted. For a moment she could have felt content. Oh, the tricks that a hot meal played on the mind! How stupid that a mug of tea could make you think everything would be all right.

Ben set down his empty cup and stared at the blank white wall. Tiffany cleared the plates and put them on the draining board, for one of them to wash up, maybe, sometime. Through the window she heard the grinding traffic, the gargle of bus engines and the hiss and whimper of their brakes. A tenant somewhere in the depths of the block was playing loud music, only the bass thud reaching them.

'Shall I see if the TV works?' Tiffany asked.

Ben said nothing so she sat down again. The TV would be rubbish anyway. The lukewarm radiators hiccupped as the long-dormant central heating revived. The noises mingled with music's relentless thump. Ben fidgeted.

'I wish we had a phone.'

'I've got mine.' Tiffany pulled it out.

'No. Don't.' He snatched it and removed the battery. 'I was only saying. I wish.'

She guessed what he meant. 'Your mum and dad?'

Ben slumped over the table.

'This can't be happening.' He groaned. 'I've done it to them again.'

There was nothing she could say.

'Last time, when they thought I'd run away,' said Ben, 'they both went to pieces. And I promised them, I *promised*…' his voice trembled, 'that I'd never do it again. No matter what happened, we'd talk it over, I wouldn't ever walk out… But I have. And they'll think… I don't know what they'll think!'

Tiffany touched his arm.

'We're protecting them,' she said. 'You told me yourself. This keeps them safe.'

Ben thumped the table. 'I *promised*.'

'We'll go back. Soon.' Tiffany bit her lip, thinking of her own parents. By eight-fifteen this morning, at the latest, they would have agreed that she'd lain in long enough. Then would have come the empty bed, the puzzled calling up and down stairs, searching the house. Then phoning her (how many missed calls? How many messages? She stared at the phone ravenously but the battery was in Ben's pocket). They would have phoned her school, the hospital (in case she'd taken it upon herself to visit Stuart) and then the police. Perhaps they'd also made a quick call to Ellen Thornwill, her counsellor, on the off-chance that she'd gone there, but of course Ellen would be as clueless as everyone else.

And now? Her mother and father would be back in their nightmare. Could such a thing happen twice to the same family? Had Tiffany been abducted again? What was happening to her at this moment? Was she already dead? It was easy, dreadfully easy, to hear Mum's terrible cries as her courage cracked around mid-afternoon, and Dad's hoarse-voiced attempts to calm her, pouring out comfort he didn't have.

Hours of this. Hours and hours.

'Actually I do know.' Ben closed his eyes. 'I know exactly what my mum and dad will think.'

'What?' Tiffany could hardly bring herself to care, she was sunk so deep in her own troubles.

'The new baby!' said Ben. 'What else could it be? They told me about the new baby coming, and that we'll have to move out of London. And now I've done a bunk.'

'But you're glad about the baby.'

'Oh, yeah, it really looks that way, doesn't it?'

'Call them tomorrow. Use a phone box.' She was already planning to do the same.

'No.' His jaw clenched. 'No breaking cover. Anyway, what could I say?'

'Okay.' Tiffany gripped his hands. 'We know we're right. So let's stop thinking about it. Please. Or we'll go bonkers.'

'Okay.' But he carried on. 'They'll think they're to blame. That they drove me away. Dad might say it's Mum's fault for wanting another kid… They'll start fighting, like in the old days…'

'Ben, stop it!'

'This is gonna break them up again!' He stood too quickly, knocking over his chair. 'I should have thought about this first. They got back together, after eight years, and now they'll split up for good and it's *my fault…*'

'No! Shut up!' Tiffany rose too, her own mind full of visions of her family in meltdown.

'Stress,' Ben blurted. 'Stress is bad for pregnant women. They can lose their babies. What if my mum – ?'

'*Then go!*' Tiffany screamed. 'Go home! Shut up and leave me alone.'

Her shout made the walls buzz. The traffic noise, central heating and bass beat mumbled on, and the tap dripped once. Tiffany stood quite still, feeling as if she were bristling all over. She could see the pulse beating in the flushed skin of Ben's neck. Shakily, she drew a breath.

'What I mean,' she said, 'is… it's okay. You can go if you want to. I forgot about your mum and her baby. You have to go home, I know. Don't worry about me.'

Ben went to suck a drink of water from the tap.

'Thanks.' He wiped his mouth. 'But that's mad. You'd be on your own.'

'It's safe for me here.' She couldn't believe she was arguing. 'Mrs Powell's flat will be safe for me. I feel that. Ben, you have to go home. Don't you?'

He nodded. 'I will. When this is over. But you don't get rid of me that easily.'

Now she was smiling, smiling like a fool.

'And they don't get rid of us,' said Ben. 'The Set killed Yusuf. And his mum and dad. Now they're after our families. No. This stops. This is *enough.*'

A knuckle in one of his fists cracked.

'Let's get them, Tiffany,' he said. 'Let's get them.'

'We will. We'll do it together.'

She stepped closer, till his face was a breath away. From the way he blinked, she could see his thought: was she inviting him to kiss her? And yes, in her heart she very much wished him to, but at this moment she knew it would be wrong. Such tender, human feelings could have no place here. This was a pact of vengeance.

Ben seemed to read her thought, and as they leaned in close it was only the sides of their heads that touched, rubbing together in the manner of greeting cats, and faint in her ear she heard the crackle of electricity between them. Before either had a chance to feel self-conscious, Ben said, 'First thing tomorrow.'

'Yes.' She hesitated.

'We go after them.'

'Yeah. Only...' She put her finger on what was troubling her. There was a rank smell in here, and it wasn't the drains or the bin, and it wasn't mice. 'Only... Ben, I would really like us both to get a fresh change of clothes first.'

15

 THE ELEVENTH HOUR

So this was how their war against the forces of darkness was to begin – with a shopping trip. After a bit of persuading, Ben grudgingly had to admit that fighting a sect of evil killers would be a good deal more pleasant for all concerned if they had clean socks and underwear. Tiffany hustled him onto the bus straight after breakfast, assuring him that they would only buy 'a few bits and pieces'.

Camden Market was heaving, the Christmas shoppers pressed so close that it was easy to confuse them with the racks of coats. Despite the crush, Tiffany browsed, chose, compared and changed her mind, holding each top, t-shirt or pair of trousers against herself (or Ben), studying every label intently.

'We only need a change of clothes each,' Ben reminded her, more than once.

'I know,' she said each time.

'Why are you looking at that party skirt? We're not going to a party.'

'I know. Here, carry these bags for me.'

And he'd thought he was ready for any horror. Worse, she was paying for all his stuff, because he didn't have a penny on him. Nor did he have a bank account, a fact which astonished Tiffany, who had over a thousand pounds in hers, she said. Last week, Ben would have called this a fortune, but things had changed. That money was all they had to live on, and neither of them knew how long it might have to last. Besides, the thought of Tiffany paying for his keep, out of her life savings, made him burn with shame. He had to watch as she bought him shirts, socks, boxer shorts, a jacket, a new tracksuit and two pairs of branded jeans, when one knock-off pair would have been fine.

He said, 'I'll pay you back.'

'It was about time you had a makeover.' Tiffany breezed between stalls of teen fashions.

'Did you hear? I said I'll pay you back.'

In a side street they found a coffee shop, where they took turns to nip into the toilets to swap their stale clothes for new ones. Back at their table Tiffany looked Ben over approvingly, and he thought she looked pretty good herself. She tightened her new sequined belt to the last notch and bought baguettes, muffins and hot chocolate for them both.

At the next table, two unshaven men were arguing in Polish. On the other side, a suited city-type sat frowning at his iPad; a young mum wiped the mouth of her chocolate-covered toddler. Ben made himself stop staring. They couldn't all be spies for the Set.

A TV on a wall bracket burbled at low volume, tuned to a news and sport channel. Here came the result of the heavyweight boxing match that Dad had been anticipating. As he'd predicted, the underdog had won on points. Ben wondered if Dad had watched it after all. Guilt soured the taste of his hot chocolate.

Then Tiffany spilled it by grabbing his arm.

'Look!'

The sport had given way to news. Ben stared at the headline banner, it read LONDON FAMILY KILLED IN FIRE, but the news was always full of stuff like that, you learned to ignore it… Then came the picture, a holiday snap of a family dining in the sunshine, and it was Yusuf and his mum and dad.

The screen cut to a shot of the street, with grim-faced residents hurrying by. A voiceover was saying how Gabir Mansour, his wife Jane, and their teenage son Yusuf, had all been pronounced dead at the scene, of smoke inhalation. A popular family, respected in the community. The causes of the fire, unclear. The police appealing for witnesses among the community. That word again.

'Idiots,' Ben hissed.

'What?'

'They think it was a racist attack. Because his family was Muslim. Or because of who his dad married.'

'How can you tell?'

'That's what "the community" means,' said Ben. 'They only say it when victims are black or – or whatever. Haven't you noticed? Almost like it's their own fault. They wouldn't talk about "the community" if it was my home that got torched…' he stopped, wishing he hadn't said that.

'Doesn't matter what they think.' Tiffany's eyes made two perfect reflections of the screen. 'They'll never catch who did it.'

Now a neighbour of the Mansour family was being interviewed. Ben recognised the thickset man who had been shouting in the street that night. Now he was subdued, his jowly face sagging as he told the reporter of everyone's shock and sadness.

'He said the funeral's this afternoon,' murmured Tiffany. 'We should go.'

'Don't be stupid. People would see us.'

'I'm not being stupid.' She almost raised her voice. 'I know perfectly well we can't go. I'm just saying. We should be there. And we won't be.'

She looked away, to weep. Ben turned his head too, and in doing so accidentally met the gaze of the lone customer at the next table, the man with the iPad and the dried-up latte mug. He too had been watching the news story with interest. Without another word, Ben seized Tiffany's arm and dragged her from the café.

'He wasn't a spy.' Tiffany sneezed at the shock of cold air.

'He might have been. He saw how that story was getting to us. Like we knew the family.'

'So? He was nosey. Ben, if we start believing that the Set are round every corner, then we've already lost.'

What she said made a lot of sense. How easy it was, to start doing the Set's work for them. In search of warmth and cheering up, they headed for the indoor market at Camden Lock, a treasure cave of impractical knickknacks, awash with sweet-smelling incense and suspicious herbs. Tiffany fingered a display of lampwork glass beads beneath the stallholder's hopeful gaze. Moving away again into the cover of the crowds, she murmured, 'Okay. Where do we start?'

'There must have been some clues on that flash drive you took.'

'Yeah, and it's back at my house. Where I can't go.'

'Well, think then! Try and remember something.'

She gave him evil eyes. 'Great, make it my fault. All I can remember is the one fifty-foot-high clue. Miles Baron's exhibition at the Tate Modern, designed by the Set. But we already knew that.'

An awful thought caught Ben off-guard.

'What's the date?'

Tiffany checked her dead phone and winced in annoyance. 'Why?'

'That clock…' Ben tried to remember what Mum's leaflet had said. The clock was a temporary exhibit. Its hands would turn through a single twelve-hour day from midday to midnight, a day that would take the giant mechanism two months to complete. A day timed to end on the true stroke of midnight, at the winter solstice. Midwinter's night. How soon?

Tiffany counted on her fingers. 'Must be the seventeenth today.'

The solstice, the shortest day, was the twenty-first of December.

'Four days,' Ben murmured.

'Till what?'

'Till that clock hits midnight.'

'And what happens then?' Tiffany demanded.

'I've got absolutely no idea,' said Ben. 'Shall we wait and find out?'

Ten seconds later they were running, weaving their way through a thousand dawdling shoppers towards Camden Town station. Tiffany yelled, 'This is the Northern line, right? What's the nearest tube to the Tate?'

'Waterloo. Hang on…' Ben staggered to a halt, and held aloft the six carrier bags of shopping and dirty clothes he had ended up carrying. 'What do you want me to do with these?'

The biting wind off the river blew warm in patches, thick with the Marmite smells of brazier carts selling roasted nuts. Hungry gulls tangled their flight paths above a concrete plain, making it seem all the more like a blustery grey beach. Ben huddled inside his new tracksuit jacket, already stressing about how he would pay Tiffany back for it.

The Tate Modern loomed above them like a vast beached whale. A slope led down towards its subterranean main doors, swallowing an endless stream of visitors, and now them too.

'Don't you dare lose that ticket,' said Tiffany.

'I've got the ticket. Stop worrying.'

A detour back to Mrs Powell's flat would have been a pain, but they could hardly pursue their mission while carrying heavy shopping. Inspired, Ben had found a launderette and ordered a service wash. The lady at the counter took all their spare clothes, both the old and the new, and gave him a numbered ticket so he could pick them up as clean laundry later. That ticket was now safe in his back trouser pocket.

The turbine hall was so huge that there was little sense of moving indoors. As the hall sloped downwards it broadened, like a river meeting the sea, and that was what the flowing crowds quickly became. The place was rammed.

'All these people,' Tiffany exclaimed.

Ben tried to elbow their way through. The noise made him think of the turbine that must have shaken this building in its power station days. After what seemed half a mile of trodden toes and cross looks, they reached a flight of steps to a viewing balcony that spanned the hall like a bridge.

CLICK CLUCK CLICK CLUCK CLICK CLUCK

It penetrated even the din of the crowd, not so much a tick as a pulse, or the slow blows of an axe. Always the pause between beats seemed too long, teasing that the next tick would never come. Always, tinny or thunderous, it came.

Ben's mind was playing tricks, for the clock looked even bigger than before, as if it had grown. People swarmed to it, like iron filings to a magnet. He jostled himself a space at the viewing rail, getting a sour look from a college-age girl who was ghosting a pencil image of the clock out of a sketchpad. Visitors of every age and nationality crammed along the balcony, staring, drawing, taking photographs or filming the huge, motionless hands. Ben heard cultivated voices behind him, a man and a woman at the nicer end of being old.

'…The Telegraph's art critic calls it a "mechanical poem" about the passing of one age and the dawning of another…'

'I can't help thinking, how awful for the artist. To miss this, because of that terrible break-in. Of course, there's never a good time to be robbed and assaulted…'

'Mm. I don't much care for Baron's work myself, usually, but people do say he's a genius…'

CLUCK CLICK CLUCK CLICK

Something moved behind the clock's smoky face, a shadow drifting from side to side. Here it came again, in time with the tick, and Ben realised it must be the pendulum. In silhouette it resembled a single, mighty oar, rowing through darkness.

'Why?' Tiffany murmured to herself. 'I don't understand. What's it *for?*'

Ben squeezed his way along the balcony, trying to see the clock from as many angles as he could. A man in a dashing Panama hat and pale suit noticed how intently Ben was peering, and offered him a peak through his binoculars. Ben knew a harmless London eccentric when he saw one, and accepted with a grateful smile. Close-up, he could see how the clock's pyramid casing was built from black metal slabs, irregular in shape, for a cracked-eggshell effect. Gaps in the carapace let visitors observe the inner mechanism. Ben glimpsed what appeared to be a second, motionless pendulum, shaped like Cleopatra's needle, hanging point-down. Then he saw an identical obelisk suspended from a parallel chain. Each must have weighed a tonne or more. Returning the binoculars, he made his way back to Tiffany.

'See those things?' he said. 'They're the weights. Like in a grandfather clock.'

Her face stayed blank.

'The weights in a clock are what drive it.' Ben tried to mime it with his hands. 'They fall slowly and turn the cogs. They're its power source.'

'So?' said Tiffany.

'Just thought that might be worth knowing.' Ben shrugged. 'In case we need to… y'know. Stop this thing.'

Tiffany gnawed at her thumb. She had the worst fingernails Ben had ever seen on a girl.

'I mean,' he gave her a prod, 'we'll have to. Won't we?'

She grimaced with uncertainty. 'But this thing isn't doing anything. It's just –'

CLUCK

'– ticking.' She shut her eyes. 'Oh, but it's bad. I know it is. My Oshtis is burning my guts. Like I've swallowed a whole baked potato. Are you getting that?'

'Er. A bit, yeah.'

'But *why?*' Tiffany almost pleaded. 'I can feel that it's evil, and I know it must be, somehow, but – ?'

'Ssh!' Ben pointed down at the crowd. They were hushing to silence. All faces turned upwards.

'What's happening?' said Tiffany.

'I think the hour's about to change. Watch.'

In defiance of the actual time, which was somewhere around mid-afternoon, the gigantic hands made a lopsided V shape, just shy of eleven o'clock. That explained why there was hardly room to move in here today. As Mum had noted, people loved to see a minute pass, for a minute on that clock face took around two hours in real time. But the turn of the hour was even more special, for an hour took nearly five days – and this one, the eleventh hour, would be the last before the final stroke of midnight. Now the only visibly moving thing was the pendulum.

CLICK CLUCK CLICK CLUCK CLICK CLUCK

There came the longer pause, one agonising extra half-second. Then –

KA-CHUNK

The minute hand advanced to 12. The hour hand jumped a notch to 11. Both hands trembled and the echo juddered up and down the hall. That sound became a soft roar as a thousand people breathed out. Then came laughter, and two pools of spontaneous applause that spread and joined with each other, till the whole crowd was clapping and cheering.

The noise settled to its natural, lively level, and the throng around the clock began to thin out. Most of the people on the balcony drifted towards the shop or the exit.

Tiffany shook herself. The moment seemed to have left her a bit mesmerised.

'Do they always do that?'

'They did before,' said Ben. 'When I came with my folks, we saw the minute hand move. Even that was a pretty big deal. Everyone stopped talking and waited for it. You know how it is in a swimming pool, just before they turn the wave machine on? When everyone gets all excited but sort of… scared as well.'

He trailed off, recalling what Mum had said.

That's the thing about these big artworks. The most interesting thing isn't always them. It's how people behave around them. It's what they make you do.

'Why him?' Ben wondered aloud.

'Who?'

'Why did the Set hire Miles Baron? They designed the clock themselves. So why use him at all?'

'Obviously, to get it on display here –'

'Why?'

'I don't know that part!' said Tiffany. 'But they must have wanted a big public exhibition, and only a famous artist could get that.'

She moved aside to let more people make their way out. Ben tried to gather his thoughts.

'What do the Set do?' he said. 'They get inside your head. Mess with your mind. And so do…'

'Well? Who?'

'Artists.'

Tiffany's mouth half-opened.

'Look at Miles Baron.' Ben warmed to his idea. 'Look at what he can do. He makes a piece of rubbish like TimeTide –'

'Like what?'

'TimeTide is a rusty nail through a piece of tissue paper. And it sold at auction for shedloads. He does all these artworks that no-one likes, but they sell for millions and people say he's a genius. Tiffany, how does he do that?'

'Your theory is that Miles Baron can control people's minds?'

'No! That's not what I'm saying…' Wasn't it? He snapped his fingers at a lucky thought. 'Okay, Tiffany. Who's the coolest girl at your school?'

'*Uh?*' She boggled. 'Well… Jenna Hepburn. She's the most popular kid in my year. She's awful.'

'Great. Now, would you ever go to school wearing a plastic ring from a Christmas cracker?'

Her eyebrows shrank from each other in concern. 'Ben, are you feeling all right?'

'*Yes*. Listen. They'd all laugh and eat you alive, wouldn't they? If you wore a tatty plastic ring. Because you're not cool.'

'I suppose, but… Hey, *not cool?*'

'It's all right, I don't mind.' Ben felt strangely daring today. 'Okay. Now let's say it's Jenna who wears that plastic ring to school. Pretty soon, all the girls are wearing them. Right?'

'You're saying Miles Baron is like Jenna Hepburn?'

'Yeah. People *believe* in him. So they believe in his stuff. Even if they don't like it.' Ben turned his back on the clock, in itself a surprisingly hard thing to do. 'I don't think he made it happen. It just… happened. Other people did it for him. They could have picked any artist, but they chose him.'

'And then the Set chose him.' Tiffany's eyes darted with thought. 'Because it's not enough that people come and see the clock. They want people to *love* it too. They want people to see it, and believe in it, and love it, because…' She faltered. 'Because what?'

Fresh crowds were already forming on the balcony, lining up to stare and murmur. The tick tapped at Ben's brain till he had to look again at the installation, Miles Baron's masterpiece, The Clock Is Set.

'Search me,' he said.

Tiffany drew in her breath. At first Ben thought he must have trodden on her toe.

'Sorry, are you – What's wrong?'

Her gasp ended in strangled words.

'He's here. I saw him.'

'Who?' Ben felt the hairs spiking on his neck. 'What are you talking about?'

Her face had paled. She said, 'I saw Set.'

16

SOUL OF THE CITY

For one terrible moment she feared she had lost her mind. She was back inside the flat at Clink Wharf, staring helplessly into a face that was part goat and part wolf, as the monstrous figure raised its sceptre and she felt her life drain from every nerve. Now she saw that same horror walking in the crowd.

'Tiffany, where? Somewhere in here?'

She pulled herself together. No, she had to be imagining it. The turbine hall was such a mix of different people, different hairstyles, different hats – the eye could play tricks as they milled together, stirring in currents, as if something was passing among them, unseen… She blinked, and this time was sure.

'There.' She spoke through clenched teeth. 'See him?'

'Tiffany…' Ben seemed to think she was fooling around.

'Don't just look. *Look*,' she hissed. 'See like a cat. There, near the man with the folding bicycle.'

Moments elapsed. Ben caught his breath.

'How…?'

'Ssh. Must be a mind trick. Let me concentrate, I'm losing him –'

If her attention lapsed even slightly then other movements, such as a little girl, running, would distract her gaze, luring it away. Visualising a green cat's eye, she drew harder on her Mandira catra, training it upon the wandering blind spot, until the phantom took shape.

Among people, the figure seemed taller than ever, taller than her dad, taller than – *taller than Ellen*, she thought momentarily, but for some reason her mind spat that thought out. He wore the same coppery tunic and white robe and carried in his fist the black sceptre, forked at the tip and crowned with a carving of his own beastly head.

Ben edged closer. 'No-one else can see him.'

It was impossibly eerie. The towering demon walked among them and nobody took the slightest notice. Wherever Set walked the crowd parted like the Red Sea, yet not one person looked at him or stepped deliberately aside. Instead, people found accidental ways not to be in his path: moving to view the clock, spotting a friend, stopping to tie shoelaces, or doubling back on a whim. In this way, without veering once or breaking his stride, the figure of Set reached the long wall of the turbine hall, and vanished.

Tiffany cried out. He had stepped through a solid concrete wall. Could he have? Or had she merely blinked and lost focus? She raked the hall with all her cat senses, shiveringly aware that nearby might be a seven-foot devil-god incarnate, perhaps closing on her stride by stride, and she would never know.

Ben nudged her in the ribs. 'Out there. Come on.'

She followed him into a claustrophobic lobby, bottlenecked with departing visitors. As they shuffled past the souvenir shop, Ben caught his breath and pulled her into the cover of its anti-theft gate. Yards ahead of them, framed in the wintry light coming through the exit doors, a man stood waiting. A smartly-suited man, stocky as a bodybuilder, bull-necked and bald.

'Isidorus,' Ben hissed.

Recognising him, she boiled inside. On and off, for many weeks now, she'd suffered dreams of the silky voice of Mister Isidorus, reciting his list of dead tiger parts. But worse than that, a hundred times worse, was her certainty that here was Yusuf's murderer. Her hatred for Miles Baron seemed childish next to this, and it was all she could do not to rush at the man with her claws.

'Ssh.' Ben kept a firm hold of her. 'Here we go.'

Mister Isidorus extended a hand as if greeting a friend, though no-one was there. Tiffany's sinuses ached from drawing so much on her Mandira catra – she refocused its waning power just as a young Japanese couple walked across her line of sight. In passing, they seemed to draw aside a veil, and there before Mister Isidorus towered the figure of Set, touching the offered hand. Oblivious visitors walked on by, like water around oil.

The lips of Mister Isidorus moved. With her hearing already boosted to the max, she caught the words.

'...by the diligence of your servants, my Lord, your temple is prepared.'

Mister Isidorus turned through the automatic doors, with the universal gesture meaning *After you*. The figure of Set stepped out into the grey light, his slow yet long strides quickly eating up the ground. Mister Isidorus bustled after him, like a servant, or a dog.

Tiffany melted into an Eth walk, pretending not to notice Ben's glance which said *Is this a good idea?* Dusk had forested the plain around the Tate with elongated shadows, making it even harder to pick out the similar shape of Set. There he was – right there – loping through the blood-tinged light, halfway to the riverside path. Then Mister Isidorus seemed to head him off, gesturing with one hand. She plucked his words out of the wind.

'...lead me on, my Lord Set.'

The figure changed direction at once, striding towards the Ray of Light bridge across the Thames. In turning so abruptly, Lord Set almost walked into a lady in dark glasses, her guide dog pulling her aside just in time. The dog cringed and snarled; the lady, puzzled, knelt to stroke its head. Mister Isidorus followed his weird companion up onto the footbridge, his words floating down.

'...I will tread in your footsteps, across these waters...'

'Hang on,' Ben muttered. 'Who's leading who?'

'Uh?' Tiffany fought not to look away.

'Isidorus. He keeps showing the big fella where to go. Like he isn't following him at all. More like he's... *steering* him.'

'No, he isn't.' Tiffany ran up onto the bridge, her view of their quarries obscured only for a second. 'Set's the leader, Ben. That's why it's called The Set.'

'So why isn't he leading?'

Tiffany ignored that. It was clear to her that Lord Set was walking in front, with Mister Isidorus meekly accompanying. Staring into the wind made her eyes water, blurring the lights of the City of London that loomed above the river's opposite bank, so that the bright dome of St Paul's Cathedral seemed to rise out of a lake of burning ice. She was suddenly, sharply aware of the river far beneath her feet, almost invisible in the dusk, transformed into a dark void across which she was pursuing this ancient Egyptian god.

Despite Ben's scowl of protest, she quickened her Eth walk, till she was only a few strides behind Mister Isidorus, close enough to taste her loathing of him. Revolted to the point of fascination, her eyes explored the folds at the nape of his neck, where the flesh bunched in stubbly rolls. The cold had turned his exposed ears candy-pink, like wads of half-chewed bubblegum. As he walked, his crabby arms swung hardly at all, and his fingers looked clumsy as sausages. But Tiffany wasn't fooled. She had seen those hands conjure bronze crescent blades to fly like deadly sycamore seeds.

The bridge made landfall on a paved square that led to a road with a pedestrian crossing. Mister Isidorus pushed the button, the traffic stopped, and almost comically the oddball pair crossed with the green man. Tiffany and Ben ran across as the lights were changing back.

'Are you seeing the same as me?' said Ben. 'Because it looks like they're going to –'

'Just follow,' breathed Tiffany. 'If we start guessing we'll lose them.'

Then she too stared in disbelief as Lord Set and Mister Isidorus approached St Paul's.

'– going to church,' Ben concluded. 'This is officially weird.'

'They're not. He's heading round the other side –' Tiffany quickened to a run. But the crowds in the cathedral plaza were lumpier, harder to see through. Tourists stood gazing up at the dome, and on every side people were either taking or posing for photographs. Two mounted police officers were keeping watch, but like the plaza's central statue they seemed mostly decorative, the horses snorting steam over the children gathered to pat them.

Tiffany swerved around a painter who was packing away his easel, dodged a hired bicycle, peered through the twilight. People hurried past in every direction, and none of them were Mister Isidorus or his master.

She rounded on Ben.

'They got away! I said not to distract me!'

'Listen, will you?' Ben broke in. 'I saw them. They went in there.'

He pointed. So close to them, in the reddening twilight, the cathedral resembled nothing so much as a fairytale mountain, some improbable rock formation flanked by two soaring stalagmites. Higher even than these twin towers rose the dome, dark against the scrolling clouds of sunset, as if the mountain were venting flame.

'In there?' she echoed. In disbelief she started up the steps at the majestic main entrance.

'Wait. Not that way.' Ben led her to a door tucked round the side of the building, which she never would have guessed was there.

'You know this place?'

'Sort of,' he said. 'My mum's got a thing about family outings. We did St Paul's a few months ago. Quite interesting, actually.' His eyes clouded with thoughts she could guess. Suddenly brusque, he said, 'This door leads down to the crypt.'

Even though she'd always lived in London, or maybe for that reason, Tiffany had managed to avoid many of its famous attractions. In fact she'd hardly ever set foot inside any church, except for weddings and Grandma Maine's funeral. The word 'crypt' led her to expect coffins, not coffee. At the bottom of the stairs she was so perplexed to find a café serving afternoon tea that she almost wandered over to get a tray. But the till had already closed, and a waitress was wiping down tables in between the few remaining customers.

The café merged into a long room like an enormous cellar, segmented by pillars and archways. That was more like what she'd imagined, only rather than being dank it was warm and well-lit, the vaulted white ceiling echoing with chatter.

Ben plucked at her sleeve.

'See? Lots of room to hide down here. Isidorus and the other guy might be meeting someone.'

'In a café in a crypt? You could be right.'

'This way.' Ben headed towards a spiked iron gate which made Tiffany think of the entrance to Mordor. Gaps in the latticework gave tantalising views of more caverns, a labyrinth of monuments and statues, like the roots of stone trees. She saw a cash register and a board of ticket prices.

'It's *how much* to get in? But it's a church!'

The young woman at the till glanced up.

'Sorry. We're closing for sightseers. Evensong starts in ten minutes.' She brightened. 'That's free. You could go in for that. There are carols.'

'No thanks.' Tiffany was in the mood to be rude. As they drifted away she said to Ben, 'When she's not looking, shin over the gate.'

'But it's a church!' Ben mimicked. Then he glanced around the café area, a bit furtively. 'Okay. We'll do that. In a sec. I just have to…' He began to edge towards a door marked with the stick figure of a man.

'Ben!' She rolled her eyes.

He winced. 'I've been holding it in all afternoon. Those two won't go far. Stay there.'

'You lightweight.' Tiffany shook her head in mock-annoyance, wondering if she too needed the loo, deciding no. Playing safe, she gave this corner of the crypt one more thorough scan with cat senses, confirming that Mister Isidorus and his master were definitely nowhere close by. In prowling, she passed an information board that caught her eye. It told the story of how this cathedral had survived the Blitz in the

Second World War. Here was a photo of St Paul's in the very eye of the storm, seemingly afloat upon the smoke of a burning city. The text below explained that, when the Luftwaffe attacked with incendiary bombs, Winston Churchill sent out the order: *save St Paul's at all costs*.

Tiffany sniffed. It didn't seem right to care so much about a building, when people were dying all around it. Yet she could see what Churchill might have meant. That proud dome towering over the explosions, impossibly intact, withstanding everything the enemy could throw at it – even now it was a sight to fill a person with courage. Churchill had known what this cathedral meant to London. It was the very soul of the city. So long as it stood, no-one would ever believe that London could fall.

Tiffany lingered by the information board, the thought dancing in her head. *St Paul's is the soul of the city. The soul of the city.* Could there be a connection? Mister Isidorus and his strange master had come here for a reason. She wondered if any famous objects or sacred artefacts were housed here, something that the Set might want to steal… until a duller thought barged in. Ben was taking long enough, wasn't he? Perhaps he had a funny tummy. That would be all they needed.

She waited outside the gents' toilet. Should she risk going in to hurry him up? Every fibre of her being rejected that plan. How absurd – she had clambered around the outside of a tower block wired to explode, yet she couldn't bring herself to enter a gentlemen's rest room.

What was he *doing* in there?

She got so far as to push at the door, only to pluck her hand back.

'Erm. The ladies' loo is over there.'

Tiffany whirled, the blood rushing to her face. One of the cathedral's tourist guides stood there, a tall young man hardly out of his teens. He wore a kind, nervous smile.

'Couldn't you find it?' he asked.

'No, it's not that, it's –' She must have been beetroot-coloured. The lad was quite good-looking, too, with wispy fair hair and a strong jaw.

'I'm, er… My friend went in there. He's been ages. I wanted to check that, um… that he's all right.'

The young man nodded, as if he dealt with such lunacy every day. He wore a simple uniform, white shirt and dark trousers, with a shirt-pocket badge that read 'Steward'. His burgundy necktie displayed a gold insignia, crossed swords beneath a symbol that she took to be a dome and cross. The radio clipped to his belt hissed and crackled.

'No problem,' he said. 'I'll take a peak for you. What's his name, by the way?'

She told him.

'Okay. Gimme a mo.' The young man spoke into his walkie-talkie. 'Dominic?' A muffled voice acknowledged him. 'Can you wait for me? I'm with a guest.'

Guest. An odd way to describe her, Tiffany thought. Maybe these tourist stewards had their own private slang.

Turning the radio over in his hands, the steward paused outside the toilet door. 'I'll pop inside and check.' He glanced over Tiffany's shoulder and pointed. 'Hey, that's not him, is it? In the café?'

Tiffany looked round, puzzled. All she could see was the waitress clearing dirty crockery from the last occupied table, at which a young Italian couple seemed to be having a muted, sad quarrel. It was possible that Ben had walked past her while she was reading about St Paul's, but why would he –

Movement stirred in her blind spot. The sense of threat came too late. She turned to see the steward make a stabbing motion, to ram the butt of the walkie-talkie into her neck.

It was over in a heartbeat. Yet for that instant she was gripped by a thousand cramps, striking at every muscle from her toes to her eyelids, like all-over pins and needles but with hammers and knives. She saw a burst of giant fireworks, felt the slam of the floor, and then nothing.

17
THE TEMPLE

With a curse Ben burst out of the cloakroom. Tiffany wasn't there. He could hardly blame her, after the stupidly long time he had spent in the loo.

He should have been back in a flash. A much-needed whizz, a rinse of his hands and he was leaving already. Then he caught his reflection in the mirror, and cringed – there was still a price tag on his jacket. He tossed it in the bin and threw out several receipts from his back pocket for good measure. Once more he turned to leave. A thought nagged him. He checked his pocket and found it empty.

The ticket from the launderette. Where was it?

He delved in his other pockets and realised he must have thrown away the ticket too.

For a moment he dithered. It didn't matter, they had far bigger things to worry about. Already he had wasted precious time. Nevertheless, he kicked himself. The launderette might not give back their clothes without that ticket. All those new clothes Tiffany had spent a fortune on, both for herself and for him. He would never live it down.

The swing-bin was inside the cloakroom wall. Grimacing, he reached in and rummaged through a repulsive papery mass, hoping the dampness was tap water and nothing worse. One by one he pulled out the receipts he had thrown away, found that label, then fistful after fistful of paper towels. There was no laundry ticket. In despair he reached again into his back pocket, and found it. The ticket had been tucked inside the seam.

It was a good thing no-one was around to hear the language he used. Leaving the contents of the waste bin strewn across the floor, he stormed out. And found no Tiffany.

The café's last customers, a couple of foreign students, were leaving. He thought Tiffany might be there, eyeing up the remaining cakes, but she wasn't. He guessed that she too had been caught short, and felt less guilty. He waited outside the ladies' loo. The girl at the cash register was transferring the day's takings into a strongbox. Tiffany didn't come out.

Girls took longer than boys, he knew that. Well, most of the time. He thought about going in to check. No, he couldn't. He'd ventured into some scary places in his time, but a ladies' lavatory was pushing the limit.

'Can I help you?'

The till girl had come over. She was dark-haired, petite and pretty, though frowning in that suspicious way that Ben, as a teenage boy, was used to. Maybe she thought he was a peeping Tom.

'Um.'

'We're closing.' The woman unclipped a walkie-talkie from her hip. 'There's still time for you to attend evensong, if you want.' She pointed over his shoulder, towards the stairs.

'Thanks, but…' Ben found his eyes followed the walkie-talkie, though he didn't know why. An uneasy heat burned in his stomach. Why was Tiffany taking so long? And if she wasn't in the loo, where was she?

'I think my friend's in there,' said Ben. 'Could you maybe…?' He gestured helplessly at the door through which no man could pass.

'Of course.' Then, with strange abruptness, the till girl pointed. 'That's not her, is it?'

'You what?' He took a step backwards. The girl had not looked before she pointed. She just seemed very keen to make him turn away from her.

The pupils of her eyes swelled in sudden fear. She raised the walkie-talkie.

'Guest,' she said to it. 'Backup, now.'

Then she flipped the radio upside-down and stabbed the end of it towards him.

Ben dodged, even before he saw the spark between two metal fangs. Missing his chest, the weapon glanced off his wrist. The result was the ultimate dead arm. A spasm through those muscles sent him staggering back, trailing a limb as heavy as a roll of carpet. His attacker lunged for his neck.

At any other time, she might have got him. But now he knew that Tiffany was in trouble. With his good hand he caught the girl's wrist and the radio fell with a clatter, its incandescent barbs flickering out. Ben dragged her into an alcove between pillars, his palm clamped over her mouth.

'Where is she?' He was shaking all over. His left arm felt like it wasn't there. 'What have you done with her?'

The young woman made mmph-mmph noises. Ben pushed her against the pillar, startled by his own brutality. Warily he released her mouth and she sucked air. He made hooks of his fingers, inches from her face.

'Call anyone,' he said, 'and they'll have to search high and low for your eyeballs. If you understand, nod very carefully.'

She nodded. Ben flexed the dead weight of his left arm, trying to get some feeling back. At present it was useful only as a crude bar with which to pin her under the chin.

'You're one of the Set?'

No nod. A sly smile.

'*Guest?*' said Ben. 'What's that? Your code word for Cat Kin?'

She kept on smiling. Her hazel eyes had lost their fear. If anything her expression now was mischievous, asking what on earth he was doing, half-strangling this pretty young woman. Ben fretted – how would this look, to anyone else? Luckily the sofas and benches had emptied with the closing of the café, though sightseers wandering the main crypt could still be seen through the black metal gates.

'Why are you here?' Ben shook her. 'How many of you are there? Who did you call?'

'What a lot of questions! Let me jot them down.' She mimed writing in the air. Ben smacked the hand away, to be safe.

'One question. Where is she?'

'Good one. Here's mine,' said the woman. 'What if I screamed?'

'Then I'll,' Ben swallowed, 'claw your eyes out.'

She giggled. 'Come off it! A nice lad like you? I could scream blue murder and you'd never hurt me.'

Experimentally, she pushed against his restraining arm. He pushed back, beginning to panic, knowing she was right. She would call his bluff. Seeing the dropped walkie-talkie, he raked it nearer with his foot.

'I know what this is.' In one movement he stooped and picked it up. 'A stun gun, right? Half a million volts, right?'

Protruding from the base of the handset were four metal studs, like fangs. His index finger found a recess behind the Talk button and he pressed the trigger inside. A blue spark fizzed between the middle pair of electrodes.

'Tell me what you've done with my friend.' He brought the spark closer. 'Or I'll zap you.'

'No.' She looked worried again. 'The current is set too high. It'd kill me.'

Ben studied her face. Was she telling the truth?

'Last chance!' He crackled the spark. 'Where is she?'

The woman gave her sweetest till-girl smile.

'She's dead.'

His hand wobbled. 'You're lying.'

'Why would I lie?' She laughed gently. 'We killed her. She's dead. She died like *this*.'

Faster than he could react, she snatched at his hand and forced the live electrodes against her own neck. Ben felt the shock kick through into his body, and leaped back. For a few endless seconds, the young woman stood bolt upright, rigid as the pillar behind her, a shapeless groan forcing its way out of her lungs. Then the stun gun dropped to the stone floor and she fell bonelessly beside it.

An unearthly dirge floated through the archways. Standing over the body in a cold sweat, it took him a moment to identify the sound. Up in the cathedral, the choir was singing a medieval carol to commence evensong, and the brass gratings in the roof of the crypt were straining the echoes down to him. Ben dropped to his knees and touched the woman's shoulder.

'Get up. Come on, get up.'

She didn't move. He rolled her onto her back and opened her airway, using those first aid skills he had made a point of practising. When he leaned close, a faint breath tickled his ear. She was alive.

Ben rubbed his arm, where the feeling was returning, mostly as pain. He rolled the woman over again, into the recovery position. Then, cursing his conscience, he searched her pockets for a mobile phone, used it to dial 999 and left it lying beside her. Finally he broke open her walkie-talkie stun gun and removed both batteries. All the while his mind was racing.

The till-girl had lied. The shock hadn't killed her. So maybe Tiffany wasn't dead either. But what if she…? What if Tiffany…? Ben checked himself. He was forgetting. *The Set mess with your head.*

He rose up, straightening his spine to stand at full height.

'I heed no words. Nor walls…'

His voice sounded strange in the cavernous acoustics, blending with the wash of ancient music.

'Through darkness I walk in day. And I do not fear the tyrant.'

'Hello?' came the burble of the woman's phone. 'Which service, caller?'

A red pulse beat in his stomach. Tiffany was alive. That was what he believed. She was alive and he would find her.

With the till-girl no longer on duty, he could simply walk through the gate into the main crypt. This was the part that lived up to its name. Stone and alabaster arches receded like reflections into the distance, in a pattern of white and shadow, branching into catacombs of tombs and monuments, paved with a mosaic stone as dark as wine or blood.

The ache in his left arm lingered as a warning. From now on, every person he saw might be an agent of the Set. At a crossroads he stopped, hearing distant voices apparently from every side. With his cat hearing he isolated the true source of each sound, and took the passage straight ahead, the empty one.

Now he invoked his Kelotaukhon catra. Reaching out with his mind, he felt for the shape and flow of his surroundings, blending them into his movements. An oblong chamber, empty save for a plinth and a sarcophagus of polished burgundy stone, seemed to stay empty as Ben passed through in a run that was no more visible than stillness, a merging of one shadow to the next. He fled on down the passage, too slippery for all but the sharpest searching eyes, like a wild creature in woodland.

Unfortunately, as a hiding place, the crypt was almost too good. He passed side rooms, vestries, chambers, cellars, tombs, too many possible dungeons. In an hour of searching he might never find Tiffany. Checking for ambushes at every aisle and transept, he forced himself to think: what would she do, in his place? Something clever, something catty. She'd sniff out the answer…

Of course. He sniffed, letting his Mandira come to the fore. There it was, like her calling voice: the smell that said, *Tiffany*. He could have laughed. She wouldn't be pleased when he told everyone that he'd smelt her from a hundred yards off.

Slowly he inhaled, trying to isolate the scent, for he himself was sweating fragrantly beneath his zip-up top. But Tiffany was there too, on the draught that passed him by. Hers was a more complex smell, a blend of the shampoo she used and that weird pear soap of Mrs

Powell's, but most of all the invisible signal that made his heart beat double-time, which he knew came from the pores of *her* skin, and from nowhere else in the world.

'Hold on, Tiffany.'

Turning on the spot he found the strongest thread of scent, and followed it downwind between statues and mausoleums, into a square hall framed with colonnades. Glass cases made a centrepiece, displaying models of the cathedral and Sir Christopher Wren's original designs. He was halfway along the first colonnade when a female voice called, 'Ben!'

He threw himself behind a pillar. Footsteps crossed the tombstoned floor and a woman in a steward's uniform strolled into view, one hand raised in greeting. Before he could decide whether to run or reply, an answer came from an unexpected direction.

'All right, Cheryl?'

A previously unseen man joined the woman by the display cases. He too wore the uniform of a tourist steward.

'Had a good day?' the woman asked him. She was fighting hard against middle age with a heavily made-up face, and styled red hair that was clearly out of a bottle.

'So-so,' said Ben-the-steward. Hidden behind the pillar, Ben breathed again. His namesake was visibly younger than the woman, but already losing his hair at the front. Handsome features could have carried off this look, but this steward didn't have them, only hunched shoulders to round off his generally sour appearance.

'I meant to ask you, Ben.' The woman called Cheryl swept her colleague along with her, into the aisle leading out of the hall. Ben stalked after them. 'Could you be a pet?' she was saying. 'Do the till collections for me tonight. It's my book group evening. I need to rush home and eat first –' She glanced back for emphasis, forcing Ben to freeze inside a stone arch. 'Or I'll get plastered and disgrace myself.'

'Um. Okay.' Ben-the-steward sounded cautious. 'The crypt, you mean?'

'The crypt, the main doors, and the galleries,' said Cheryl. 'You know the routine by now. Keys are in the common room, on the hook.'

Ben darted to the next pillar, and the next, keeping them in sight. Fortunately he didn't have to choose between them and the scent trail, for as far as he could tell, the stewards were moving with it, through a series of archways. He was close to Tiffany now, very close.

'Fine. I suppose.' The man sagged gloomily. 'How long's that lot gonna take me?'

'It takes five minutes, tops.'

'Well, then,' Ben-the-steward looked crafty, 'if it doesn't take long…'

'Ha ha.' Cheryl was ready for that. 'Five minutes is for eye shadow and lipstick, matey. Which I'm not doing on the bus.'

Ben weighed his options. One thing was clear to him by now – these two weren't Set agents, they were the cathedral's regular tourist guides. So they'd know every inch of this building, wouldn't they? Including parts that were off-limits to the public. In short, they could be highly useful in finding Tiffany… if he could only think of a way to approach them and ask for help.

Cheryl put on a flirty face. 'Come on, Ben. I'll owe you.'

Ben-the-steward nodded, reluctantly. 'You already owe me a Sunday morning for –'

He was interrupted by a burble from his walkie-talkie. He answered. 'Rory? Go ahead.'

The radio voice was crackly; the word Ben overheard sounded like: 'Khyan?' The face of Ben-the-steward changed almost imperceptibly. Those sulky shoulders squared off and his eyes caught a gleam.

'Go on, Herihor.'

'Tell your stewards to dig in for the night,' rasped the voice. 'No-one leaves the temple. Understood?'

'No-one goes home. Got it.' Ben-the-steward glanced at Cheryl with satisfaction.

Cheryl looked mildly peeved. Into her own radio she said, 'Merres here. What's happened?'

'Small problem,' the voice crackled. 'There's a guest loose in the crypt.'

Ben dry-swallowed. That had nearly been a bad mistake.

'You sure?' said the other Ben – or Khyan.

'Yes,' the voice responded. 'Tjan took care of one but Satiah couldn't manage her friend. Watch out, he could be close.'

'Thanks for the warning,' said Khyan, sourly. 'Got any kind of description?'

'No. Tjan says he might be a teenage boy. Called Ben.'

The woman – Cheryl, Merres, whatever she was called – gave her partner a wry look.

'Great,' said Khyan. 'What now? Do we search?'

'No,' crackled Herihor. 'You're breaking up…'

'It's the lead lining of the dome.'

'I know what it is. I'll move inside.' The next words were clearer. 'If you see him, report. Don't approach. We're sending stewards who are trained to fight guests.'

Thanks for the warning, thought Ben.

'Satiah's training didn't do her much good,' said the woman.

'He caught her off guard,' Herihor retorted. 'You get to the common room. That's secure.'

'Understood. Out.' Khyan lowered his walkie-talkie and reversed his grip on it. The pair set off briskly, brandishing their radios now as weapons. Stumbling, the woman swore, took off her high heels and hurried on in nyloned feet. More choir music floated down from above, louder than before and muddier, smudged with so many echoes that the carol was impossible to identify.

The stewards reached a plain white door with a combination keypad lock, near the statue of a reclining lion (Ben dived behind this). The common room, presumably. Even evil agents needed a place where they could have tea and a biscuit – and perhaps lock up their enemies, too. The scent trail had grown as clear as if he was on top of it. His heart leaped and he was sure: Tiffany was being held prisoner behind that door.

The steward named Khyan pushed four buttons on the keypad. Ben strained to see what numbers they were, but cat vision wasn't telescopic. Khyan pulled the door open and the pair disappeared inside, as Ben vaulted over the stone lion's head and made a desperate lunge, getting there just as the door clicked shut again. Locked.

He winced in frustration, not despair. A plan was already forming. Nose to the keypad, he got a complex bouquet of human skin grease, which as expected was particularly pungent over certain keys. The correct buttons would of course be pressed more often than the wrong ones. He picked out 1... 3... then 4 and 9. What his nose couldn't tell him was the right order to push them in, but with only four buttons he reckoned he could work through them all. Clenching a fist at his own awesomeness, he got pressing. 1349 – no. 1394 – not that one either. 1439, 1493, 3149... he strained to keep track of which ones he'd tried, wiping sweat from his upper lip.

With his hand underneath his nose, he froze. The scent of Tiffany was stronger than ever. Too strong. He smelled his hand, then the sleeve of his tracksuit jacket. He touched his t-shirt, ran a hand through his hair, trying to hold back terrible, crashing thoughts.

He thought of how Tiffany had helped to choose all his new clothes. How she had brushed them down once they were on him, and straightened necklines and fussed over his appearance, in a way he rather enjoyed. He thought of all the times she had grabbed his arm for reassurance, or pulled at his hand to drag him this way or that. Of how they had sat together on the sofa, shared meals, rubbed their heads together, even fought – done almost everything, in fact, except kiss.

She had left herself all over him. Her smell was his smell.

Ben had to lean against the door, or fall down. She wasn't here. Like Winnie-the-Pooh, he had been tracking himself.

He could have howled. Where was she? Where *was* she? In one wrench she went from being near to being nowhere, perhaps no longer even alive. She might have died, alone and terrified, while he was down here among these tombs, chasing after a phantom. Tears of rage and fear squeezed from under his eyelids. He could not lose her now. It would be like dying himself. The torment of it was a physical pain, a cramp in his stomach, tearing at him, tugging, pulling…

Pointing.

Although Tiffany was a great believer in the Oshtian Compass, Ben had long been suspicious of the mystical side of pashki, and as for that mysterious feline ability to find one's way home, no matter how unknown the road – well, there wasn't much use for it in London. But the Compass could also work a more remarkable trick, which no map could do. It could help you find a person. Not just any person, though. It had to be someone who was dear to you, someone you had lost, someone – yes, he might as well admit it – someone you loved.

Ben let the pain inside him become his Oshtis catra, blood red, a lone magnetic pole. All at once it arc-jumped to connect with green Mandira, and his mind went like a weather vane in a gale, twirling in every direction. With a shudder it came to rest, and he could feel the pointing of the Oshtian Compass, as surely as he knew which way was up.

He looked up.

Whether by chance or by some guiding force, he was standing beneath a round grating in the roof, like a decorative doily cast in brass. Its curlicue holes sieved the image of a vast space above it, a space that churned with music from a choir that now sounded almost on top of him. Ben stared up through the grating, into the gloomy heights of what could only be the inner dome of St Paul's, seeing almost nothing, but knowing.

'Got you, Tiffany.'

18
🐈 THE TEETH OF SET 🐈

An ache in place of her head. One side of her neck all bruise, like the last banana in the bowl. Her limbs felt disconnected, not her own. A tangy taste from the rag of cheek that her clenching teeth had chopped out.

Tiffany became aware that her eyes were open, focused upon something inches from her nose. Now and then it made a sound. *Tink.* Rufus's bell, dangling from the cat collar on her left wrist. Even in her pain and confusion, the old grief cut her.

'Oh…'

But the collar had company. Her wrists wore hoops of black metal, tethered by a chain link that clinked as she tried to scratch her nose. Someone had put her in handcuffs. The reflex action was to yank and yank at them in panic.

'I wouldn't do that.' A shadow blocked the weak light. 'If you struggle you'll hurt yourself and your wrists will swell.'

Scrambling to her feet didn't work. She flopped like a stranded fish.

'Your feet are in cuffs too,' said the voice, helpfully.

Tiffany blinked at an electric lantern that dangled by a stout chain from the ceiling. The room in which she lay seemed about the size of her bedroom at home, and was almost perfectly round. The only furniture was a stone bench set into the wall. Two narrow doors faced each other across the room, and to her left stood a larger door with an iron frame painted in flaking gold. All of this she took in with a glance as she rolled towards the voice.

'You…' she croaked.

It was the tourist steward who had been helping her. From this angle he looked even younger, for she could see the acne spots under his chin. The walkie-talkie in his hand triggered a horrible rush of memory.

'Don't be afraid.' He followed her gaze. 'I won't hurt you again if you lie still.'

Out of sheer stubbornness she tried to sit up. Surprisingly, he helped her do it, though he kept his radio close. The stun gun. Tiffany sat hunched over, her cuffed hands laid heavy upon her shackled feet.

'What do you want with me?'

The young man sat on the stone bench.

'You must know. Isn't that why you're here? You're Cat Kin. We are the Set.' He might as well have added, *You lost*.

She had to ask. 'How old are you?'

'Twenty-one,' he said, primly.

'Well, I'm fourteen,' said Tiffany. 'You proud of yourself? Electrocuting a girl and chaining her up?'

'Yes. I am proud of myself,' said the steward. 'I have done the bidding of my Lord Set.'

Tiffany shivered, only partly with cold. But truly, it was freezing in this strange round room. She could see only one small fan heater, vainly whirring. Where was this place? Was she still somewhere inside the cathedral?

In the centre of the floor was a curious feature, a circular brass plaque. With her pinioned feet she shuffled herself closer to it. A dark spot in the middle turned out to be glass, like the pupil of a great eye. She craned to see through it. The young man rose, handset at the ready.

'Move back where you were.'

She'd seen enough to guess. A window in the floor meant there was something to look down upon. So this room probably wasn't in the crypt. And then there was the icy temperature, and a disembodied moaning that might have been the wind. No, this place didn't feel like it was underground. More likely, some considerable height above it.

'My name's Olivia,' she said, giving her middle name. She took heart when he didn't correct her. So the Set weren't sure exactly who she was, and didn't know she was the same girl they had been texting. That was something. She had another idea. 'What's yours?'

'I am Tjan,' said the steward.

'T-yan?'

'Tjan Sethemhat,' he elaborated.

'Set-hem-haat?' Tiffany was sceptical. It was a poor match for his fair hair and Scottish jawline. He looked more like a Callum.

'Tjan Sethemhat. Steward of Lord Set.' He touched one fist to his breastbone.

'Look,' sighed Tiffany, 'I've already got a headache. Can't I use your real name?'

'That is my true name.'

'John. How about John?' Tiffany forced a smile. 'That's close enough.'

Tjan returned to his bench. 'I shouldn't talk to you.'

'Why not?' she pressed.

He didn't reply.

'Come on, John. There's no harm in smalltalk.' Tiffany sat up straighter. 'Interesting job you have. Tourist guide and assassin. Are they all like you?'

A stonewalling shake of the head.

'Okay, that wasn't smalltalk. Sorry.' Carefully she lied, 'I'm at City of London School. Are you a student?'

'I'm not at college. I'm twenty-one.' Tjan coloured slightly.

'Sorry. I forgot.' Tiffany faked her friendliest smile. It dawned on her that she was trying to do something, she didn't yet dare imagine what. 'So! How long have you been a... a... you know, a Set person?'

'Always.'

'Really? Since you were born?' Tiffany had a surreal vision of Set schools, Set nurseries, a Set maternity ward.

'The life before does not count.' Tjan absently picked off a long hair that had clung to his shirtsleeve. One of Tiffany's hairs. 'I have always been a steward of Set. Ever since I died.'

Tiffany lost the power of speech.

'To serve the Lord Set, one must die,' said Tjan, matter-of-factly. 'He will suffer no servant of his to be alive. For life is an abomination, the handiwork of Ra.'

With the clear vision born of sudden terror, Tiffany saw again the gold emblem on the steward's necktie: the crossed swords beneath the shape she had thought was a dome. It wasn't a dome. That was the ankh – the Ancient Egyptian symbol of life – turned upside-down.

'Death is forever,' said Tjan. 'So how can there be a life before? Once dead is always dead. I have always served the Lord Set.'

Her panic ebbed. Of course this young man was no zombie, no vampire. He looked as alive and warm as herself – warmer, for he sat nearer the heater. When he talked of his own death, of dying to serve Set, he had to be talking figuratively. Didn't he? It was symbolic, she told herself, symbolic. A crazy belief, nothing more.

She rallied. 'And your parents? Are they alive? Do they know what you are now?'

He looked at her askance. 'Do yours?'

'No, but… no.' Damn him. 'I'm just interested, John. You seem like, y'know, quite a good bloke. A nice guy. Do you have a girlfriend?'

In response he gave a smile that was almost sad.

'That's the way,' he said. 'Call me nice. Call me ordinary. Make me into that person. Try and *reach* me.' He advanced on Tiffany with dreadful suddenness, raising his stun-gun, the spark blazing inches from her face. She cowered.

'Have you forgotten who we are?' he asked. His voice was soft and terrible. She stared at the electrodes paralysed with fear, until the spark winked out to leave a crack across her vision.

'I'm s-s-sorry…'

'It's all right.' He waved a hand, almost apologetic, and sat back down. 'I'm just a little… insulted, I suppose. We are the Set. We can do to your mind what the Aussies can do to a cricket ball. And you think you can bowl me out with an easy lob like that.'

'I w-wasn't trying to…'

'Oh yes, you were.' Tjan chuckled. 'You still are. Even if you don't think you are. You can put away the whimpering and the tears, Tiffany. You're tougher than that.'

She caught her breath. So he did know her name.

'You can't appeal to my better nature.' Tjan Sethemhat shrugged. 'This is it.'

He pulled the fan heater closer to himself. Tiffany's side of the room grew chillier. Through the walls came the wailing of the wind, like someone using a vacuum cleaner in the next room. Then, with almost magical strangeness, she heard music. A melancholy carol, welling up from the eye window in the floor.

'There's a service going on!' She had thought it the middle of the night.

'Evensong,' Tjan confirmed, shortly.

'Why are you lot here?' Tiffany burst out. 'This is St Paul's cathedral!'

Tjan Sethemhat nodded – yes, he knew the address. She was more cunning with her next question.

'What a stupid place for a base!'

'Lord Set must have his dwelling,' said Tjan. Thank you, thought Tiffany. Now she made the connection. Something Mister Isidorus had said to his masked companion. *My Lord… your temple is prepared.* It was crazy. Yet neat. Convenient, even. What religious cult would say no to a ready-made temple? She had wondered what was here that the Set might want to steal. The answer was, simply, St Paul's.

'You can't do it, you know,' she murmured.

Tjan raised a quizzical eyebrow.

'You can't bring back Set,' she said.

'Of course we can,' said Tjan.

'But that's mad,' she said. 'You know that's mad. Set's not real. He was a myth. You can't bring back something that never existed.'

Tjan regarded her in a puzzled way. 'But you're Cat Kin.'

She wondered what that had to do with it.

'You worship the goddess Bastet,' Tjan prompted. 'Don't you?'

'That's different. Pasht,' Tiffany used the name she preferred, 'she's not like a real person to me. It's the *idea* of her. That's what I follow.'

Her captor smiled, triumphant.

'Tell me the difference,' he said. 'What is a god, except an idea? You can't see them, you can't touch them, yet they can shape or destroy whole worlds. An idea can last for eternity. An idea cannot be killed. An idea may rule over millions. What is an idea but a god?'

Tiffany shook her aching head.

'You want proof? Look around you!' In his excitement, Tjan Sethemhat spread his arms. 'This cathedral! It feeds no-one, it shelters no-one, it doesn't buy or sell. It serves no practical purpose whatever. Yet it's the grandest building in London. All because of an idea.'

'But,' Tiffany protested, 'no-one believes in Set anymore.'

Tjan only smiled. Sick of feeling so helpless, Tiffany blew on her fingers, staring at the heater, receiving not a breath of its warmth.

'So what's the deal with the clock?' she sighed.

She'd been trying to avoid direct questions, but the effort was exhausting. To her surprise, he answered.

'The Teeth of Set,' he said.

'What?'

'They were lost. Then they were found.' Tjan leaned forward. 'The Teeth are a sacred mechanism. The first of its kind. The ancient priests of Set turned its wheels to direct the movements of the stars, and so command the fate of the world below.'

Tiffany coughed. 'Really?'

'Yes. But the last surviving mechanism was looted from Egypt by the Romans, more than two thousand years ago. Set, in his wrath, avenged the theft by sinking the plunderers' ship off the Greek coast.' Tjan's voice had become flatter, as if he was reciting lessons learned by rote. 'At the dawn of the twentieth century its remains were discovered. Now, by the wisdom of Set's minions, the fragments have been reconstructed and copied. This is what the world flocks to see. The Teeth of Set.'

He seemed to expect her to be as thrilled as he was. Not for the first time, she was struck by his youthful good looks, and how nice his smile might be if not for the mad glitter in his eyes. A feeling almost of pity came over her. What had they done, these twisted people, to turn him into this? Had they made him kill for them? Might he even be the one – No. She wouldn't think that. It would break her, to be chained here at his feet, thinking that.

'So what happens –' She cleared her throat. 'What happens when your clock hits midnight?'

Tjan looked sly. 'Wait and see.'

'Whatever you think will happen, it… won't!' said Tiffany. 'That thing is a bunch of mechanical parts. All they do is move.'

'All you do in pashki is move,' answered Tjan.

'It's a lifeless machine!' Tiffany snapped.

'Yes. And thousands upon thousands come,' said Tjan, 'to worship it.'

'Pretentious twerps.' Tiffany made a face. 'I came, I saw, I yawned. What, you think midnight will strike, and suddenly everyone bows down to your Lord Set?'

'Oh, no.' Tjan smiled. 'It will be far greater than that.'

'Huh?'

'You will see for yourself,' said Tjan Sethemhat. 'You will be there.'

'Yeah, I'll be there,' Tiffany shot back. 'You try and stop me.'

But her fetters clanked and she fell silent, losing hope, not knowing what he meant, but suddenly dreadfully afraid.

Oh, Ben, she thought. *Where are you?*

19
WHISPERING TO STONE

The Christmas tree was nicely invisible. Positioned so as not to obscure the choir, it nonetheless dominated this side of the nave, tall as a steeple, gleaming with tinsel and icicle lights and baubles of red and gold. Needles at the tips of its shaggy boughs tickled the carvings on the wooden pulpit, or slowly rained onto the chequerboard marble floor. The tree was the single biggest object in this place and yet, for all its size and glitter, no-one in the congregation was really seeing it.

Even a careful observer might have struggled to notice the lithe figure climbing beneath the foliage, causing brief squalls in the rain of needles. Few eyes would have detected the quivering of the star on top. Baubles swung, swilling tiny, bulbous reflections of the cathedral's interior. Where the branches tapered towards their starry pinnacle, the tree seemed itself to be hanging from a giant bauble, an immense decorated orb. One blink, and that illusion popped inside-out, the orb becoming the inside of the dome.

Ben planted his foot in the face of a cherub. As the upper branches grew too weak to bear him, he continued his ascent up the transept wall, trying to match the stonework with his stealthy climb. He supposed he must now be in full view of the congregation, but he heard no astonished shouts to interrupt the singing of 'In The Bleak Midwinter'. Wedging his fingertips inside a gargoyle's jaws, with the rest of his weight on one toe and an angel's wing, he tipped back his head. There, above that daunting overhang, was the Whispering Gallery.

It had been the highlight of that family excursion. The Whispering Gallery was a balcony that ringed the inner dome, a hundred feet above the chequered floor. Visitors could gaze up in wonder and mild vertigo at the sepia frescos, or at the statues standing at intervals among the belt of tall windows. But when people weren't gazing, they whispered. The acoustics of the curved walls meant that the tiniest sound could be heard on the walkway's far side, thirty metres away. Ben had seen grown men and women giggling, as enchanted as their kids, carrying on remote conversations about nothing, as if phones had never been invented. In the Whispering Gallery, everyone got the chance to hear like a cat.

Though not at this hour. The dome was closed. Sunk in shadow, illuminated only by the light diffused from below, the walkway rang with a solitary set of footsteps. A steward was on patrol, pacing the gallery. A stout man, grey with middle age, he put a little pomposity into each slow stride, content to be the master of his lonely domain.

The steward stopped and spoke into his radio.

'Whispering to Stone. What's the weather like up there?'

The radio's reply garbled into its own echoes, inaudible from a distance. Whatever it was, it made the steward smile.

'Oh, are you? Well, it's warm and dry in this bit.'

After patrolling a few more steps, the steward radioed again.

'Stone Gallery? Everything okay on your watch?' Another distorted interlude. 'No, nothing much. Just wondering. Thought I saw someone up here, that's all.'

The radio crackled a question.

'Nah. It wasn't anyone. Trick of the light. Right across from me, on the opposite side. Turned out to be a railing with a shadow coming off it!' The man wheezed his amusement. 'Thought it was a bloke in a hood. Standing still, y'know. Staring.'

Another crackle.

'No, relax. They nabbed the guest downstairs, that's what I heard. I'm looking both ways now. See? No-one here.'

The radio seemed to chuckle. The steward smiled into the mouthpiece.

'Yeah. This place likes to have a laugh sometimes. All those holy statues standing up there between the windows. Sometimes you can swear they're watching you.' A crackly reply made the man scowl. 'Oh, shut up, Kanif. Try being here on your own for two hours. I'll catch up with you and the lads later. Whispering out.'

He put away his radio, seeming to chew his cheek as he swept another glance around one hemisphere of the gallery. He frowned, then without moving his feet he looked the other way, scanning the remaining hundred and eighty degrees. Satisfied, he smiled to himself and resumed his dignified walk.

Almost immediately he spun round again, as if towards the memory of something he had seen, which his brain had been late taking on board.

'Who's that?'

No-one. Nothing was there. The steward went for his walkie-talkie. Ben came up behind him and put him in a Vermin Choke.

Although the gallery offered no cover to speak of, the railings and the upcast shadow had been enough. Several times the steward had looked straight at him, the way that Mum could stare at her lost keys on the table and not see them, as Ben stood absolutely motionless, balanced in the Siamese Stone freeze. Every time the steward turned away, Ben trimmed the gap between them, moving in his most silent Eth walk so that even the whispering walls could not betray him. As in a game of Grandmother's Footsteps he worked his way closer, till he could slip an arm round the man's neck.

The Vermin Choke, like the more heavy-duty Lion Jaw, compressed the carotid arteries to starve the brain of oxygen, causing swift unconsciousness. Usefully, it also squeezed the larynx, so the victim could not utter a sound. Ben got his grip good and tight but didn't really cram it on yet – he wanted the man awake for a bit.

The steward's flat leather shoes scrabbled at the floor as Ben dragged him off-balance. In this freaky place even a breathless squeal was dangerously loud, so Ben squeezed harder to silence it, while twisting the man's head round to meet his eyes. He dared not speak aloud, not in here, but with a glare Ben asked his silent question.

The bulging eyes flicked up involuntarily, towards a halo of light at the dome's zenith. Ben saw a round window at the top, like the pupil of a giant eye. The Oshtian Compass gave a tug of confirmation and he tightened his Vermin Choke. The man abruptly increased in weight and slid to the floor, taken out as quietly as a library book. Ben stepped over him.

A passage led off the gallery to a red-carpeted landing, from which wooden stairs climbed in a broad spiral. Ben ran up them two at a time, bounding from the edges of each tread so that the elderly, warped boards would not squeak, listening for other feet, his Mau whiskers alert for tell-tale tremors. After what must have been a hundred steps, a draught sank past him and he knew he must be near the top of the flight, a doorway to the open air.

He froze five steps below the two men who stood in the threshold, touching cigarettes to a shared lighter flame. Over their steward uniforms they wore black coats, flapping in the wind. Beyond them Ben could see the night sky above stone balustrades, at the edge of a broad promenade. That was where he'd stood with Dad on a crystal clear October afternoon, gazing over the city from the base of the outer dome.

Lighting their fags, the men stood side-on to him; he would be shading the edges of their vision. Reluctantly, he fingered a toggle on the hood of his new tracksuit jacket, snipped it off with a Mau claw, and flicked it past the men at knee height to land, *skit-skitter*, on the floor of the gallery outside. They turned towards the sound, away from him.

'You hear that?'

'Pigeon, I think.'

Ben stepped between them, plucked the radios from their belts, crossed his arms and jabbed each with the other's stun-gun. The men went rigid, slammed into the door posts and tumbled almost peacefully down the stairs. Ben dropped the weapons and walked out into the Stone Gallery, letting the wind blow his hood off.

Tiffany shivered. She had worked out that this round room must be at the very top of the cathedral, inside the cupola on the peak of the dome. That was why high winds moaned on every side, leeching every drop of warmth. Her captor must have carried her up a heck of a lot of stairs.

'Hope I gave you backache,' she murmured.

'Oh. You're not heavy.' Tjan seemed to know at once what she meant. 'I keep fit.'

'You play cricket?' It was a shrewd guess. Tjan's eyes lit up – another flicker of a normal person.

'Yes, actually, I do! Are you a fan?'

'Oh, yeah…' Well, she knew that cricket wasn't the one with the off-side rule. 'I stayed up all night to watch the Ashes.'

'The last Ashes series?' Tjan inquired. She nodded; the interest evaporated off his face. 'That was in England. Not Australia. You didn't watch it, did you?'

So much for that line of conversation. She struggled to think of others, some ordinary topic, but her brain refused. It could only dwell on her terrible plight, slowly drowning in the fear that deepened with every passing minute. She flexed her shackled ankles to keep her legs from going to sleep.

'Why the stunners?' she asked, purely for something to say. 'You all use those sparky-jabby things. Why not –' *guns or knives*, she almost added.

'Easy to hide.' Tjan unclipped his walkie-talkie to show it off, and sure enough it still looked harmless. Even the electrodes at the base could be mistaken for a charging socket. 'And there are other reasons.'

'You don't want to kill people?'

'Well, of course we do,' said Tjan, blandly. 'But the actual spilling of blood is forbidden to us. Blood is the fluid of Life, and Life is an abomination. Blood is therefore not to be touched. Lord Set permits only his closest minions, the Divine Adoratrice and the prophet Isidorus, to wet their hands in blood.'

'The who?' asked Tiffany. 'The Divine what?'

'Our high priestess,' said Tjan. 'The Divine Adoratrice of Night. By her devotion did Lord Set become incarnate again.'

Tiffany had a feeling she was on to something, perhaps a clue about that huge masked man who walked around in the guise of the god Set. However, when tried to ask a follow-up question, her mind started playing silly beggars. She found she couldn't form a clear thought about this Divine Adoratri– Adora– what was the word again? Tiffany closed her eyes. She had lost the thread of their conversation.

'Because we may not shed blood,' Tjan was saying now, 'Lord Set gives us leave to use his sacred weapons instead. The lightning bolt,' he crackled his stun-gun, 'and fire.'

Fire. Tiffany's throat closed, as for an instant she smelled the fumes around Yusuf's gutted house. Sick with horror she gazed at Tjan, wondering again if he had lit the match, disabled the smoke alarms, sealed the windows… Then her nausea changed to something else. A knot of heat in her stomach, like coffee drunk too fast, burning and yet not unpleasant, wonderful in fact, melting through her fear.

The pull of the Oshtian Compass was unmistakeable. And this feeling was different from the one she knew, because this Compass wasn't her own. It belonged to someone else. Someone who cared deeply for her and was coming to find her.

Ben! She managed not to yell it out loud. *Come on, Ben*, she thought, desperate, delighted. *I'm here, I'm here. You can do it. Oh, thank you, Ben. I'm up here…*

Already she was looking smugly around the room, trying to guess which door he would come leaping through. Then a thought began to rankle. Hold on. This was a very odd prison cell, wasn't it? *Why* would the Set keep her here? Why cart her all the way up hundreds of steps, when any locked room would have done? They had imprisoned her at the very summit of the building, like a cat stuck up a tree… Yes. *A cat up a tree*. Because they *knew* she wasn't alone. They *knew* she had a companion. And of course they would want to chase him up a tree… or *lure* him up there.

Tiffany understood. She was bait.

By drawing him up to the high, confined space of the galleries, the Set could surround him on all sides and cut off his escape. As a trap it was lethally simple and now, thanks to the bond that she and Ben shared, Tiffany was helping to spring it.

No. She strained at the cuffs on her hands and feet. *No, Ben! Go away! Get out of here!*

But the Oshtian Compass didn't work like that. It was not like telepathy, or texting. It was as mindless as hunger, a mad, blind thing, a need that did not know defeat or despair.

Go away, Ben! she screamed inside her head. Then, as the pull grew even stronger: *I hate you! I can't stand the sight of you. Never want to see you again. Hate you. Hate you.*

But the emotions that overflowed from her felt more like the opposite, and they poured into the mystic link between them, like petrol onto a fire.

The cathedral's clock and bell towers, not-quite-identical twins, stood like misshapen, half-melted candles against the backdrop of city lights. Ben stalked on round the Stone Gallery, keeping close to the inner wall. Up here it was sky-quiet, silent but for the wind, high above the roarings of traffic which the sleety gusts whipped away. Like a flying mountain, looming preposterously close overhead, the cathedral's outer dome nosed towards the clouds. At the sight of it, his Oshtian Compass flared bright as magnesium. There she was, up there. The hundred stairs remaining between them seemed like nothing. He felt he could reach out and take her hand.

But on seeing the entrance to the final staircase, he switched his Eth walk into reverse. At least a dozen men stood there, barring the threshold. Some wore the uniforms of cathedral stewards, while others were dressed more like the smugglers at Clink Wharf. He saw sticks like police batons resting in folded arms, stun guns clipped to belts, and gloved hands brandishing menacing-looking objects he could only guess at. He would never get past that lot.

Ben shrank into the shadows and ran back the other way. It would have to be Plan B: climbing up the face of the dome. The lead lining would be soft enough to let his Mau claws gain purchase; he tried not to think of how slippery the sleet would make it. Hunting for a patch of fancy stonework to give him footholds, he was pulled up short for the second time that evening by someone calling his name.

'Ben!'

A man's voice. Cultured and clear-cut, like the Prime Minister's.

'Ben Gallagher! Delighted to make your acquaintance at long last.'

Flanked by armed and darkly suited men, Mister Isidorus was walking towards him. His bald head shone beneath the glowing dome like a crude replica of it. Ben fled back the way he had come, only to see the guards from the final staircase now fanned across the width of the gallery. Mister Isidorus and his stewards closed in from the other side, the second claw of the pincer.

'I was beginning to wonder if you had spurned my invitation,' said Mister Isidorus.

There was no escape in front or behind. Ben vaulted up onto the balustrade. Below the precipice he saw the giant statues of saints keeping watch over the city, and far beneath their limestone feet, the lead-lined roof of the south transept.

'You should be most disinclined to jump from here,' Mister Isidorus advised. Ben was forced to agree. The shallowest drop on offer was at least fifty feet, into a jaggedly unpredictable roofscape. One bad landing and this lot would be on him to finish him off. Better to dash past them along the balcony rail – but two stewards had already second-guessed him and stood blocking his path, as much at ease on their perch as scaffolding workers.

With exaggerated patience, Mister Isidorus brushed sleet from his jacket sleeve.

'Step down, Ben Gallagher. Look around yourself and – what is that popular saying? – *do the mathematics.*'

Ben met the piggy eyes, full of loathing.

'Where is she?'

'She? Whom do you mean, *she? She* is the cat's mother.'

Mister Isidorus twitched the corners of his lips, a valiant stab at a smile, acknowledging his own witticism. In that apparently unguarded moment, his sleet-brushing fingers twitched and emitted a glint and a hiss. Ben swayed aside, as automatically as blinking, and a moment later understood that a flying blade had cut the darkness near his ear. His heart gave a thud of delayed fright.

Someone whistled, as if impressed. Mister Isidorus pointedly drew another bronze crescent from his jacket sleeve. Ben steadied his balance and said, 'Where's Tiffany?'

Mister Isidorus placed the blade between two fingers of one hand, produced another, and slipped that one beside the first, like toast into a rack.

'At a time like this,' he said, 'a cleverer boy would be worrying about himself.'

The other men raised their weapons. Ben saw stun-guns, night-sticks, stubby things like futuristic pistols. The hand of Mister Isidorus whipped, sending one glimmer at head height, another lower. Ben felt a blade skim over his ducking head, while the other – he winced in relief – buzzed between his legs as he swan-dived over it, into a momentary handstand. He bounced back onto his feet, wobbled once on the stone rail, was still. He drew a deep breath.

'*Where. Is. She?*'

'Dead,' said Mister Isidorus. 'You are too late.'

Ben watched, a fascinated spectator, as his own hand batted aside another flying blade, even as he pivoted over the sheer drop to dodge two more. Sparks splashed on the stone. The ham-like face of Mister Isidorus could no longer hide his frustration.

'My advice is that you surrender now, while your body and your dignity remain intact.' Mister Isidorus had raised a finger; his men stood ready. 'A glance about your person will confirm that you are outnumbered and hopelessly outmatched.'

Ben was hardly listening anymore. The sense of Tiffany so close, desperately calling, overwhelmed everything else. She was coming through as clear as a lighthouse beam, as clear as a scream. He clenched his fists.

'If you've hurt her…'

Unexpectedly, as in a waking dream, he saw a wildcat, under lock and key in some dark cave of his mind. This was how his Mau body had always seemed to him, as a wild thing, a beast timid yet terrible, untameable, best kept on a tight chain. More than once he had regretted ever waking it up, for he had seen for himself what calamities could happen if it writhed out of his control. And now, maddened by the blazing scream that his Oshtian Compass had become, the wildcat was working itself into a pitch of fury, savaging the bars of its cage.

Mister Isidorus and his men moved in. But they were now less frightening than the thing inside of him, the cornered wildcat with its fur up in spikes. The Mau claws leaped unbidden from his fingertips and for the first time he heard them rip the air.

'*If you've hurt her…*'

He opened his mind and let the cat out.

20
UNCAGED

Hanging her head to seem a picture of despair, Tiffany studied her two sets of handcuffs. Those on her wrists were linked by the shortest chain – it was wearying, always having to move both hands together. The chain on her leg-irons was slightly longer, but any walk beyond a shuffle would be impossible. Discreetly, she rotated one wrist inside its cuff, finding a sliver of space between the metal and the skin. She squeezed her hand as slim as it would go, scrunching her palm like a folding umbrella... The slipping cuff stopped dead at the base of her thumb, no matter how she pulled. Pashki had made her supple, but bones were bones. Real despair took a step nearer. Every moment she spent here, she was leading Ben into a trap.

Footsteps approached the nearest door and a man entered without knocking. He wore a pinstriped business suit and Tiffany knew him at once, for his hair was the rare shade of pure black that made the stubble on his cheeks look blue.

Tjan stood. 'Sabu? Anything wrong?'

He was the bathroom man, the one that Yusuf had choked unconscious. Seeing Tiffany he smiled, then scowled.

'Why isn't she gagged?'

Tjan ignored that question. 'What's happening down there?'

Sabu, who was visibly the older of the two, looked at him with disdain.

'Nothing. Waiting in the cold.'

'You're not meant to be in here with me,' said Tjan. 'You know the orders.'

'You know the orders!' Sabu mimicked. 'I'm relieving you early. You can go down to Stone. Leave her with me.'

Sabu squatted beside Tiffany.

'Hey.' He smiled. 'How's it going?'

She swallowed, afraid.

'Do you miss your friend?' he asked. When she didn't reply, he produced a book of matches. One match, still attached, was suddenly lit. She watched, hypnotised, as it burned down its length, finally igniting the remaining matches to turn the whole book into one big flame, which he flicked at her. Crying out, she shook it free of her hair before it could tangle there.

'Spoilsport.' He stamped out the smouldering scrap. 'Don't you want to know what it feels like? How it feels to burn?'

Tjan had not departed. 'Sabu. We can't both be in here.'

'Down you go, then.' Sabu leaned so close that Tiffany could smell his aftershave. He said, 'To perish in fire is to die at the hands of Lord Set himself.'

'It was you,' Tiffany blurted.

'It was the will of the Set. But prophet Isidorus granted me the honour of setting the flames. As payback for a certain... prank your friend committed.' Sabu twisted his mouth, as if at a lingering bad taste. 'He should not have upset me.'

This time Tiffany couldn't stop it. The tears spilled from her eyes. All her attempts at spitting curses came out as sobs. Tjan stepped forward.

'That's enough.'

Sabu turned irritably. 'Can't I make your prisoner cry?'

'As you say,' answered Tjan, 'my prisoner. Handover's not for another ten minutes.'

Sabu peered at him. 'What's the matter, novice? Getting fond of her?'

'I'm fond of my orders. Go.' Tjan opened the door. Sabu hesitated and then, to Tiffany's surprise and relief, obeyed. In departing he looked back.

'See you soon, girly. And Tjan? Prophet Isidorus will be having a chat with you.'

Tjan murmured, 'Oh, put a sock in it.'

'*What?*' Sabu returned up the steps.

'I said, I look forward to it,' said Tjan. Sabu left, his face like thunder. Tjan shut the door firmly and sat on his bench.

Tiffany couldn't stop trembling. It was as if her long-held courage had finally cracked, to let all the pent-up terror and grief come flooding out. She huddled on the floor and found it all too easy to weep, for herself, for Ben, for Yusuf's mother and father, and most of all for Yusuf.

There were far too many enemies to fight. They pressed in upon him from every side, night-sticks clubbing, electric barbs crackling, a bombardment of gloved fists and booted feet, bronze blades ricocheting off the masonry, and mysterious wires that hissed through the air like the webs of giant spiders. No-one would be able to think fast enough to keep up with such an onslaught. It was like running down steps four at a time – you couldn't count them, you couldn't watch where you put your feet, and you certainly couldn't think. You just did it.

Although lately Ben had been outgrowing his old pinball addiction, the thrill of play remained a vivid memory. Those special times, when he'd been operating on a table for half an hour straight, when his score was racheting up into the millions and he was batting at not one ball but four or five or six, cannoning them off bumpers and kickers, flinging them through slingshots till the playfield was pure fireworks; when his fingers were numb to the first knuckle from the hammering of buttons, when his eyes were glazed and watering and he could barely see – and yet he kept on striking the targets, never dropping a ball, scoring and scoring with a demonic skill that seemed hardly to belong to him… Ben felt a bit like that now. Only this thrill wasn't fun. It was fury.

With the same feverish detachment, he saw men crumpling to

the stone walkway, clutching at bloodied noses and mouths, the sight seeming almost unrelated to the bone-crunching impacts through the soles of his feet. Only the tatters of jacket sleeves flapping in the wind, the tell-tale trails of his Mau claws, allowed him to guess where his hands had recently been. He found himself whirled and flung about with the engineered violence of a theme park ride, a mere passenger inside his own body as it leaped, slashed, tumbled, punched, twirled on the ground like a breakdancer and kicked another steward in a painful place.

On every side of him, men fell squirming in agonies. Some of them, he was sure he never touched. Reflexes kept him dodging the wires that spat, *tiss-tiss*, through the darkness, and when these missed him they would often hit someone else, and that steward would stiffen, shudder and collapse. They were Tasers, stun guns of a more dangerous kind, firing electric barbs on wires to bring down victims at a distance. But Ben did not think any of this consciously – he simply ducked, and another man dropped.

With the little control that he still had over himself, he was trying to hew a path through his foes to work his way closer to the stairs. He hardly felt the glancing blows that occasionally broke his defences, or the thickening crop of bruises on his arms, legs and flanks. Nor did he heed the first symptoms of weariness creeping through his muscles. If he thought at all, it was only of reaching that staircase, running up it, finding Tiffany. As for what they would do then, he had not yet had time to wonder.

Into the round room rose a familiar melody, the words now twisted in Tiffany's mind to take on new and nasty meanings.

O come, let us adore him…

O come, let us adore him…

Tjan Sethemhat sat resting his chin on his fingertips. Tiffany let herself shudder and sob, sprawled on the floor, her tears dripping to a puddle between her chained wrists. Tjan awkwardly cleared his throat.

'My guard duty ends in a few minutes,' he said.

Tiffany hardly raised her face off the floorboards.

'Sabu takes over from me,' said Tjan.

'D-don't let him,' Tiffany sobbed.

'My orders.' Tjan frowned, just a flicker. 'We both have orders. You must be kept alive for now.'

It sounded almost as if he were trying to reassure her.

'Don't let him,' Tiffany pleaded again. She made a clumsy, failed attempt to sit up. 'You stay and guard me. Please.'

'No. I can't. I – prophet Isidorus –' Tjan made a helpless gesture. 'It'll be all… I mean, I can't. That's that.'

Beyond the walls the wind lamented. A draught blew strong enough to make the ceiling lantern swing on its chain. Tiffany struggled feebly into a sitting position and hugged her knees. Her cat bell jingled with her shivers.

'It's s-so cold in here,' she moaned.

Tjan stooped to check the fan heater.

'This is turned up as high as it'll go,' he said. Tiffany broke into fresh sobs. Tjan moved the heater a bit closer to her, to the limit of its short electric cord.

'It's still freezing,' Tiffany complained, through chattering teeth. 'Doesn't it go any hotter?'

Tjan shook his head.

'Then g-get a longer cord,' she begged. 'An extension lead. Please.'

That was patently absurd. With a sigh Tjan rose from his bench and came over.

'Oh, shut up. I'll pull you a bit nearer.' He bent to drag her by the legs. Tiffany seized his neck between her cuffed feet and with a twist of her whole body slammed his head into the floor. His arms and legs puppet-jerked. Tiffany pressed her feet crushingly tight, anchoring the chain of the cuffs under his chin. After a slow count of ten she oh-so-carefully released her grip on the unconscious Tjan, and had just enough breath left to gasp, 'Howzat?'

With her sleeve she mopped the tears and sweat off her face and sat up, instantly dry-eyed. The first thing she did was check that the young man was breathing. A gurgling snore reassured her.

'Sorry,' she murmured in his ear, and started frisking him for the keys to her cuffs. Tjan, or whatever his real name was, would be okay. In five or ten minutes he would wake up, with a splitting headache, and she hoped that he would then come to his senses, realise his mistake, and run for his life until the Set were far behind him.

'Come on, come *on*. Where do you keep them, you must have the – Gotcha!' Her fingers found a scrunch of metal in the trouser pocket he was lying on. Heaving, she rolled him over and pulled out a crowded keyring. There were house keys, a car ignition key, small keys that might have been for windows or a bicycle lock – the ordinariness of the collection was somehow eerie. At last she found a simple, round-shafted key, the only one that could possibly fit the holes in her cuffs.

She tried it on the leg-irons first. It didn't fit those, so, bending her wrists awkwardly, she poked the key into her handcuffs and… it didn't fit there either.

'Oh, Thoth and Horus…!' She tried again. And again. It obviously wasn't the right key, yet she made two more attempts, in disbelief, before she understood.

The Set were too clever. Hadn't Tjan reminded Sabu that they should not be in the room together? It was to ensure that something like this couldn't happen. One steward stood guard over the shackled prisoner, while another steward kept the keys safe. Sabu had the keys.

'No, no…' Frantic, she searched again for what wasn't there, until a noise made her drop the bunch onto Tjan's snoring body. Footsteps on the stairs.

'Novice?' Sabu's voice came through the door. 'Down to the Stone Gallery. Now.'

The doorknob turned. Tiffany crouched, utterly at a loss. There was nothing to hide behind. She couldn't run to either of the other doors, she could barely shuffle. Her only chance was gone, had never really existed. Then, as the door began to open, she thought of looking straight up. The lantern hung from the ceiling by its iron chain. She could still jump.

Lucy Gallagher hadn't liked the look of this final staircase. The Stone Gallery was high enough for her, thank you, and she'd baulked at the tight spiral of iron steps that led to the very crown of the dome, the Golden Gallery. But Ben and Dad had dared her to give it a go, because the view from up top would be worth the vertigo and claustrophobia, and after all, they were only stairs.

But now it was like trying to fight his way up a drainpipe clogged with rats.

Stewards of the Set had taken positions higher up, jabbing their batons through the gaps between steps. Others swarmed from below, clutching at his heels. Half-blind in the confined space, he had to rely on his Mau whiskers probing the air, and on Mau spurs conjured around his hands and feet. These ethereal feelers mimicked the hairs behind a cat's paws which let it sense prey at close quarters, and as he kicked and swiped and dodged, his spurs and whiskers traced a sketch of the mayhem around him. This enabled him to know that there was a steward right behind him, swinging a baton to break his shin; and to know that if he hopped just *now*, the stick would find another victim more deserving; and that if he grabbed the banister rail, to cartwheel over the stricken man, he could sweep out the legs of the attacker three steps higher – and that the two falling men would knock heads.

Something zinged past like a metal wasp, and a pain deadened his left biceps. He saw a rip in his sleeve, skin through the fabric, and blood. And Mister Isidorus, aiming another blade, squinting up the spiral staircase as if through a telescopic sight.

The cut was shallow, but in flinching he had broken his flow. Ben stumbled, ducking the next punch only by luck, and the spectre of exhaustion stole over him. He could not keep this up. Sensing weakness, the stewards pressed their attack. A man one stair above Mister Isidorus levelled his Taser, looking for an opening. Ben flung up his hands and cried, 'Don't shoot!'

The steward fired. Ben sprang into the air and jammed himself with hands and feet in the space between the walls, as the electric barbs flew beneath him to snare in the banisters. The men on the steps found themselves clinging to a handrail suddenly flowing with half a million volts. For a moment they stood as rigid as dominoes and then, like dominoes, they fell. The human landslide down the staircase finished far below in a twitching, groaning heap, with Mister Isidorus buried somewhere towards the bottom. Ben dropped back onto the stairs.

'Told you not to shoot,' he said.

He ran on, up and round, higher and higher, towards the door at the top.

'Tiffany!' He burst through, rolling, and rose in the Arch On Guard. He blinked. Tiffany wasn't there.

On the floor of this curious round room lay two Set stewards, unconscious. They were chained together with two sets of handcuffs in a cat's cradle of limbs, and one of them was hamster-cheeked with a huge, bulging gag. Ben recognised this man by his jet-black hair. His shoes were off and his feet were bare, because somebody had pulled off his socks and stuffed them both into his mouth.

'*Tiffany!*' he yelled, but she was already gone. He pumped his fist in delight, then muttered, 'Typical.'

From the doorway rose a thunder of feet. The Set had regrouped. Ben ran to the downward staircase and found the noise was in stereo. They were coming from both sides. And his muscles were burning – he couldn't beat them all a second time. He was trapped. Unless…

The third, biggest door led outside. When Ben had climbed to the Golden Gallery with Dad, to look out from its external balcony, they had peered over the railing at the dome below, plunging like a waterfall, and Dad had joked, 'I wouldn't like to slide down that, would you?'

Ben burst out into the night sky and leaped the rail, as if to plunge into the sea of city lights. *Thanks, Dad,* he thought. *You and your big mouth.*

A gentle slope near the summit quickly became almost vertical, until only the friction of his tracksuit kept him sticking to the wet lead. As if tugging a parachute's rip-cord he drew hard on his Ailur catra, to try and soften his landing in the Stone Gallery that came rushing up to meet him – and there in his drop zone was Lord Set.

Ben's heart caught between his ribs. The figure stood black against the glowing night, impossibly tall, impossible in every way. With its wolf-goat face tilted back almost nonchalantly, watching his fall, it lifted up one bare arm to point the beast-headed sceptre at him. Falling now as if in a nightmare, Ben saw the tip of the staff stab the air. A coldness impaled him, snuffing the indigo catra like a candle flame. He hit the limestone walkway on one foot and one knee.

The howl that broke out of him was wholly animal. There was nothing but pain, appalling pain. His kneecap, his kneecap... surely it was smashed.

Ben rolled upon the stone till his breath was gone, and his howl became coughing sobs. When at last he was able to open his eyes, he wished that he had kept them tight shut.

21

THE BELL

Fear and pain collided inside him like two huge waves, wiping each other out. It was in that momentary, death-like calm that he got his first proper look at Lord Set.

It began with toenails. Two feet away from his face were two feet. He saw a row of huge bare toes, clawed with things like oyster shells, ridged and calcified. They looked as if they had never been cut, only worn down by years (*centuries?*) of barefoot walking.

The huge feet, calloused almost into animal paws, grew up into shins as long and lean as a horse's cannon bones. Above muscular calves came the hem of the white robe, which Ben could now see was of very coarse cloth, its pallor ingrained with grime. Then came the massive torso in its coppery tunic, the arms in their bronze warrior-bracelets, and the great black monster head. Ben no longer thought it was a mask.

The eyes peered down like suns of coal. How long he lay pinned beneath their blank and pitiless gaze, he would never know. But as he clutched at his left knee, trembling so hard that the sweat rained off him, he sensed movement nearby. Feet approached along the gallery, slow and reverent. Little lights came bobbing, lines of stewards with pen-torches, gathering before Lord Set. At the head of the assembly stood Mister Isidorus, smoothing his suit lapels. His voice rang out.

'Hail, Set.'

In unison the stewards chimed in.

'*Spear of night.*
Master of the starving sands.
Lord of the last day.'

The figure cocked a blade-like ear towards the chant, at once gracious and disdainful. Mister Isidorus spoke again.

'My Lord is wroth.' His penetrating baritone had to compete with the wind. 'We have failed him. Must the Spear of Night exert himself to catch one slave-boy of Bastet? Lord Set, we bend ashamed.'

Mister Isidorus sank to one knee, as the crowd behind him grovelled on both.

'The fault is mine.' Mister Isidorus bowed low, uncreasing his bulldog neck. 'My Lord, wreak your justice upon me. Let my death in you be complete.'

Lord Set took a step towards Mister Isidorus and raised his sceptre. Ben winced, but could not look away, as the staff came down to touch the back of that shaven skull. The wind itself seemed to hush. Ben waited for the body of Mister Isidorus to fall dead upon the stone.

Mister Isidorus stood up.

'My Lord has delivered me a new death.' He bowed once more. 'I am ever yours in darkness. We will not fail you again.'

The assembled stewards rose to their feet. Ben looked on, bewildered by all this talk of death from a man who was so evidently alive. Experimentally he tried to move, and got fresh crippling pain through his knee.

Mister Isidorus went on. 'Our task is half-done. The other vassal of Bastet has escaped.'

The stewards sank into another fearful silence.

'You slaves,' said Mister Isidorus, 'you have proved incapable. My Lord himself will hunt down the girl. You must secure the Temple. Expel any lingering visitors.' He added, 'Politely, please.'

Lord Set remained where he was, standing motionless, like – Ben didn't know where this thought came from – like someone who wasn't sure what to do. Then Mister Isidorus said, 'My Lord, I give her to you.'

Now the god responded, gliding towards the downward staircase. Ben cried out, 'Tiffany! Run!'

Lord Set whipped round, pointed his sceptre, and Ben's shout became a shred of air. The tall figure stalked towards him, the sceptre poised like a dagger, and Ben was suddenly stone-cold certain that these were the last seconds of his life.

Lord Set stopped, the toenails close enough to kiss. Ben had to look up. The god bent low and then it was in Ben's nostrils – a foul smell, a stench like blocked drains. Ben gagged. What was this thing? What hid behind that mask, if it was a mask? Something dead? A crumbling mummy? No, no, such things were impossible. But then, pashki had once seemed impossible.

The fork of the staff touched his chattering teeth, and they shut. In his mind he called out to Tiffany once more, but his ears heard no sound. He could not shout; he couldn't even moan. It was as if Lord Set had plucked out his voice and eaten it.

By the time he dared to look up again, the monstrous figure had departed, as had all but two of the stewards. A dishevelled pair, they were getting a talking-to from Mister Isidorus.

'Sabu. Tjan. You will take him to the crypt and make him safe. I trust that *this* one will not escape you?'

Both shook their heads. Poisonous glances passed between them. Now Ben recognised them as Tiffany's guards, the ones he had seen shackled together. Both had bruising to the sides of their necks, and the younger had a bump on his forehead. Good old Tiffany. If only he could warn her of what was coming to get her. *Don't try and save me,* he pleaded silently, hopelessly. *Get away.*

The black-haired man touched his fist to his chest.

'Prophet,' he said, 'I beg the honour –'

'No, Sabu.' Mister Isidorus cut him off. 'The Divine Adoratrice requires them alive. Go.'

The stewards hauled Ben to his feet, and as his weight pressed through his injured knee he felt a scream burst from him – but even now, no sound came out. He writhed in silent agony.

'We need more handcuffs,' muttered Sabu.

'The spells of Lord Set are stronger than chains,' said Mister Isidorus. 'Take him down. I shall join the hunt.' He looked up at the dome. 'They say the cross that stands atop this edifice is hollow. A person might fit inside. It does make one wonder…'

He headed for the iron stairs. Ben stared up at the golden cross, wondering if Tiffany was indeed hiding up there, alone and afraid. He tried his Oshtian Compass, but his catras stayed dead, and then the stewards were dragging him away. Struggling was futile, and in any case his leg hurt so much that he was almost glad of their supporting arms.

The descending stairs were broad, each taking up a full stride or more, and with every downward jolt Ben felt sicker. The stewards weren't enjoying it either. Sabu grumbled at the younger man, Tjan, for letting the girl escape. Tjan remarked that Sabu had done no better. But he'd had no chance, Sabu growled – she had dropped on his head from above. Ben almost smiled.

At last they reached the foot of the stairs, or seemed to. Then Ben recognised the red carpet of the landing beside the Whispering Gallery, realised there were still two hundred agonising steps to go, and soundlessly groaned. Through a short passage he could see the gallery's safety rail, at the brink of a pool of darkness like a volcanic crater. In those unseen depths lay the cavernous cathedral, deserted now and silent.

'Take a breather –' With a grunt Sabu let go of him and Ben crumpled to the floor, winded with pain.

'Only a minute,' said Tjan. 'The prophet is already displeased.'

'Yeah, well so am I *displeased* –' Sabu retorted. Tjan raised his hand. 'Sssh!'

Only his eyes were moving.

'What?' Sabu hissed.

Tjan pointed to the threshold of the Whispering Gallery. In that moment Ben heard it too. An irregular sound, high and faint. His first rush of relief turned to terror and despair.

Sabu frowned the question. Tjan swivelled his wrist, where a watch might be.

'The girl,' he said, under his breath. 'She had a… bell thing. Cat bell. Wearing it.' Another ghostly tinkle floated off the gallery. Tjan's eyes glinted. 'That's her. She's on the walkway.'

Ben tried with all his might to call out, but could not. The touch of Lord Set had deadened his mouth like a dentist's needle. He thought in agony of all the times he could have made Tiffany get rid of that stupid cat collar. Now it was too late. He sat and listened to Tiffany making her fatal mistake.

She had boasted about it – how she had trained herself to move so stealthily that the bell hardly stirred. She had never reckoned on acoustics like those in the Whispering Gallery. The round walls of the inner dome were catching those vibrations and magnifying them. Didn't she realise how loud they were? Perhaps not. That was another strange thing about the gallery – you could hear everyone else's whispers, but your own seemed to be at normal volume.

'Got her,' breathed Sabu.

Tjan seemed to waver.

'She is Lord Set's prey. If we interfere –'

'My Lord can have her. But I'm delivering.'

Maybe Tiffany would overhear them. But the gallery would not pick up whispers from this side landing, only sounds from within its curved space. Ben went to slam his fist against the wall's wood panelling, but Tjan was ready, catching his arms and pinioning them. *Tink. Jing-tic.* The bell came two steps nearer.

Sabu drew something from his pocket. It looked like a cigarette lighter. Tjan blinked in alarm.

'The orders are not to kill her!'

Sabu sneered. 'Thunderbolts don't kill. It's just a bang.'

'A stun grenade, in there, it could –'

'It'll wreck her inner ear and she'll lose her balance and fall over. Any more objections?'

Ben tried to bite Tjan to make him cry out, but the spell of Lord Set seemed to have leeched his strength away, and the pain from his knee did the rest. He wilted on the carpet. Still holding him, Tjan turned one ear to the wall and covered the other. Wretchedly Ben followed his example, sticking fingers in his ears and blocking out the last tinkles of the bell's approach.

Crouched low, Sabu weighed the Thunderbolt device in his palm, his thumb touching a yellow switch. Like a sniper he watched the gallery entrance. A shadow eased into the threshold. Sabu pressed the yellow switch and skimmed the stun grenade across the floor, just as Tjan bellowed, 'No!'

The figure on the gallery was Lord Set.

Sheet lightning whitened the air. There came a boom, and a succession of ear-splitting echoes, like the climax of Fireworks Night. Beyond the white hole that the flash had burned in his vision, Ben saw a tall silhouette reel against the safety rail and pitch over it. In apparent silence, Lord Set tumbled off the gallery and fell out of sight.

Sabu remained absolutely still. Tjan's mouth had frozen open in its O shape. Ben fought a wave of dizziness as he looked from one to the other, watching the blood drain from each face till both were near transparent. As his deafened ears began to recover, he heard the fading thunder of the boom, still drumming around the cathedral and the dome. Sabu made a curious sound. It was the sort of weak squeak a rat might make as a cat bites its neck. Then he flopped over in a dead faint.

Tjan wailed like a terrified child. He scrambled to his feet, fell down, got back up and ran for the stairs. In his panic he missed the top step, slithered down on his back for a bit and yet kept running, and Ben could hear his crashing downward flight, bouncing from wall to stair to banister, until the din of it was far below him.

Ben sat beside the unconscious Sabu and wondered what to do.

A new shadow stepped into the gallery threshold. Tiffany rushed towards him.

'Found you!'

She gathered him in a hug. Ben screamed. Tiffany recoiled.

'*Ben...?*

'My...' he spoke through clenched teeth, 'knee. I think it's broken.'

As the flare of pain ebbed, he realised he could speak again.

'Oh no.' Dismay crossed her face. 'Uh... Don't worry. You'll be okay, Ben. You hear? I am going to see to it. We're getting out of this place.'

'What...' He was still dazed from the bang. 'What happened? They heard you coming. Your bell. And then...'

She looked more like a smug cat than ever.

'Mm. That worked better than I expected.'

'What worked?'

'I buckled Rufus's collar onto Set's robe.'

Ben stared at her.

'I wanted a decoy,' said Tiffany. 'I thought if my bell was on the big fella, he might distract the others, so I could reach you. I crept up behind him on the stairs. I figured he couldn't hear so well inside his monster mask.'

Ben tried to imagine the courage that must have taken.

'And then of course they tried to blast me to kingdom come...' Tiffany winced and rubbed her ears. 'Haven't these guys got some vicious hardware?'

'They need it, with you around.'

'Look who's talking, Bengal tiger! How many of them did you shred on your way up to see me?'

'Lost count.' Ben inspected the cut on his arm. It had scabbed over. 'And you weren't even in!'

'Yeah, sorry about that. I was afraid you might rescue me.'

'You what?'

'Haven't you noticed?' Her grin was mischievous. 'Every place you save me from gets demolished. I couldn't let that happen to St Paul's!'

'It's still standing, isn't it?'

A kind of tipsiness had taken hold of them, an urge to crack jokes, as if they were larking about in town together, and not stranded in the heart of an enemy's lair. Ben tried to haul himself up onto his good leg, and Tiffany ('Don't be stupid! Let me –') helped him.

'I can try giving you a fireman's lift,' she said.

'Down these stairs? I'd rather hop.'

Ben put his arm around her shoulders, purely for support, and so began a staggering, painful descent. At around the ninety-stair mark he tried flexing his left knee, and though it made him gasp he dared to wonder, for the first time, if the bone was really broken or not.

Expecting an ambush with every turn of the spiral stairwell, he jumped in fright at shapes that turned out to be jackets on pegs. They had reached the galleries' ticket gate and cash desk, on the ground floor. Warily they shuffled out into the nave. St Paul's was one big gloom. High windows gleamed no brighter than pennies, and emergency exits glowed in distant corners. There was no other light. Silence filled every aisle and arch, a deep stillness, as if the entire cathedral had been sunk underwater.

'Where is everybody?'

'Gone, I think,' said Tiffany.

'Yeah, right.'

'Seriously.' She scented the air. 'No-one's here. Except –' She broke off.

'Except what?'

She looked away, then said, 'It makes sense. After all, they can't carry on without him.'

Him. The thought startled Ben like a spider in the bath. He had almost forgotten about Lord Set.

'Where is he? He fell –'

'Over there.'

Ben turned too fast, almost toppling. They had emerged beside the broadest part of the nave, a chessboard of black and white marble directly beneath the dome. On the far edge of this otherwise empty board lay what looked, at this distance, like a fallen piece, a knight. Its long-nosed head rested on a white flagstone, twisted at an unnatural angle.

Ben swallowed. 'Dead?'

'I can't hear him breathing.' Tiffany stepped nearer.

'Wait! What are you doing?'

'Checking.' Her face hardened. 'And getting my collar back.'

She was out of her mind. Ben tried to get in front of her and stumbled to the floor. '*No!*' he hissed, through the pain.

'It's all I've got left of Rufus.' She walked on. 'I have to keep it. Back in a second.'

Ben crawled in pursuit. Lord Set had fallen a hundred feet onto a marble floor. Few could have survived that. Few mortals.

'Get back,' he gasped.

Now Tiffany stood within grabbing distance of Lord Set's motionless hands. Ben saw the cat-collar trailing from Set's white robe. Tiffany stooped to detach it.

There was a sound. The merest whimper, seeming to come from the black beast head.

Help…

Sweat-soaked, faint with pain, Ben tried to convince himself that he had imagined it, that it had been a creaking door somewhere. Then it came again.'

'Help…?'

Tiffany drew back in shock as Ben reached her. The body lay still.

What made him do it? Perhaps it was the thought that, if they ran away now, he would be haunted by that cry forever. Or he might have had another, simpler reason. Either way, Ben found himself kneeling on his one good knee, reaching behind the beast head and beneath its thick black mane – which turned out to be a weave of horse hair – and unfastening leather straps from buckles. Tiffany joined him, tugging at the head, till the mask (after all, it was a mask) lost its shape and slipped off like a boot.

Ben looked at the face underneath.

Many features remained hidden by hair. A beard had overrun the cheeks and the oblong chin, a growth that was matted with unspeakable gunk around the mouth. Chapped lips parted to reveal ruined teeth, either missing or brown and crooked. Pale grey eyes rolled lopsided beneath a sloping forehead.

With his mask gone the man heaved a sigh, and at the whiff of his breath Ben flinched – there it was, the stench of rotten teeth like a dead thing, which had so terrified him before. Yet staring at this man's dirty, misshapen features, Ben no longer felt any fear, just a horrible, fascinated pity. The massive jaw worked, till the dry lips found each other.

'Muh –' The man's eyes seemed to see, then glazed again. 'Mother?'

'Ben,' Tiffany said, hoarsely. Ben stooped lower, trying to hear.

'Mother. Please.' The man gurgled air. His enormous body lay freakishly still. 'Mother… let me go.'

'What did you say?' Ben leaned close.

'Mother…Please. Let me…'

The words dissolved into a long snore, as the man's chest sank and kept sinking, till the noise ceased. Ben saw his eyes; they were like glass.

His fear had only been biding its time. It came flooding his veins, as strong as any anaesthetic, and he was up on his feet, stumbling away from the dead body and its empty mask.

'Tiffany,' he gasped. 'Come on.'

Snatching up the cat collar she took his arm to support him and they fled the cathedral, not daring to look back, too shaken to speak.

22
ABANDONED

Ben spilled his mug of water as the front door clicked. It was only Tiffany returning. She plonked her shopping bags on the kitchen table and he watched as she unpacked a bag of frozen peas, followed by another bag of frozen peas, then another. He said, 'What's for lunch?'

'Tuna sandwiches,' said Tiffany. 'The peas are for your knee.'

On close examination, his knee injury had turned out to be just one almighty bruise. Ben hobbled to the bathroom where he took off his trousers, sat in the bath and pressed the first bag of peas in place. His yelp echoed through the flat.

'You'll be running up crocodiles again in no time,' Tiffany called from the kitchen.

Ben gritted his teeth. 'Go take a flying leap.'

As the shock eased off he moulded the peas around his knee and let them slowly thaw. The joint had swollen almost to a ball, a private little planet of pain. Chill water trickled down his legs to the plughole. He sat and shivered, listening to Tiffany unpacking her other groceries. She seemed better this morning. That much he could be glad about.

Getting back to Mrs Powell's flat yesterday evening had been not so much the end of it as the start. The moment they were safely inside, with the door locked and bolted behind them, was when things had got really bad.

The first thing that happened was that they both started shaking. Neither of them could hold a glass without spilling it – for a while, it was almost funny. Then it wasn't. They tried sitting against radiators, bundling themselves in blankets. Nothing helped. Tiffany had brewed cups of tea, but they couldn't swallow more than a few sips. Ben made toast which dried in the toaster. Strangest of all, they hardly spoke beyond a few glib words: *Are you okay? It'll be all right. Have we got any sugar?* They couldn't talk about what they'd done, what they had seen.

For hours they had sat on the kitchen's hard chairs, staring down the hallway at the front door, jumping at every gurgle from the central heating. When Ben got up to limp to the loo, Tiffany followed and lingered outside the bathroom. And Ben waited in dread when she made a trip downstairs to check the main apartment door was locked.

By a quarter to midnight it was obvious that neither of them dared go to bed. They retreated to the lounge and watched mind-numbing TV. Every time Ben's eyelids grew heavy, he would see in the blackness the mask of Lord Set, or the face of the dying man beneath it, and snap awake. Now and then Tiffany fell into a doze, only to moan and kick out feebly, disturbing them both. So they simply sat on the sofa, no longer noticing what programme was showing, waiting for nothing, not even morning, only trying to bear the fear of each minute that passed.

In the end, sleep had taken pity on them. Ben awoke to the face of a newsreader he had never seen before, to find Tiffany fast asleep on his shoulder, and his arm around her. He would happily have stayed there, like that, for a year, but he needed the bathroom and his leg was seizing up, so with great care he extricated himself and let Tiffany sink full length upon the sofa to sleep more comfortably. Returning after his shower, he found her awake and confused, grumbling, 'When did we agree to swap rooms?' But she didn't mind Ben taking the bed last night, she said, on account of his injury. Ben said nothing.

The bag of peas felt as good as cooked. With the pain frozen out of his knee, for now, Ben hauled himself from the bathtub, dried off, and reclaimed his trousers. Walking into the pashki studio in the manner of Long John Silver, he found Tiffany pinning tinsel around the notice board.

'Ugh.' Ben sat on the floor, head in hands. 'Christmas. I forgot.'

'Don't worry. We'll be home by then.' Tiffany stood back to admire her decorations. The gleam was decidedly forlorn.

'Want to bet?' Ben sank deeper into gloom. 'My parents hate me by now. They'll shut the door in my face.'

'Home. By Christmas,' Tiffany insisted. 'It'll be the best ever.'

She tried to fluff up the tinsel.

'When you were younger,' she said, 'did you ever lie awake at night, listening for the sleigh bells in the sky?'

Ben had to smile. 'What, in Hackney?'

'Why not in Hackney? Santa visits every house in the world.'

'We lived in a flat. No chimney.'

'Doesn't matter. I always guessed he could open front doors. With a special key.' Tiffany chewed her lip. 'I used to listen, every Christmas Eve. Some years I was sure I could hear them dashing overhead.' She jingled Rufus's bell, snugly back on her wrist. 'Then when I was eleven I was going to stay up all night and look out of the window, but... *what?*

Ben tried to stop laughing.

'You believed in Father Christmas till you were *eleven?*

Her cross face gave way to a grin. 'Yeah. I think so.'

'You're telling me that the year before you first met me, you still thought – ?'

'Yes. Sort of.' Tiffany had blushed a lovely festive red. 'That is, I did and I didn't. It's hard to explain. Obviously, I'd worked out ages ago that he *couldn't* be real. Not in the way I used to think. But you know, when it's Christmas Eve, and the last person's gone to sleep and even the buses have stopped, and the radiators have gone cold, and you're full of it, the weeks of writing cards and wrapping presents and decorating the classroom and the tree... Even though you know it can't *actually* be true, you still want it to be. And you try in your head to make it true. At least, I do. I did.'

Ben no longer felt like laughing at her. He twisted round so as not to see the tinsel.

'We *can* go home soon.' Tiffany sounded like she was trying to convince herself. 'Because... It's over. Isn't it?'

'Is it?'

'Yes. It must be. Lord Set's dead. So the Set will have to give up. With no leader...' She trailed off.

It was time to say what had been preying on his mind.

'Tiffany –' He flexed his leg and winced. 'Was he really their leader?'

Her hesitation was an answer.

'That man...' Ben found it all too easy to picture his face. 'He looked like he might be a bit... different. Y'know. Like he wasn't all there, in the head.'

'He was dying.'

'I know. But...' His suspicions hardened. 'Tiffany, what if he was a sort of – of puppet? That the Set were using?'

'You mean a decoy?'

'No, not exactly, more like –' Ben shut his eyes, 'like a figurehead. They take some poor guy who doesn't know any better, put him in that mask, and make him believe he's Lord Set.'

'Why?'

Ben shrugged. 'To keep their people under control. Or to hide who's really in charge.'

Again he saw the man's face, bearded, ravaged. But not old. Forty at most. Who was he? Probably they would never find out. He might not even have a name. But somebody, at some time in the past, had taken this person and forced him into that mask, and left him in it.

'He said *mother*.' Ben sat up straighter. 'He said, *Mother, let me go.*'

'Don't let's talk about him anymore.' Tiffany grew restless, prowling around the pashki studio, rubbing at imaginary marks on the floor.

'Yeah, right.' Ben decided she must be joking. 'This could be the answer. If he said *mother*, then maybe his mother did that to him. Which means *she* might be the leader. Whoever she is.'

'You're guessing.' Tiffany had become almost ratty. 'Dying people often call for their mothers. Well-known fact.'

'So what are you saying?' Ben looked hard at her. Something wasn't right. 'Lord Set's dead, so we've won, now let's go home and eat mince pies?'

'No, but…' Tiffany gave an explosive sigh. 'I'm tired, Ben! I'm so tired. I want to go home. I want to see my mum and dad, and Stuart, and… and…' She caught her breath and a moment later Ben was alone in the studio. The bathroom door slammed and he heard the sound of Tiffany locking herself in. Ben limped to the kitchen to fetch a fresh bag of frozen peas.

With his knee still resembling an exhibit from the London Dungeon, all they could do was lie low. Mostly they stayed in with the curtains drawn, Tiffany waiting for twilight before venturing out to buy food and recharge the energy card. Ben spent the next day watching TV with his knee frozen, while Tiffany cleaned the kitchen and the bathroom just for something to do, and made their simple meals. When Ben looked up to ask her for a cup of tea, she finally snapped and told him to get it himself.

The flat's small size meant that Ben could not help being under her feet. He, in turn, grew irritated to find Tiffany always there, flicking the TV channels or telling him to exercise his bad leg. Most wearisome of all, she made him practise the Pur meditation every hour, because it helped to speed up healing. He obeyed, though he had never felt less like purring. He wished with all his bored soul that he could go out for a walk – or that she would.

The hours passed, horrendously slow. Yet every second seemed like one they couldn't spare. In the long, moody silences that soured the air, Ben would hear the clang of a warming radiator, and imagine it to be the tick of a clock. The midwinter solstice was two days away.

'What are we going to do about it?' he asked.

'About what?'

'You know.'

Tiffany turned a page of her book. 'Hurry up and get better.'

'We could call the others.'

'No,' said Tiffany. 'They wouldn't come. Not after what happened.'

'Yes they would.'

'Even worse.' She sighed. 'I can't let it happen again. Besides, what would I say?'

'Tell them we have to stop that clock or the world will end.'

Tiffany stopped reading and looked up. 'You don't believe that.'

'No, I don't. And you don't,' said Ben. 'But I think we might be outvoted.'

'What do you mean?'

'Half a million people have seen that clock,' said Ben. 'What if it… hypnotised them, or something? So they end up worshipping Set?'

'So? Worshipping something can't make it real.'

'Maybe it can,' said Ben. 'Think about it. The Set hate *life itself*. What would happen if half a million people had the same idea? That'd be real enough for me.'

Tiffany was silent a moment. Then she murmured, 'Ideas are gods.'

'What did you say?'

'That was Tjan. The steward who took me prisoner. He was banging on about how gods like Set are real, because ideas and gods are really the same thing… But he was a nutter.'

'Hang on…' It didn't sound that crazy to Ben. 'That does make sense. Kind of. If everyone behaved as if Set was real, then he *would* be real, wouldn't he? As good as.'

'People would stop wanting to be alive,' Tiffany mused.

'More than that. They wouldn't want *anyone* alive, would they? Not even their friends, their families… it'd be a bloodbath.'

'The end of the world.' Tiffany stared into space.

Evening came, then a foggy dawn. Ben woke up certain that he couldn't even move, but after a hot bath with frozen peas on the side, he managed to Eth walk across the studio without stumbling. He even dared a gentle Chasing the Bird manoeuvre, though it wouldn't have caught a sick penguin.

'Tomorrow,' he reminded Tiffany. She hadn't risen by lunchtime. 'Midnight is tomorrow.'

Her hand waved from the mess of sheets on the sofa, saying both *I know* and *Go away*. Later, hunched over a mug of coffee in the kitchen, she continued to be sleepy and distracted.

'I'm phoning them,' said Ben. 'We need help.'

'What's the point?' Tiffany almost whined. 'Susie won't come. And the others won't know how to stop that clock any more than we do.'

'*I* know how,' Ben insisted. 'If we can get close enough. It's powered by those two massive weights. As the stones fall, they drive the mechanism. Stop them and the clock stops.'

Tiffany shook her head. 'They'd be much too heavy for us.'

She really didn't seem like herself today. Her eyes had a cloudy look. Ben guessed she was exhausted.

'We'd put something under them,' he said. 'A pile of bricks would do it. There's bound to be a pile of bricks somewhere in the Tate Modern.'

Tiffany gazed into her coffee. Ben had never seen her as low as this. He had a vague idea that for a few months she had been seeing a counsellor, about her problems at home or school, but he'd never been brave enough to ask her about it. Maybe these depressions were normal for her. He was resigning himself to another day of going nowhere when she set down her mug.

'Okay.' Her eyes had lost their cloudiness. 'We'll do it. Now.'

'I'll call the Cat Kin,' said Ben.

'No. I will.' Grimly determined, she stood up. 'This was my fault. I need to make it right.'

They had no phone. Ben had thrown away the batteries of their mobiles. How stupid that seemed in hindsight. Thinking he was outwitting the Set, he had instead cut their only lifeline – escaping one trap by walking into another. Tiffany would have to go out and find a phone box. She was in the doorway when she wailed, 'I can't remember anyone's number! They were on my SIM.'

'Hang on.' Ben found a shopping receipt and scribbled a London number on the back. 'Call this. He'll give you Daniel's mobile.'

'Phew.' She took it. 'His landline?'

'No. His dad's building firm. That number was painted on the crane that demolished my home. Kind of sticks in the memory.'

Watching her descend the stairs, sinking farther and farther away from him, he called down, 'Be careful out there.'

'I'm only popping round the corner,' she said.

Tiffany caught her reflection in the glass wall of Clissold Leisure Centre and stopped in shock. How gaunt she looked, how pale. Almost like her own ghost.

The first public telephone box she reached was clearly no longer in use, or at least (if her nose was any judge) not for its intended purpose. She hurried past. The dawn's fog had only partly lifted, and a single clammy shade of grey seemed to blur the pavement into the sky. Turning the corner onto Albion Road she crossed the greasy air flowing from a kebab shop, a warmth that was not comforting so much as disconcerting, like someone weeing in a swimming pool.

A second phone box outside a barber's shop looked more or less intact. Inside the shop were men lounging in chairs drinking tea, none of them having haircuts. Keeping one wary eye on them, she stepped into the phone box and delved in her belt for change.

It was only her third time inside one of these boxes – they had always seemed to her like the loneliest places in the world. Chilly inside the cracked plexiglass walls, she touched the handset and worn-down number keys, hearing the sounds of her own breath above the muffled traffic. Lifting the receiver, she was seized by an urge to call home. She longed to hear Dad's voice, to talk to Mum, to tell them both she was all right – no matter how big a lie this was.

Her fingers fumbled a pound coin to the slot. How had she even come to be here? All she had wanted to do was save the tigers. Was that so much to ask? Somehow, she had become ensnared in something else, and the more that she and Ben struggled against it, the more entangled they became.

She missed sleeping in her own bed. She missed the smothering love of an interfering mum who thought she knew what was best. And feeling safe. She couldn't remember how that felt.

Or being happy. When was the last time? Not since she'd run away to Dartmoor to find Mrs Powell. Feeling, that fluttering excitement of adventure that her friend Joy must know so well. One day, when she was older – yes, she had made up her mind! – she would get on a train and let it take her away, to other trains, to ships, to planes, to rickety buses bumping down dirt roads, just her and her backpack and bedroll, heading who-knew-where. For hadn't Mrs Powell herself once lived like that? In the long-lost days of her youth, when she was only Felicity. Bedding down beside beach-built camp fires on the far side of the world, trekking through China, then down to Zambia to look for lions.

I could do that. But it was only a thought, with no hope behind it. *I wish. I wish.*

A motorbike snarled past. The noise jolted her back to the moment: a precarious coin at the tips of her fingers. She told herself off for daydreaming. Time to call Daniel.

She unfolded the scrap of paper with the phone number. Within minutes, she could be speaking to the other Cat Kin. Including Susie. At the thought of her, Tiffany misdialled. It was less than a week since Yusuf's death. She herself remembered going out of her mind with grief, and that had been over a cat. Susie had lost her boyfriend. Tiffany slammed down the phone.

She couldn't do it. To call any of them would be madness. Susie must hate her. They all must. Now that she was thinking clearly, at last, it was obvious that even Ben must hate her, for the mess she had made of his life. How could he like her after that? No wonder he had never tried to kiss her. He was just too nice to abandon her.

Tiffany hugged herself, breathing her own breath inside the phone box windows till they clouded over. Now she was truly alone, she had no-one: not her family, not Mrs Powell, not the Cat Kin, certainly not Ben. She had thrown it all away, and for what?

A sob escaped her. She wanted to go home. She couldn't go home. And then the idea popped into her head, as unexpected as a cuckoo.

There was someone else, wasn't there? Someone she had almost forgotten. A person who might comfort her, who had always seemed to know her so well – someone who was, most importantly, sworn to confidentiality. Suddenly it was obvious. Who better, in all the world, than a professional counsellor?

Tiffany retrieved her pound coin and pocketed it. Her head was clear, as if at the breaking of a spell. She wouldn't go back to the flat yet, and neither would she go home. She would go and see Ellen first. Ellen would tell her what to do.

23
CATATONIC

How long, Ben wondered, was too long?

He made toast to distract himself. Tiffany couldn't stand being mollycoddled, it was what her parents did. So, instead of worrying, he cut the toast into quarters and nibbled slowly. She'd be back before he finished all four. She wasn't.

Ben performed his knee limbering stretches, then decided it was time for his ten-minute Pur mediation. This forced him to relax. Nothing could have happened to Tiffany. She had only popped out to make phone calls. No doubt Susie was taking some persuading. His ten minutes up, his throat hot from purring, Ben listened for her feet on the stairs. Even she could not be that silent.

How long was too long?

Anxiety became anger. She might have strayed into the corner shop to browse the magazines. When she knew he was waiting! He told himself not to be so pathetic. This was Tiffany, she could take care of herself. Ben put the TV on and watched golf. He hated golf.

As a windblown ball trickled into a bunker, it dawned on him that, *if* something bad had happened to her, then by the time he decided he had waited too long, the bad thing could have happened some time ago. So he might already be too late.

With a curse he jumped up and turned off the telly, ignoring the nail of pain through his patella. Grabbing his new jacket and the door key he headed out, silently deciding that if she *was* loitering in that magazine shop, then he'd catch a rat and leave it in her bed.

The first phone box reeked like toilets, but in the second was the scent he knew, the one that quickened his pulse. She had got this far, at least. He lifted the receiver and ran his nose over it, in case a clue might be lurking there. All he got was her shampoo, tainted with an acrid trace he had come to recognise as the smell of angst.

The view from here took in Albion road, the bus stop and off-licence, and a Turkish barber's shop. Nothing to hint at where Tiffany might have gone. Tentatively he reached for his Oshtian Compass, trying to make the accident happen on purpose. The catras fused to become the needle, spinning... but it would not settle on a single direction, jerking instead this way and that. Ben guessed it was trying to send him not towards Tiffany, but home to his parents. It took an effort of will to shut it off.

So much for feline instincts. He still had a brain. If the call of home was so strong for him, then maybe Tiffany had felt the same. Ben left the phone box and crossed the road to the bus stop.

Thanks to pashki and those peas, his knee had held up well for most of the day, until the last cold, gruelling mile back to Mrs Powell's flat. His breath rolled phantom snowballs under the streetlamps, where the night air seemed to prickle with frosty pins. Shivering, he let himself in the main door and limped up the stairs, alone.

Tiffany had not been at home. By the time he'd reached her house, he had convinced himself that she could only be there, *had* to be there. He was wrong. From behind the hedge he had a view through the bay window to the dining room table, where Tiffany's mother sat. Beside her was the handset of a cordless phone, a cup, and a cafetiere of something green, perhaps herbal tea. Ben saw Cathy Maine and knew. She was waiting, still waiting.

After that he panicked. He roamed random streets, searched for her in shops and cafés. She wasn't in the library, nor wandering the park. His Oshtian Compass continued to be worse than useless, pointing in two or three directions at once. At dusk he returned, shattered, to the only place he had.

Opening the door of the flat he caught his breath, not daring to hope. Then he stepped inside, sniffed again, and his fears blew away. Tiffany was here. She was back. He heard faint sounds, as of somebody moving about, and wiped the smile off his face. She deserved to get the third degree for messing him around.

'Tiffany? You'd better have bought me a Chinese takeaway at the very least.'

His hung-up jacket missed the peg and flopped to the carpet. He let it lie and gave his bad leg a stretch.

'Where the flaming hell have you been? I've walked halfway across Hackney…' The sounds of movement had stopped. Light leaked from the bedroom. Peeping at first nervously round the door, he found Tiffany lying on top of the bed covers. She had not even taken off her trainers. Should he wake her with crashing saucepans? No, she looked dead to the world.

Then he saw that her eyes were open.

'Tiffany?' His skin shrank with goosebumps. She was waxen, her breathing shallow. When he leaned over her, she stared through him.

'What's wrong?' She didn't respond. 'Tiffany, where have you been?'

She lay upon the quilt as still as a girl in a fairytale, the Sleeping Beauty, or Snow White.

'Tiffany! Wake up.'

Her eyes stayed empty but her lips moved. She mouthed a word. *Ben.*

'Yes, it's me! Wake up. You're creeping me.'

Her mouth shaped another word, a narrow one. Then a rounder sound. *Ow… Ouch?*

And again. *Ben…* The second word might have been *Get*. And finally, *Out.*

'You what?'

At a noise he whipped round. Mister Isidorus stood in the bedroom doorway. In his right hand he held a black staff, the sceptre of Lord

Set. Mister Isidorus pointed it towards him.

'Sleep,' he said.

Ben was already in the Arch On Guard, his sinews drawn like bowstrings ready for battle. Jumping high was still a painful prospect, but a low, sweeping attack like a Ratbane Lunge would sway Mister Isidorus off-balance, to be picked off with a choke-hold from behind. Not even that bulldog neck would be able to resist a Lion Jaw.

However, instead of kicking away those stout legs, Ben found himself unaccountably down on all fours, staring into the shine of two black shoes, wondering if they were Clarks or Hush Puppies. The carpet between his fingers felt soft, deep, so inviting. But he had to ignore that, he was meant to be attacking someone… yes, he would… as soon as he had found out how it felt to lie down on this lovely, plush, velvety rug. As he had expected, it was bliss.

A faraway voice in his head was screaming that he must get up, he must fight, defend himself, save Tiffany. He brushed it away as a pesky dream. Ben curled up, closed his eyes and sank into delicious warm blackness.

🐈 24 🐈

THE DIVINE ADORATRICE OF NIGHT

When she was very young, probably not yet four because Stuart wasn't around, Tiffany had flown on a plane for the first time. She had hardly any recollection of that holiday, except for a gathering of friendly stray dogs of all shapes and sizes, which Mum later told her must have been among the ruins of Pompeii. Her only other memory was of the plane trip – or rather, of forgetting it. In her own mind they had made an impossible journey: boarded a taxi in north London, driven for a while (she may have dozed) and then rolled to a stop outside a hotel overlooking the Bay of Naples.

According to family legend she had fallen asleep before they reached Heathrow, stirring intermittently during the flight to wail and grizzle and drink a little diluted juice, but only waking fully when they reached their resort. For years thereafter she had lived with the vague notion that her house was a mere half hour's drive from Italy. Yet she was left also with a sense of those missing hours, those dimmer-than-dim snapshots of the plane, of thirst and bewilderment and frightening faces, uncomfortable arms lugging her about, all parcelled up like a bad dream and put aside.

Here was that feeling again; the suspicion of time cut and spliced. Tiffany was aware of herself, after a gap in which she had seemed not to exist. Sounds pushed in on her, voices and a clank of machinery, and in hearing these she knew she was alive and thinking, though not where, or when.

In the darkness she groped for her last memory. She had been phoning Daniel (no, she hadn't) – she had been walking home (no, not that either) – of course! she had decided to go and see Ellen. What then? Had she wandered across the street and been hit by a car? It seemed unlikely. There was no pain save a headache with a slow throb, like waves thumping a breakwater.

Her body clock fretted over many hours, even days unaccounted for, yet she wasn't thirsty or hungry. So she must have drunk and eaten. It was nowhere in her memory. All she could recall was a single dream: that she could sense Ben close by, and was trying to warn him of a terrible danger, shouting at him *Ben, get out...* The dream had melted away before she learned the ending.

Tiffany opened her eyes.

The light was dim, nothing in focus. She lay on her back upon a hard surface, which her fingertips reported to be smooth stone. A floor? She tried to sit up. Something prevented her.

The blur resolved into shapes like storm clouds, stacked in ranks, turning into great toothed wheels. Above these sloped a black tented structure, echoing with the throb of her headache... a heartbeat... a tick. The tick of a clock that sounded louder than ever because she was inside it.

Terrified, she tried to move. Nothing seemed to be touching her, no ropes or chains, yet something pinned her flat to the stone. In struggling, she noticed a blind spot. On either side she saw the machinery of the clock, but at the centre of her vision was a void. The void spoke.

'How lovely to see you again, Tiffany. I'm so glad you could keep your appointment.'

Her mind corrected itself. The voice had come from somewhere to her right. And she had heard it before, many times. A figure stepped into view, looming at a weird slant because Tiffany could not raise her head. This tall person wore an ash-grey robe, with a headdress of dark beads half-covering her silver hair.

'Can you hear me?' the woman asked. 'Say my name.'

'Ellen?'

The woman looked and sounded so much like her counsellor,

Ellen Thornwill, that Tiffany blurted out this absurd reply. She did not expect to get a nod.

'That will do.' The woman addressed someone outside Tiffany's field of vision. 'Isidorus. She wakes. How about the boy?'

'Her young henchman remains insensible.' The silken tones rang inside the clock's gloomy pavilion. Exerting all her strength Tiffany turned her head, and saw Mister Isidorus, resplendent in a black robe trimmed with gold. Beside him stood a block of stone like an altar, dappled with the slowly shifting shadows of cogs. The shadows crawled over a human figure, lying still as death. It was Ben.

Tiffany's cry died at once, smothered by the unseen weight upon her. She and Ben lay upon identical, parallel altars. Above Ben there seemed to hang an optical illusion, a pillar suspended in mid-air. Except this was no trick of the light. It was a huge stone weight, she realised – one of the two weights that Ben had told her about, the ones that powered the clock. The lowest point of it, sharp like Cleopatra's needle, was poised above his chest. Tiffany's heart clenched in horror at the sight, and almost stopped beating altogether when she realised where the second weight was.

That explained her mysterious blind spot – the stone hung almost too close above her to see. From this angle, it seemed that only her breath was holding it up. Thick as a post box and twice as tall, the stone looked heavy enough to bury itself in the slab on which she lay. Frantic, she tried to squirm aside.

'That won't help.' Ellen Thornwill stooped beside her, all bedside manner. 'Funny, isn't it? How the weight isn't even touching you yet, and still you feel it. Every… last… ounce.'

Tiffany found herself gasping for air.

'And even though you can't see it moving,' Ellen murmured, 'you know it is. Moving like the hands of the clock. Lower and lower – there! – can't you feel it dropping? Just a millimetre. Don't worry. Not much longer. Midnight is almost upon us.'

Ellen gestured to someone behind her. Tiffany heard the clank of a lever. She winced, sure that the weight had been released to drop. But she opened her eyes to find the gloom dispersing. A pale dawn spread through the innards of the clock as panels around the base fell open.

The light was carried on a surge of excited voices. Outside, the turbine hall was one enormous crowd. People pressed against the rope barriers, their coats discarded amid the heat of packed bodies. At the front was a tidemark of sleepy but excited children, getting the best view with their parents ranged behind them; other children farther back perched atop their fathers' shoulders. Students tried not to jostle pensioners, a young mum rocked her baby in its sling, and an old woman in a wheelchair soothed the head of the large dog in the fluorescent jacket that lay on the floor beside her. Rows of phones and cameras were taking aim, like the rifles in the front lines of an army. All of this Tiffany took in at a glance. The shock must have been written on her face.

'Yes,' said Ellen. 'It is that moment.'

Tiffany gaped, uncomprehending.

'You have been,' Ellen frowned, choosing her words, 'out of action since the day before yesterday. This night, in your ugly Gregorian calendar, is the twenty-first of December. More properly, it is the winter solstice, when Ra the sun god lies at his most weakened. The Teeth of Set are turning full circle.'

Tiffany stared aghast at the familiar face beneath the strange black headdress. The face that had frowned so sympathetically as she poured out her troubles, week after week.

'Who are you?'

'I am both mother and consort to the great god Set,' said Ellen. 'I am the supreme commander of his legions of darkness. I am the Divine Adoratrice of Night.'

You're mad, Tiffany silently translated. Aloud, she said, 'And the counselling?'

The corners of Ellen's mouth twitched.

'A position of great strategic value,' she said. 'Human minds are the weapons of the Set, and our battlefields. Most of the time they are like fortresses, walled in and defended. But to a counsellor…!' She smiled. 'How many weak minds have I captured, without stirring from my chair! How many loyal stewards have I recruited from the legions of the lost and troubled. And what fascinating things I have learned. Take, for instance, the poor woman who used to come to me, tearful with worry over her daughter, who was neglecting her schooling for some strange obsession, a fitness class, a kind of yoga… she thought it was called pakshi, pashki, something like that… Well! That got my attention.'

Ellen paused, no doubt for the pleasure of seeing Tiffany's dawning understanding.

'So anxious, she was. I could almost feel sorry for her. So I suggested that she send you along.'

'You used my mother to get to me?' Tiffany tried to thrash out. Hardly a muscle would move.

'Of course,' said the Divine Adoratrice. 'I did not enjoy hearing that word *pashki*. Too many times I have been assured that Felicity Powell and her Cat Kin friends are gone, dead, destroyed, and every time the rumours turn out to be…' she paused and stared at Tiffany hard, 'exaggerated.'

The effort of trying to break free had drained her strength. Tiffany could only gasp, 'I trusted you.'

'And in a moment you will die,' replied the Divine Adoratrice. 'You can hardly expect mercy, when the blood of my son is on your hands.'

My son. The words seemed to pile on blocks of extra weight.

'I bore him and reared him from infancy to be the one in whom Set would live again,' said the Divine Adoratrice. 'I raised him in darkness, cleansing him of corrupting Life, my one, my only. And you killed him.'

Tiffany swallowed. 'I didn't mean for him to die.'

'Die?' Ellen uttered a light laugh. 'Set cannot die. Hark! Do you hear his footsteps?'

The sound of the crowd was now a rustling hush, as in a theatre between the dimming of the lights and curtain-up. Tiffany could not see the clock's hands from here, but the sound alone told her they were poised to converge, standing at a minute to midnight. A muffled public announcement warned people to keep their belongings with them at all times. That was it – of course! She could call out! If she could see and hear the crowd from here, then those in the front rows could see and hear her. Someone would come and help –

'You can give up that hope.' The Divine Adoratrice seemed to read her thoughts. 'Seeing is not the same as noticing. You are of no importance in the eyes of these people. They see only the Teeth of Set.'

Tiffany heard a weak shout.

'Let her go!'

Ben was struggling to rise from his altar, pinned by the unseen force of the weight above him. The Divine Adoratrice moved from Tiffany's side.

'Ben! Dear Ben Gallagher. I have heard so much about you.'

His bewildered, darting eyes found Tiffany's. In that glance she tried to send him a message: *Don't listen to her. Whatever she says, don't listen.*

'Your leader, Tiffany, she was easy,' said the Divine Adoratrice. 'A lucky catch. You were the tricky one! No wonder she kept you working for her.' Ellen stroked Ben's arm. 'Are these the new clothes? Did she buy them? How sweet.'

'Tiffany –' Ben spoke breathlessly, 'who is this?'

'Their leader. You were right,' Tiffany gasped back.

'Hasn't she told you about me?' Ellen sounded hurt. 'Ah, but there was so much she never told you. And so much she let you think. To keep you close. Where you could be useful. It's the cat way, isn't it? Cats are the great deceivers. I know you've never liked them, Ben. You're very wise.' Her gaze moved between him and Tiffany. 'Cats will let you love them, and they'll make you believe they love you back – but it's only so they can get what they want.'

Tiffany watched Ben digest this. She cried out, 'Don't listen to that witch!'

'Oh, but do listen, Ben,' said Ellen. 'For only I know her true thoughts. Tiffany has opened her mind to me, she has told me *everything*. How she deliberately strings you along, trailing after her like a lovesick fool, because she knows you're a useful lad to have around. And that's all you are.'

Ben writhed on the altar, as if the weight upon him had redoubled. Tiffany drew breath to scream a denial – she did love Ben, she *loved* him – but the futility of it overwhelmed her. What use were mere feelings now?

Besides, Ellen was right. She had led Ben on. Would he have abandoned his parents for anyone but her? And in return she'd treated him like a lackey. Yet that was nothing to how she'd treated her own family. She had turned her back on Mum and Dad, and she had even put Stuart back in hospital. In finding pashki, she had lost everything else. And on top of all that there was Yusuf.

She moaned as the weight became unbearable. It felt as if the full mass of the obelisk was on her ribs, though it still appeared to hang a full two inches above her. She saw Ben, straining beneath his own stone's invisible force, and understood.

'You see?' Ellen was there again, looming like a mad surgeon. 'It is you who have done this. The weight that crushes you is of your own making. You have only yourselves to blame.'

'Ben!' Tiffany cried out. 'Listen to me! I –'

Ellen clapped a hand over her mouth.

'Forget it,' she said. 'He'd never believe you now. Did you think you could escape by thinking happy thoughts?'

The clock's tick seemed to grow in strength, knocking like a fist upon a door, and the crowds pressed closer, bumping the woman in the wheelchair and almost stepping on her dog. Yet for all the flashing cameras and staring eyes, the people here inside the clock remained unseen, as ignored as actors in the wings.

'At the stroke of midnight, the stones will fall.' Ellen showed her crowned teeth. 'Set will rise from the darkness and break his fast by devouring two minions of Bastet.'

'Tiffany!' Ben called out. 'It'll be okay… Our friends, remember our friends! You called them, didn't you? If we can hold on…'

'I –' She shut her eyes. Had she called them? 'I can't remember!'

'They'll come.' Ben was wild-eyed, struggling to escape. 'They'll know we're here. Believe it, Tiffany!'

Mister Isidorus moved in, pointing his staff just as Ben seemed on the point of writhing out from beneath the stone. With a groan, Ben lay back on the altar. But Tiffany clutched at her last remaining hope. Yes. What if they had guessed? Daniel or Susie might be leading the others here now. The Divine Adoratrice, mysteriously, smiled.

'And so we come to it, at last.' She leaned closer. 'Actually, Tiffany, I don't need to kill you. How about a deal?'

Tiffany would not trust her. But she had to ask. 'What do you mean?'

'You tell me something,' said Ellen. 'Your last secret. Trade it for a life.'

Tiffany had no idea what she was talking about.

'You've hidden it from me very well,' said Ellen. 'Even when I put you in the deepest trance, you stuck to your story. But I'm afraid you slipped up. So tell me the truth at last, and save a life. Yours or Ben's. I wonder which you'll choose.'

'Tell you *what?*' Tiffany demanded. Ellen's eyes blazed with sudden anger.

'I will not leave old enemies lurking where I cannot see them. Why else do you think I let you and your friends run around free for so long? Don't flatter yourselves! I could have plucked you off the streets or from your home at any time, if it had been only you I wanted. No! I hounded you to make you run to safety, to the only person who could help. I hoped that you might leave a trail my stewards could follow, but it was not to be. No matter. You will tell me now, Tiffany. Where is she? Where is Felicity Powell?'

Grief crushed Tiffany almost to silence.

'She's dead.' Tears beaded at the corners of her eyes. 'I must have told you that. She died in the tower.'

'Yes, you told me that.' Ellen jabbed her with a finger full of rings. 'Ten times, you told me. But do you think I am a *fool*, Tiffany? Do you think I can't *count*? Sitting on my sofa, eating *my* biscuits, you have given me the whole story, every last detail. So I know about the tower block that collapsed. And I have watched the news reports a hundred times. The police pulled two bodies from the rubble. Two, Tiffany! So if one was your treacherous Geoff White, and the other was the Ferret man who fell from the roof… then *where is Felicity Powell?*'

For a moment Tiffany lay still. Ellen Thornwill was, of course, insane. Yet as Tiffany replayed the speech in her mind, it made sense. Two bodies had been recovered. This she knew. But she had always been too sick with sorrow ever to include Martin Fisher in her arithmetic. So she had never thought to check – as Ellen surely had checked – whether both of the bodies had been male.

It flashed through her like summer lightning. With her scream of joy, the crushing weight melted away, and Tiffany sprang off the altar, light as a kitten. She bounded to the slab where Ben lay.

'Ben, she's alive!' she cried. 'Mrs Powell didn't die! She's alive!'

Tiffany kissed him hard on the mouth. There was time to think: *Wow.* Ben blinked, looked dazed, then pulled a huge grin and rolled out from beneath the hanging weight, as if it simply wasn't there anymore.

'Isidorus!' cried the Divine Adoratrice. 'Restrain them!'

'Stewards!' bellowed Mister Isidorus. Tiffany turned on her heel. Through the gaps in the clock's structure she saw black-robed figures, pouring in along the maintenance walkways. She moved back-to-back with Ben.

'Phew –' Ben turned his head to murmur in her ear. 'Nice kiss.'

'Yes. By the way, did you hear what I said?'

'Yeah, but… are you sure? If she survived, then where – ?' Ben broke off. 'Look out. Here they come.'

The robed stewards deployed on three sides of them, their battle lines forming a triangle, which tightened. As they drew their weapons, Tiffany unleashed a Rauthkhon hiss, like *ptah* but longer and drawn out, with a sound like breathing fire. The stewards faltered as Ben hissed too, whipping them back with pure distilled rage.

'Contain them!' commanded Mister Isidorus. He was jabbing his sceptre towards Ben and Tiffany like a remote control with a dead battery, turning bug-eyed in frustration when nothing happened. But all around them night-sticks were being raised, and Tasers were taking aim.

'Look after yourself, Ben.' Tiffany's heart was pounding, for too many reasons. 'Don't try and protect me.'

'Stop telling me what to do,' Ben muttered back.

The Divine Adoratrice stepped through the lines of her footsoldiers.

'We can kill you now,' she said. 'Set will be reborn whether you live or die. At my command you will be slain where you stand. Tiffany Maine, I give you one last chance to save your friend. Tell me. Where is the Grey Cat?'

This might be the last time she ever used her Mau claws. Tiffany made them good and sharp. A voice came from the crowd. She turned to see the woman in the wheelchair rising out of it, to stand with the aid of a stick.

'I am here.'

25
THE SECOND COMING

Ben sprang after Tiffany, straight through the ranks of stewards who were too startled to react, bursting out onto the dais beneath the clock. Maybe he had never quite loved Mrs Powell the way Tiffany loved her, but when he saw the flash of those green eyes, saw the person he had known to be dead standing there in the front row, he felt sure that if he leaped now, he would fly.

Tiffany howled as if in mortal pain. '*Mrs Powell!*'

'Tiffany. Ben.' Mrs Powell nodded calmly. 'You make it very hard for a person to rest in peace.'

There was that twinkling half-smile, the one that said *Yes. I know it's impossible.* Mrs Powell wore no face-print, just a simple grey trouser suit, and her right hand rested on a jade cat's head that was the top of a walking cane. Though many of the people around her stood much taller, she seemed to tower above them, as if smiling down from a great height. Her grey hair was tied back in a young woman's ponytail, and as usual Ben gave up trying to guess her age.

A few seconds' amazement was all he could afford. Swivelling to guard his exposed back, he saw the weird woman who called herself the Divine Adoratrice emerging from the clock's main portal.

'Nine lives? More like twenty.' Her voice simmered with hate. 'I killed you years ago, Grey Cat. Then my sources told me that you had been shot by your charming son. Later still, I learned you had been buried alive. This is pure impertinence.'

'Ellen.' Mrs Powell redirected her gaze. 'What is it this time? The end of the world again?'

'I thank Set for keeping you alive long enough to see it,' replied the Divine Adoratrice. 'It was Set who preserved you when the tower fell on your enemies. He was keeping you for me. So you could witness your final defeat.'

'It's a theory,' said Mrs Powell.

Ben was only half paying attention to this. He was more concerned to see how the ranks of stewards had reformed to bar any possible escape. The only way out would be through the crowd, and he wasn't sure he fancied that option. Something about this mass of people utterly unnerved him. Never had he been in any place that felt so... empty. He could hear the sea-like murmur of two thousand pairs of lungs, could feel the heat coming off them, and could see them plainly, human beings filling every inch of the immense floor space as far back as the distant doors – yet he had the overpowering sense that no-one was really here. Every face was as drained of life as a passport photograph. The parents and the students and the photographers around Mrs Powell hardly blinked, oblivious to the confrontation taking place before them. They saw nothing but the clock, heard nothing but the clock, waiting there as still, blank-eyed and patient as piranha fish.

The Divine Adoratrice visibly relaxed, delighted at the closing of the trap.

'You old fool,' she said. 'It was you I wanted most of all. Thank you for coming. What do you hope to do, run me down with your wheelchair? You think I will be scared of you now?'

'No.' Mrs Powell rapped her walking cane upon the floor. 'I think you will be scared of Frieda.'

Beside her wheelchair the recumbent animal, which Ben had already half-noticed and dismissed as a dog, a very large one – sprang to its feet, as Mrs Powell ripped off its fluorescent jacket. That was no dog. Out of its mouth broke an extraordinary noise, a giant's cough. Mrs Powell clung to the loose skin at the nape of its neck as the Divine Adoratrice stepped smartly backwards.

'Ellen, I must warn you.' Mrs Powell was struggling to restrain the huge black-and-tawny cat. 'I have almost no control over her. But she sees me as family and you know, these mother cats can be fearfully stroppy when it comes to defending their loved ones.'

With a visible effort Ellen stood her ground.

'A jaguar?' She stared, incredulous. 'How did you get a jaguar into central London?'

'She paid the congestion charge,' said a familiar voice. Someone shouldered his way through the crowd to stand at Mrs Powell's side, a burly teenage boy dressed all in black, his face camouflaged with a pashki print.

'Olly!' Tiffany cried.

Three more figures emerged like cats from dense forest, Daniel, then Cecile, and finally Susie, glowering up at the soldiers of the Set. Ben couldn't speak. Daniel caught his eye and winked, as Cecile pointed an accusing finger.

'Tiffany, I been trying to reach you,' she said. 'You turned off your phone! We thought you might be dead or anything. I didn't dare sleep in case you called.'

'Yeah.' Susie gave them some of her glare. 'Don't you dare leave us out of it again.'

Olly just grinned and pointed repeatedly at Mrs Powell, in case Ben and Tiffany had missed the fact that she was standing there with them, alive. Frieda the jaguar loosed her coughing roar.

'What now, guys?' Daniel coiled like a dancer ready to leap. 'Do we get them?'

'Too late!' The scream of the Divine Adoratrice drowned him out. 'Midnight is upon us! The Teeth of Set turn full circle!'

Dimly visible through the clock face, the pendulum floated for a moment at the end of its arc, then swung back.

CLICK

'Mrs Powell!' Ben seized on a desperate idea. 'Throw me your cane! I can climb inside the clock and jam the gears!'

CLUCK

'You can do nothing.' Ellen flung up her arms. All her minions, including Mister Isidorus, fell to their knees either side of her.

CLICK

'The hour comes round at last,' cried the Divine Adoratrice. 'Behold the Second Coming of Set!'

With the echo of her shout another tick boomed. The pause that followed was slightly too long. Then the clock's sword-like long hand joined the hour hand on twelve.

KA-CHUNK

The reverberations took perhaps a quarter of a minute to die completely. Even then, when the last lingering rumour of the sound had decayed and disappeared, nothing came to replace it. And this was a nothing that was deeper than silence, far beyond the simple absence of sound. It seemed to Ben that the very molecules of the air had stopped moving, that the light had frozen and set like pale yellow glass around them; that time itself ceased to flow. He could no longer hear his own heart beating. The only movement he could detect was the trickle of his thoughts, running on under their own momentum, like the final futile flight of a headless bird.

It had happened. They hadn't been able to stop it. Midnight had come.

Feet shuffled near the back of the hall. The crowd was stirring. Whispers crawled the walls in a growing swarm, the tiny sound of an indrawn breath multiplied by thousands. Tiffany stood white-faced. Ben promised himself that he would die before her.

Mrs Powell sighed theatrically.

'Yes, but… is it art?'

'Set is reborn!' Ellen called across the multitude. 'He walks in you. Rise up!'

The crowd began to move in swirls and eddies. Faces turned to look at one another. A ripple of blinking broke out, uncertain smiles, nervous laughter. Phones were raised to take a few more snapshots. A baby in a carrier sling awoke and commenced a crotchety wail.

'Rise up, my slaves,' thundered the Divine Adoratrice. 'Tear to pieces the minions of Bastet!'

'Oh, Ellen, give it a rest,' said Mrs Powell. 'Did you really think that would work?'

Ellen's jaw slackened.

'You're a devious hypnotist, I admit,' said Mrs Powell. 'Good enough to pin your victims to altars, powerful enough to make Miles Baron try to hang himself. But honestly.' She shook her head. 'Capturing the soul of an entire city? Even the ancient priests would never have attempted that.'

From his vantage point on the dais, Ben watched the crowds flow towards the rear and side exits, the visitors picking up bags, putting on coats. The show was over, it was late, the night was bitterly cold, and most of them had tiring tube and bus journeys between themselves and a warm bed. They had seen what they had come to see. Now they were leaving.

'Do you understand, Ellen?' Mrs Powell spoke sharply, as if to a difficult child. 'They are going home. You and your pet artist have kept them enthralled for a few months, that's all. They have lives, you see. Lives that are far more important to them than any demon you can conjure up.' She winced with sudden effort as her jaguar tugged to get loose. Bracing herself on her walking cane, Mrs Powell stood as straight as the beast would let her. 'Ellen. As a sorely missed friend of mine might have said, if he were here: you fail with a big fat zero.'

At that, Susie raised her head, all ten fingers curling into hooks. Daniel and Olly moved in like bodyguards to flank her. Ben summoned his Mau claws. The Set stewards looked at each other in dismay as Frieda coughed another roar. Ellen backed away.

'Tiffany?' called Mrs Powell. 'Over to you.'

Tiffany drew herself up. 'Cat Kin! Get them.'

The Set were in no frame of mind to fight back. Frieda bounded forward, breaking their lines, and many dropped their weapons on the spot and played dead. The one brave steward who turned his Taser on the jaguar received a gentle-looking pat with a paw that laid him out cold. Others flailed ineffectually as the Cat Kin swept among them. The most fanatical closed in a protective ring around the Divine Adoratrice, a formation that was blown apart when Olly leaped from the slopes of the clock to stomp two of her guards, and Tiffany pounced.

The biggest danger, after all, turned out to be the crowd. People were at last beginning to grasp that strange and frightening things were afoot, and those closest to the battle began to push to get away. A surge towards the exits threatened to become a crush. Mrs Powell shouted a warning, but Cecile was already on the case. Climbing to the balcony, she found a service desk with a PA system, and soon a soporific rumble was droning from the loudspeakers. Cecile was intoning Pur into the microphone. It had a magical effect. In all but a few isolated pockets the shoving died down, and the people padded serenely towards the exits, filled with a mysterious calm.

Ben had to hear about this later. Of all the Set, Mister Isidorus alone seemed unfazed by their failure. He did not cower from Frieda, warding her off with jabs of his sceptre, and when a raging Susie flung herself at him, he coolly chopped her down with the edge of his hand. Daniel darted in to protect her, which gave Ben time to fight his way to their side. Swiftly running out of bronze blades to hurl, Mister Isidorus flung instead a handful of loose change and fled inside the clock. Ben went after him.

Mister Isidorus moved with extraordinary speed and grace for such a thickset man, and the whirling staff gave him a much longer reach. Ben relished the chance to pull out all the stops. In a full-on wildcat blitz he drove his foe backwards, up and up the maintenance walkways, until Mister Isidorus, his face scratched and his robe in tatters, could retreat no further. Cornered against the inside of the translucent clock face, his thrashing figure resembled a furious man in the moon. Ben, deciding playtime was over, lunged beneath the staff to disarm him, and stumbled at a twinge of pain. Mister Isidorus noticed and kicked him in his injured knee.

Ben rolled on the steel platform, felled as if by an axe. Through the agony his own thoughts mocked him: *You idiot. We've won. The Set failed, Mrs Powell is alive, Tiffany just kissed you – and now you're going to die.* He had forgotten about somebody.

Mister Isidorus put his foot on Ben's throat.

'As the prophet of Set,' he declared, 'I have the privilege of spilling your blood.'

From his gold-trimmed robe he drew a dagger, slender as a reed. Lying there half-choked, Ben thought he was hallucinating, for the clock's pendulum hung not in its usual place, but had drawn far back behind Mister Isidorus and was moving, swinging this way, travelling with the deceptive slowness of an aeroplane. The round weight on the end of the cable grew to the size of a fridge, at which point Ben realised that the shape riding it was Susie, yelling, 'This is for Yusuf, you son of a –'

Bits of glass made a blizzard around Mister Isidorus as the pendulum punched him through the clock face. Shards broke from the ragged rim of the hole, tumbling swords of plate glass crashing down as deadly hail.

Then Susie was there, helping Ben to his feet, carefully flicking sharp fragments off his clothes – she had jumped clear, and was unscathed. Side by side, they stared down through the shark-mouth hole in the clock face, to the body of Mister Isidorus, sprawled beneath a pile of bloodstained glass. Ben had no wish to look any closer.

'Ten out of ten, Susie,' he murmured. Her almond eyes glistened.

When the two of them emerged from the base of the ruined clock, the battle was over. Any stewards too slow or stubborn to flee were now face down on the floor in two rows, watched by Cecile and Mrs Powell but mostly by Frieda. Olly and Daniel had one arm each of the Divine Adoratrice, restraining her half-hearted struggles. Tiffany stood before her, smiling.

'You know the funniest thing, Ellen?' she said. 'Without you, I could never have beaten you. I felt so lost and alone, and then you came along. You really should have stuck to counselling.'

Ellen curled her lip in a snarl. Ben had the feeling he was missing something.

'This… woman,' he stammered. 'You know her?'

Tiffany threw him that glance: *It's a long story.*

'And Ellen knows me,' said Mrs Powell. 'Once, many years ago, she even tricked me into working for her. I didn't see through you for a long time, did I? But then I was younger and not nearly so brilliant. And Ellen Thornwill can be very persuasive.'

'You think you've won?' Ellen laughed as if trying to regurgitate a fishbone. 'What have you won? No, Cat Kin, you have lost *everything.* All that you hold dear, I have taken from you. And I will take more, before this night is over.'

'Strictly speaking,' said Olly, 'you can't take more than everything.'

'Mystical nutcases can,' said Susie. 'For they speak in riddles, for they find it terribly amusing.'

'You don't believe the world will end, Felicity?' Ellen's headdress was crooked, her silver hair mussed into wisps. She looked demented. 'I myself will end your world!'

Daniel shoved her. 'You and whose army?'

Ellen's army, such as it was, lay petrified with fear. Frieda was plodding up and down the line of them, like a cat bored with too many feeding bowls. The last of the bemused visitors had trickled out of the main doors, leaving the turbine hall echoingly empty. Down its length came a distorted whoop, rising and falling. Ben pricked up his ears.

'Don't tell me that's a police siren.'

'Olly begged me to let him call them,' said Mrs Powell. 'I said yes. Must be getting old.' She clicked her fingers. 'Taxi for Miss Thornwill! Don't worry, Ellen. Since you failed to bring about the apocalypse, they'll only want to talk to you about murder, kidnap, arson, trafficking protected species and serious professional misconduct.'

Ellen's smile grew more poisonous still. She threw back her head and chanted to the empty space.

'Hail, Set! Spear of Night! Master of the Starving Sands! Lord of the Last Day!'

The walls took up her cry. Ellen inhaled and doubled the volume.

'Hail, Set! Spear of Night! Master of the Starving Sands! Lord of the Last Day!'

'Oh, shut up,' sighed Tiffany. 'Don't you get it? Your silly spells don't work on us anymore.'

Ellen said, softly, 'It wasn't meant for you.'

Ben had already turned his head towards a noise, a tinkle and scrape. He saw Mister Isidorus rising like a lake monster from beneath the heap of broken glass, his bald head a cross-stitch of cuts, his pig eyes blazing through a wet red mask. Mister Isidorus drew a long glass sickle out of his own thigh and threw it. The blade whistled through the air.

Ben couldn't even shout out. As a smear of light the glass knife flew at Mrs Powell. Then Ben saw a blur and it was Tiffany, leaping, arm outstretched in a desperate goalkeeper's dive. She hit the floor at Mrs Powell's feet, slithered to a stop and lay still.

'Tiffany!' Mrs Powell dropped beside her. In an instant Ben was there too. Tiffany's eyes were screwed tight shut. She gave a faint, creaking cry.

'Don't move her!' Mrs Powell commanded. Her face had aged shockingly, every line deep as a scar. She swept aside fragments of the shattered glass blade and touched the front of Tiffany's sweater. Her fingers came away red. Ben's guts knotted up.

'Tiffany.' Mrs Powell clutched at her. 'You foolish… Foolish girl. You didn't have to do that for me. Not for me, Tiffany…'

Ben was dimly aware of Cecile and Daniel rushing to secure Mister Isidorus, but he had already collapsed, having spent the last of his strength. Olly knocked Ellen Thornwill to the ground and sat on her, where she kept up a low, gurgling laugh. Ben knelt down as Tiffany continued silently to writhe.

'Tiffs? It's okay. You're going to be okay. Hold on.' He swallowed. She was pressing her left hand to her chest. When he tried to take a look, he almost lost it, lost it completely… Her palm was wet with blood.

Oh no, he thought. *Oh no. Oh no.*

'Put pressure on the wound,' ordered Mrs Powell. 'The police, they'll be here soon, don't worry, they carry first-aid equipment…' Her hands flapped, frantic. Mrs Powell was never frantic. For the first time since Ben had known her, she seemed to be in despair.

But he gritted his teeth and did as he was told, pressing both his hands to where he guessed the bleeding must be, praying that he would not push a glass shard deeper into her heart. Tiffany squirmed.

'Hold still,' he begged. She caught her breath.

'Get off, you!' She struggled harder. 'It's not my chest, it's my hand. My hand's cut!'

It took him a moment to process that. She was only holding her chest because she'd landed flat on it, and the fall had been a bruising one.

Ben snatched his hands away.

'Thank you.' Tiffany sat up, cradling her wrist.

'Let me see.' said Mrs Powell. The colour was flooding back into her face. 'A wound to the wrist can still be dangerous.'

'No.' Tiffany seemed puzzled herself. 'I don't think so. It's not deep. Something turned the blade. My sleeve – no, it cut through that…'

She pulled up the ragged sleeve and something fell *ching* on the floor. Mrs Powell picked it up. It was a cat's collar. The leather near the bell was severed, and stained with two kinds of blood.

Mrs Powell frowned. 'Rufus?'

Tiffany nodded. From the far end of the hall came a wash of radio crackles.

'The police.' Mrs Powell put the collar in her pocket. 'Punctual as ever. Let's be off.'

26

🐈 WILD AND TAME 🐈

FAR I WANDER
SLAYING YOUR ENEMIES
SEEKING YOUR HOUSE
I SLEEP BY YOUR FIRE

Coffin text, Egyptian cat burial, c. 600 BC
Translation: Matthew Toy.

It was hard to recognise their old pashki studio. Its bare wooden floor, on which not a stick of furniture nor a speck of dust had ever been permitted, was now strewn with plastic bags, vinegary paper, cartons, pizza boxes and crumbs. There was no way the seven of them could have fitted in Mrs Powell's kitchen so, with a tiny sigh, she had said they might as well eat in here. Though it was now the early hours, nearer dawn than dinner, all were hungry as lions. Finding no food in the kitchen except an absurd supply of frozen peas, Mrs Powell had sent Olly and Daniel to the all-night takeaway, for pizzas and fish and chips.

Raw meat had not been needed, thankfully, for the Cat Kin's honorary extra member was no longer with them. In the back street outside the Tate Modern, Mrs Powell had flagged down an unmarked black van. Its driver, a young Indian man, had opened the rear doors onto a roomy, straw-lined cage. Mrs Powell coaxed Frieda inside, and the jaguar went straight to a half-chewed pig leg in the corner and lay down. The driver spared the Cat Kin one conspiratorial smile and a thumbs-up as he pulled away. When the van was out of sight Daniel asked, 'Who was that?' Mrs Powell replied, 'Backup,' and said no more.

Then they had ridden the night bus all the way back to her flat.

'*You?*' Tiffany spoke through a mouthful of haddock. 'Mrs Powell, *you* put spyware on my laptop?'

'*Spy* is a nasty sort of word.' Mrs Powell picked an anchovy from a discard pile and ate it. 'Yes, I did.'

'But you could have seen anything!' Tiffany turned her best shade of pink. 'I could have been emailing my… my boyfriend or something.'

'Your boyfriend?' Ben prodded her, teasing.

'Well… You know. Some things are private.'

'Just keeping an eye,' said Mrs Powell. 'You were risking your neck because of what I'd taught you. I couldn't walk away. I thought I could.'

Tiffany shook her head, amazed.

'I can't believe it. All that time, on the forum… You were my friend. You were Joy!'

'Well.' Mrs Powell gave a bashful smile. 'An old-fashioned way of saying joy, or happiness, or luck…'

Susie twigged. '…is felicity!'

Tiffany stroked the gauze dressing on her cut hand.

'I was talking to you all along.'

'Yes, you were,' said Mrs Powell. 'Though you mustn't think Joy wasn't real. Everything she told you, all those stories of her travels… those were true. That's who I used to be. You were talking to me, but the twenty-year-old me. Felicity the silly and carefree.' She paused. 'There are many days when I think of her.'

'I never knew.' Tiffany had stopped smiling. 'You didn't tell me.'

Mrs Powell looked away, pretending to notice the tinsel on the noticeboard for the first time, and made some remark of forced jollity. Ben could sense the strain between her and Tiffany. There was so much they had to say to each other, but not yet. Neither of them wanted to spoil this – whatever this was.

'Anyway,' Mrs Powell resumed, 'to cut a long story short. When

I saw the files on the dongle that you'd stolen from Miles Baron, I realised what you were up against. So I came. Though not, of course, in tip-top condition.' She indicated her walking cane.

Daniel chipped in. 'But you knew the Set's plan would never work, so why – ?'

'Why did I bother?' Mrs Powell gave him a blink.

'It was real enough from where we were standing,' said Ben.

'Lying down,' Tiffany corrected. 'Under two-tonne stones.'

'Exactly,' said Mrs Powell. 'The Set are mad and deluded. Does that make them less dangerous? No. It makes them more dangerous.'

Susie bit her lip. Ben saw that her vegetarian pizza was almost entirely uneaten.

'The Set are deadly,' said Mrs Powell, 'not because they might succeed, but because they never can. So they will never stop trying.'

The rustlings of greasy paper and cardboard subsided.

'You mean they could be back?' said Olly.

'They will be,' said Mrs Powell. 'Not soon. I hope not soon. But one day. In ten years' time, in a generation… Ellen will be sent to Broadmoor rather than prison, when they realise she's insane, but even if they manage to keep her there, the Set won't disappear. They've been around, in some form or other, for at least three thousand years. But then, so have we. So have the Cat Kin. We can last for another century or ten, I'm sure. As my old teacher Mr Singh used to say, as long as there are rats, there will be cats.'

He would have such indigestion in the morning. It was morning already, officially. Ben helped Cecile crush their cola cans to put out for recycling, stacked the pizza boxes and bundled up the sea of salty paper. The pashki studio reeked of fish and chips, a smell that ever after would make Ben think of goodbyes. Mrs Powell had no more need for this flat in London, she said. She was retiring to her house in the heart of Dartmoor, to care for her menagerie of big cats, support

Liverpool FC from a distance, and... well, who knew what she would do. But she would try to grow old gracefully. Would they ever see her again? Ben hoped so. He tried to freeze this scene in his mind, the littered, unfurnished room with the seven of them lounging about, the drooping tinsel, this farewell smell. Batter and vinegar.

Mrs Powell vanished into the kitchen and told Tiffany to come and help wash up. No-one else was asked, and they were shrewd enough not to offer. The studio quietened, and Ben felt that a gap had appeared among them, a space for the person who wasn't here. Cecile huddled closer to Susie, talking in a low voice, and Susie was sniffing and wiping her cheeks. The boys withdrew, mumbling random chat so as not to overhear, but inevitably their talk drifted back to Yusuf, and to Susie herself. That trouble over her school exams, Olly said, was all sorted. The school's head teacher, after learning how close Susie and Yusuf had been, had dropped the allegations of cheating. She would not be expelled, thanks to Yusuf.

'Great,' muttered Daniel, sarcastic. 'She must be over the moon.'

'That's Yusuf all over, though,' said Olly. 'Always trying that little bit too hard.'

Ben elbowed Olly, but gently. Yusuf would have laughed at that joke.

Tiffany had been in the kitchen a long time – long enough, Ben thought, for her and Mrs Powell to have cleaned every plate and glass, and the cooker and cupboards as well. He stretched himself out on the floor, hearing the others carry on soft conversations as he closed his eyes.

When he woke, he was alone in the studio. Everyone had gone. He sat up, bleary and indignant. How could they have left him lying there? What time was it? Tiffany walked in. She looked very, very tired, and when she spoke her voice had a rough edge, as if she had recently wept. In spite of this she seemed curiously at ease, giving a great yawn and stretch, laughing when the tendons of her shoulders cracked. She moved with a lighter step, freed from the tension Ben had sensed earlier.

'Oh dear,' she said. 'It's late at night and I'm a girl on my own. I hope you're going to walk me home.'

He was still fuddled by sleep.

'Yeah, of course. But –' From the kitchen came the lonely rattle of cutlery being sorted and put away. 'I haven't said goodbye to Mrs Powell yet.'

'Say it, then.' Brusquely, Tiffany made for the front door. 'I'll be waiting downstairs.'

They took a short cut through Clissold Park, clambering over the railings as the gates were locked. Crossing the bridge through the duckponds, Tiffany slipped her hand into his.

'Well?' she said.

'Huh?'

'What did you say to her?'

Ben slowed to peer through the wire of the deer enclosure. It was utterly still, the animals sleeping unseen. The wood-chipped earth twinkled under a layer of frost, catching the glow of the low, lopsided moon.

'I said I would,' said Ben.

'You would what?'

'She said –' Mrs Powell had said a great deal to him, much of which he was too embarrassed to repeat. 'She told me to look after myself. I said I would.'

Tiffany shivered and got them moving again. 'Is that all?'

'No.' Ben squeezed her hand. 'She asked me to look after someone else as well. Actually it was more like an order. You know what she's like.'

'Yes.' Tiffany did a bitten-lip smile.

Their path took them out beyond the sheltering trees. A chill wind that had taken a run-up across two playing fields blasted them from the side. They moved closer together.

'Okay,' said Ben. 'Your turn.'

'For what?'

'Come on. You took an hour to wash up seven plates. You must have talked about something.'

'Oh…' Tiffany waved a hand. 'This and that. Y'know, her travels, when she was younger… all the stuff she did before she discovered pashki. Did you know her family used to be rich? Even as a teenager she'd been to so many amazing places…' Tiffany trailed off, as if her mind wasn't really on what she was saying.

Ben waited.

'And we talked about why,' Tiffany resumed, 'why she let me go on thinking she was dead. I mean, it's obvious to me now. Because, of course, she almost *did* die, didn't she? She started telling me how… I didn't really want to listen. Anyway, when the explosives detonated and the tower came down, she ended up in a little space under a broken section of the stairs. She had cracked lower vertebrae and a shattered femur in her right leg and quite a lot else, but she could still wriggle. She managed to crawl downwards through the ruins into the basement, which was only half caved in, and found a drain cover leading to a sewer…'

Ben grimaced.

'I know. Yuck,' said Tiffany. 'Eventually, she dragged herself out through a storm drain into the gutter, where a homeless man found her. By that time she was in a coma. So after she'd spent weeks in hospital, recovering, she…'

'She took the hint?'

'Right. And I think she hoped I would, too. That I'd stay safe from now on, if I thought she was dead.'

'She doesn't know you very well.'

'Oh, she does. So she spied on me online. Curiosity, you see? It always pays off.'

The park backed on to the main road that led to Tiffany's neighbourhood. Reaching a corner within sight of some imposing Georgian houses, Ben stopped walking.

'Go by yourself from here,' he said. 'If your dad sees me…'

'Mum and Dad'll be asleep. Come on. When I get in, I'll phone a taxi for you.'

'No.' He stayed where he was, standing on the other side of the sign that said Riversmead Drive.

Tiffany sighed. 'If it's the money again…'

He shook his head. A dreadful and strange fear had rooted him to the spot.

'Don't get dignified on me now,' said Tiffany. 'Let me pay for your taxi home.'

'I'm not going home,' said Ben.

'Pardon?'

It had shocked him too. He ran back over what he'd said.

'I… can't.' As he spoke he began to understand. 'I can't go back now. To my parents. It's not fair.'

'Okay, you've lost your mind,' said Tiffany. 'Understandable. You're knackered. Go home and sleep for a day or two.'

'I mean it,' said Ben. 'Of course I want to go home. More than anything. But…' His voice choked up. 'It's better, don't you see? If I'm there I'll only mess with their lives again. Something'll happen and I'll have to disappear. It's not fair on them. And… it's dangerous. With the baby on the way. What if someone tries to come after me? I can't put my little brother or sister through that. I need to stay away. They can start over again, just the three of them. Like it was always meant to be.'

'Ben,' Tiffany interrupted him. 'They're your mum and dad!'

'I'll be around.' Ben took deep breaths. He wouldn't cry. 'They just won't see me. I've got to be nearby, right? To protect them. And you.

You heard what Mrs Powell said. The Set haven't gone. They'll keep coming back. They'll never give up.'

Weary though he was, his mind was perfectly clear. He knew what he had to do. There was no alternative.

Tiffany drew breath to argue, but didn't. Her eyes glinted with understanding.

'Ben. You really are like a cat, aren't you? Even more than me, I think.' She stroked his hair, as if demonstrating the point. 'And cats, Ben… Cats are special. Do you know why?'

He said nothing.

'Because they're domestic,' said Tiffany. 'And they're wild animals too. They're the only thing that's both wild and tame. They've got the choice. Whether to curl up safe at home, or run out of that door into danger.'

She paused, fingering the bandage on her wrist where the collar used to be.

'But sometimes,' she said, 'I think you can't choose. You can't stay safe at home, because you have to go out and fight that danger, before your home can be safe.'

Ben took the hand she offered him.

'So I will too.' Tiffany squared her shoulders. 'I'll go with you.'

'You will?'

He could have collapsed from sheer relief.

'Yes,' said Tiffany. 'We'll carry on leading the Cat Kin and make sure it survives, even after we're gone. And we'll tear apart the Set wherever they are, until they never dare come back. And while we're at it, we'll find those tiger poachers too, and the traders in rare animals… and the crooks who smuggle children to make into slaves, and the drug dealers who wreck people's lives, and the men who get rich by sucking people dry…Oh yeah. We'll make a list. And we'll hunt them down one by one, even if it takes forever. We'll do it, Ben. You and me.'

She stopped and squeezed his hand.

'But not yet.' She looked along her street, where the elegant houses slumbered in a blanket of freezing mist. 'First I want to do some other things. Go to school. Concentrate in class and pass my exams. Make Mum proud of me and get Dad to stop losing his hair so fast. Hang out with friends who maybe can't balance on chimney pots. Spend a few more Saturday afternoons at the cinema, find out what music I'm meant to be into now. Stay in bed all Sunday, reading. Buy too many shoes. Take care of Stuart, for as long as I can. Get him interested in something besides comic books. Help him have fun. Go to university and train to do something – I don't know, what degree lets you be a journalist?'

'Um. I think you just need to be pushy.'

'Oh. Good,' said Tiffany. 'And I'll get out and about, like Felicity did. Take the Greyhound bus across America, visit those pyramids in Egypt. Come back here and get a great job. Find another cat who sleeps on my pillow. And… other things.' She held him in her gaze. 'I'll do all that first. Because, Ben, the way I see it… you know, it's all very well being able to fight like a cat, and fall off cranes and get up again, and dodge bullets and outrun collapsing buildings… It's good, being able to protect the things you love. But what's the point, if you've got nothing worth protecting?'

The windows of the nearest house pulsed with Christmas lights, casting patterns across the brickwork and gleaming on the wet trails that ran down Tiffany's face.

'What's the use of nine lives,' she said, 'if you don't even have one?'

She was shivering. Ben put his arm round her and they continued down her road. And as they fell into step he understood why she had to go home – and why he had to go home too. He would go home, though it scared him more than crocodiles and demons and death. He would go home even though nothing else in the world had the power to hurt him so much, and he would rather wander alone for the rest of his life than bring harm on the people he loved. He would go home because that was where he lived.

Tiffany spoke in his ear.

'It'll be okay,' she said. 'I don't know how, but it will.'

They walked under the bare poplar trees.

'Sure you don't want that taxi?' asked Tiffany.

'Thanks. I'll walk.'

She looked anxious now. Her own house was in sight.

'Your parents… What'll you tell them?'

Ben shrugged. 'Dunno. Everything, I suppose.'

'You mean the truth?'

Yes, why not? He was tired, so tired of lies. The truth could be no worse. John Stanford, Doctor Cobb, Martin Fisher, Geoff White, Mrs Felicity Powell… Mum and Dad would hear it all. And when they knew, when he had left them no choice but to believe those tales, they would know something else too. They would know that they were not, after all, the awful parents they believed themselves to be, but that he, Ben Gallagher, was just a very strange son.

'The truth,' he said.

'Good enough plan.' Tiffany stopped by her gate. 'Well. This is me.'

'Night then. See you soon?'

'I think you just might.'

They said goodbye.

The emergency key was in its usual place. Tiffany unlocked the front door and replaced the key in the air brick under the porch. The house was so quiet that the thumping of her heart sounded like a late-night party next door. She climbed the stairs careful not to creak the floorboards, until she realised she was Eth walking, and stopped doing it. The stairs could creak if they liked. On the landing she dithered, shaken by bizarre doubts as to which of the five closed doors led to her bedroom. Even when the foolish moment had passed, she wondered if she had the right to go in. She felt like an elf or vampire, unable to cross a threshold unless invited.

Perhaps it was that superstitious qualm which made her tiptoe to the next door along. This one was covered with forbidding notices such as PRIVATE – KEEP OUT and ENTER AT OWN RISK, which were welcoming enough to her. She touched the door handle, a specially fitted one that would turn at the slightest pressure, and pushed. She wouldn't wake Stuart. All she wanted was to stand by his bed and see him sleeping, real and warm and alive –

'Who's there?'

She stood still. It was the merest whimper, poised between fear and terrible hope.

'It's okay, Stuart.'

'Who – ?'

'It's me,' said Tiffany. 'I'm back.'

'Tiff…?'

She could see the shape of him, struggling to sit up. His hand found the controls of his motorised bed and he elevated himself to a more upright position.

'Come here,' he begged. 'Come closer.'

She sat on the edge of the bed. Stuart drew back his fist and punched her on the shoulder. The blow was startlingly hard, for him. Before she could gasp in surprise he had thrown his arms around her, squeezing with more strength than she would have believed.

'I thought you were dead.' His voice was fierce, furious. 'You never called, you never answered your phone. I thought you'd at least find a way to email or message me but you didn't. So I knew you must be dead. Why didn't you tell me? Why didn't you? And it's almost Christmas and I haven't got you anything because I thought you were…'

His words became weeping. She hugged him back, tentatively at first, then with a growing conviction that, no matter what the future might hold, she would not let him go without one hell of a fight.

27
CAT'S CRADLE

A smidge of dawn glowed through the curtains but it was crazily early, no time for her mobile to be playing a song at her. And the first of her summer exams was today. What idiot would dare to wake her up…? The penny dropped and she groped for the phone.

'Ben? Ben! What's happening?'

Ben was sitting on his windowsill, feet on bed. It had been a night of sleeping in snatches, waking often to the silence that told him he was alone in the house. He clasped the phone to his ear with both hands.

'My dad called,' he said.

'Yes? *Yes??*'

'It's a girl.'

Tiffany made a *squeee*– noise, bounced out of bed and capered around her room, swinging an imaginary dance partner. Ending up at the window, she parted the curtains. Enough light came from the sky to show the green of the poplar leaves above the dark street.

'A baby sister!' she squealed. 'Ben, you've got a baby sister. A baby –'

'I know.' He smiled. Her reaction was thawing him out. All night he had been churning with worry and dread, yearning only for it to be over. Now she was reminding him that he could feel happy and proud as well.

'How's your mum?' she asked him.

'Worn out, I think. But okay.' Ben had spoken to her briefly, as Dad held the phone to her ear while she fed the baby. Her voice had cracked with exhaustion, yet she had also sounded calm, at ease, as contented as a person could be.

'It all kicked off yesterday afternoon,' he explained to Tiffany. 'She was cleaning the bathroom when the pains started –'

Tiffany was shocked. 'You let your heavily pregnant mother clean the bathroom?'

'Couldn't stop her. She said that sort of thing is meant to work. And it did. Anyway, it took nearly all night,' said Ben. 'But she said this one was easier than I was.'

'I bet.' Tiffany perched on top of her desk so as to stare more comfortably out of the window. She touched her wrist, long since healed, rotating the charm bracelet that Ben had given her at Christmas.

'Is that a car alarm I can hear?' asked Ben.

'No, it's my local blackbird,' said Tiffany. 'Don't suppose they make that noise where you are now.'

'Not so much, no.'

'Anyway, Ben, details, details! You haven't told me anything yet. Does your baby sister look like you? How much does she weigh?'

'I dunno. Why do people always ask that? Dad said eight-something. Eight kilos?'

Tiffany winced. 'Pounds, I think. I hope. What about pictures? Send pictures!'

'Ain't got any yet.' Ben hesitated. 'She does have a name.'

'A name!' Tiffany knocked over her porcelain cats. 'Come on, spill it!'

Ben braced himself, because he knew what was coming. 'Mum and Dad called her Catriona.'

'Oh! Cat! What a great name.'

'Catriona,' said Ben, patiently.

'I bet people will call her Cat, though.'

'Yeah. I'm sure some will. Wait a sec –' His phone tinkled. He went to his Inbox and found a new message from Dad. His stomach lurched, irrationally – as if Dad would send him terrible news by text! He opened it and found a photo. He stared at the picture and forgot where he was and what he was doing.

'Hello?' said his phone. 'Ben, are you still – ?'

'Yeah.' He put it back to his ear. 'Catriona's cute.'

'What? You got a picture? Send!'

'I will. In a mo. She's got blue eyes.'

'They all do, to start with,' said Tiffany. 'I expect they'll turn green, like yours.'

'What?' said Ben. 'My eyes aren't green.'

'You obviously haven't spent long enough staring into them,' replied Tiffany. 'I can tell you, there's some lovely shades of emerald mixed in there.'

'Aww.' Ben tried to sound mocking, even as he felt his insides melt like chocolate.

Tiffany switched the phone to her other ear. The thought of her looming Chemistry module niggled her, like a sensitive tooth. After the exam it would be such a relief to hook up with Ben in Clissold Park, where he could reassure her that she must have done brilliantly – and the fact that she wouldn't be able to meet him was a torment.

'So.' She made herself not think about that. 'Will you have to share a room with Cat, or what?'

'Catriona. No way! She's got her own room here. Well, she will have. She'll sleep in Mum and Dad's room at first. And there's a cute little nursery next to mine. First job is to paint it pink.'

'Don't make her into a pink girl,' Tiffany pleaded. 'So, um, how's it all coming along? The new house and everything?'

'Oh. Fine,' said Ben. 'My room's huge. Almost as big as yours. And we've got a garden now and somewhere for Dad to park his van. You wouldn't believe how quiet the village is. Especially at night. It actually gets dark.'

'What about your new school?'

'Yeah. It's fine.' His eyes strayed to his new blazer and tie, hanging on the wardrobe door. After a shaky first few weeks he had settled in well, meeting lots of new mates around the basketball hoops, where he was careful not to be too good. The kids here were scarily bright, so in most subjects he was bouncing along the bottom of the class, but he liked his teachers and sat with his cleverest friends, and his grades were slowly cranking upwards. Dad had promised him a new bike if he didn't fail any exams.

'It's fine,' he repeated.

The line went quiet. Ben tried to think of something else to say.

Tiffany tried to think of something else to say.

'I don't suppose –' they both began, together.

Tiffany laughed. 'What? Go on, you first.'

'I was wondering,' said Ben. 'You've got to study next weekend as well?'

'Yes. But those papers will be easier.' Tiffany paused. 'Why d'you ask?'

'Only that you could catch the train down here. See the new house. And baby Catriona. And me, obviously.'

'Obviously.'

'Except… we both have to revise, right?'

'I'll bring my books.' Tiffany hopped down off her desk and browsed the make-up stand on her dressing table, fingering a couple of likely lipsticks. 'We can test each other. My form teacher says interactive revision is the best kind.'

'I think she's probably right,' said Ben.

He rubbed off the mist he had breathed upon his window and saw a familiar shape in the driveway beside Dad's van, sitting with its tail curled round its paws as it watched the birds in the crabapple tree. The neighbours' tabby was always hanging around their house.

'Have you got yourself a new cat yet?' he asked.

'Uhh. Not quite. Soon, though. I'm making lists of names.'

Ben chuckled.

'Oh, look.' Tiffany returned to her window. 'The sky here's a lovely pink. Is it there too?'

'Course it is. We're not that far away. But I might see the sun a few seconds before you do.'

'Okay, I'll time it.' She peered through the chimney pots, keeping one eye on her bedside clock. 'Such a pretty sky. What a great morning for a birthday.'

'Whose birthday is it?'

'Your baby sister's, dumbo! Write down today's date before you forget it. And ping me that photo.'

'Yes boss.'

'Hey. I can see the sun already. You must have missed it at your end.'

'Sorry. Got distracted.'

'Never mind. Send the piccie.'

'Okay.'

'A new little baby! I can't believe it.'

'Nor me. It's scary.'

'Wow. Look at her. Tiny, tiny fingers! Will your mum let me hold her?'

'Rather you than me, I bet.'

'You know, Ben,' said Tiffany, 'I've been thinking. Don't laugh, but… maybe, in a few years' time, when we're older, after we've left school, you and I could get together, the two of us, and we could…'

Ben felt his phone starting to sweat.

'What?' he whispered.

'We could teach her pashki,' said Tiffany.

Ben laughed until he coughed.

'Go take a flying leap,' he said.

They sat at their separate windows and together watched the sun rise.

THE END